T0196075

THE LIVES SOME PEOPLE LIVE

Uncovering One Family Killer

T.J. Gray

iUniverse, Inc.
New York Bloomington

The Lives Some People Live
Uncovering One Family Killer

iUniverse books may be ordered through booksellers or by contacting:

iUniverse
1663 Liberty Drive
Bloomington, IN 47403
www.iuniverse.com
1-800-Authors (1-800-288-4677)

ISBN: 978-1-4401-1844-9 (pbk)
ISBN: 978-1-4401-1845-6 (ebk)

Printed in the United States of America

iUniverse rev. date: 01/27/2009

DEDICATION:

This book is dedicated to all of the families that suffer from the pains and stresses of adultery. I hope after reading this book, you find some once of strength to move on and put your lives back together again. Just to say that someone out there understands my situation and years of sacrifice devoted to my marriage is more than all of the money in the world. This book attempts to reach those horribly affected and give them a way to express what they've been feeling perhaps for many years.

ACKNOWLEDGEMENT:

I would like to acknowledge everyone in my family that has stood by me in my quest to write and publish works that enlighten and lift people up to a higher level. Thank you all!

Chapter One

Felicia's veins in her neck thumped and throbbed vigorously as her well-developed chest heaved in and out with such force that the top button on her brand new silk blouse popped clear off its tightly stitched placing. The infamous photos, sent by a private investigator, had revealed what she suspected for at least a month or so. Her selfish, no good, slyly, unsophisticated, uncouth husband Dennis Lamont Patrick III was cheating, and now she finally had the proof of it! She and Dennis married at a young age. Felicia was only 18 and he was 21. The two of them ran off and was secretly married by a justice of the peace that wasn't so cognizant of the two young and nervous people standing before him, still quite wet behind the ears, however. He was only interested in one thing- getting his fee for performing the ceremony. Felicia stood about 5′6″ tall and had a body that could stop the heart of a man ten miles away. From head to toe, this woman was a woman. With full, round lips and curvy hips to match, she would utterly command the streets she walked down. A single pair of jeans could hardly contain the package she carried quite handily, and other women made her presence very difficult. Once, Felicia walked just two minutes to a neighbor store to buy a few household items. Not only was she ogled by almost every man who saw her but most, if not all of the women who saw her, turned away and shook their heads with such force that you could literally see the extra pounds of skin flapping on their faces and necks in a stiff wind. Not deterred, Felicia kept walking and eventually made it back home unmolested. Why Dennis would cheat on his wife with someone else is beyond many, but he did.

Anyway, the front door opened and Dennis entered the small foyer area with their young, precocious daughter, Tara.

"How was your day, baby?" she stepped gingerly over to her eight year old, smiling.

"Fine. I have a science project due in a week," she slowly walked into the living room area, dragging her brand new Little Mermaid book bag behind her.

"Cheer up, babe. I'm going to help you with it, remember," Dennis quickly took off his coat and cut his eyes over at Felicia, grinning.

"Take off your coat, Tara, go into the kitchen and get some cookies before dinner. Not too many, though. And don't forget to wash your hands."

"I want cake, Mommy," she frowned, one raised eyebrow signaling a change of pace.

"Cake. All right. One piece," Felicia nodded, with a slight tilt of the head.

"Yes," Tara tore the tiny leather coat off, scarcely watching it hit the floor before heading straight for the open kitchen area.

"Wait," Felicia flinched, her body suddenly and rapidly contorting and creating spasms.

"Yeah," she stopped, looking back to only glimpse a cold stare in her mother's eyes.

"Look at that coat, girl. Pick it up. Your clothes are too expensive to throw around."

"Sorry, Mommy," Tara hurried back and snatched the coat up off of the floor before finally running into the kitchen.

"How was your day? Good, I hope," Dennis started up the stairs, carrying the mail.

"Not as interesting as yours apparently."

"What?" he turned slowly, with deep ridges in his forehead and sunken in joules.

"I received a package today. It contained some pictures."

"Pictures of what?"

"You and another female," she grimaced, gritting her teeth and lowering her eyebrows casually.

"What female? What are you talking about?" Dennis backed up and stood directly in front of Felicia.

"This," she walked into the living room and grabbed the pictures from the ivory mantle.

"Oh, I see," he dropped the mail and extended his hands.

"What were you thinking, Dennis? How could you? Who is she?"

"A colleague," he nodded, taking the photos from her.

"I want an explanation, Dennis?" she finally allowed the built-up tears and anguish to cover over her face as a cascading waterfall would envelop a steep and mighty cliffside.

"There is no explanation, Felicia. I provide very well for you and Tara. I deserve to be rewarded for all of my hard work."

"What?!" She stumbled away from him with her breath, literally, stuck in her throat.

"Mommy!" Tara came running from the kitchen covered in white icing.

"I'm fine, baby. Go back into the kitchen. Me and daddy are just talking," she turned her back to her and choked on every word.

"All right," Tara turned slowly and walked deliberately back into the kitchen.

"Let's not do this, Felicia. Actually, I'm glad you know. No more sneaking around. No more late lunch meetings at some far away motel in the boondocks. I can simply tell you that I'm going out to see Vanessa for a few hours, and I'll be back when I'm through with her. Everyone knows everything. No one is hurt by this," he sighed deeply, thoroughly crushing the photos in his hands.

"Are you insane? Do you really believe I'm going to stay in this relationship with you seeing this other woman? Either you leave this house or I will. And if I leave, I'm taking Tara with me. You will not have her," Felicia swallowed, glancing at his hands the entire time.

"No one is leaving this house. Can't you see this is a good thing, Felicia? I don't have to bother you anymore with sex. I can get all of that from Vanessa. You can stay in this nice four-level townhouse we've built together and live the life you've grown accustomed to. I ask you for nothing but trust and understanding," he exhaled slowly, while peering at her and dropping the pictures onto the floor.

"You are crazy, Dennis. I have no intentions on staying in this house with you here. I will take my daughter and go. You disgust me," she started to walk away before he suddenly reached out and grabbed her, very hard.

"Let go of me!"

"You're not going anywhere. This is our family, and you will obey what I'm telling you now. Get upstairs!" he pushed her towards the stairs and raised his tightly clinched right fist.

"You are not going to hurt me anymore, Dennis. I want out of this marriage. I want you out of this house," Felicia turned and huffed, never taking her eyes off his hands.

"You still don't get it, do you?! I control the money and everything else that happens around here. Do you actually believe I would let you take my daughter and walk out of this house? I would see you dead first," he grunted, with a slight growling hush in his voice.

"What?" she whispered with raised eyebrows and her right hand tightly clutching her heaving, exhausted chest.

"I won't allow you to leave this house tonight or any other time with my daughter, Felicia. I would take my gun and shoot you, Tara, and myself. Do you understand?"

"Yes, Dennis," she nodded very slowly, her jowls hanging lifelessly towards the floor.

This wasn't the man she married so many years earlier. Fifteen years later and he has changed for the worse. An animal is what he has become. A cold-blooded murderer, if pushed to the extreme.

The Hendersons lived not too far away from the Patricks. Sean was a devoted father who worked very, very hard to provide the necessities and a little of the comforts for the family. His wife, Jessica, also worked but truly felt that all of the money she made was hers to keep. Sean never insisted she spend her paychecks on anything other than herself. Over time, Jessica accumulated a lot of funds and found the extra time to hang out with her friends that were both married and single. Before long, though, Jessica was spending much of her time in downtrodden bars and away from her family altogether. Once, she didn't make it back home until seven-thirty the following morning. The kids were getting ready for school when she finally decided to casually stroll through the front door. Of course, by this time, Sean had already left for work.

"Mom, why are you always out so late?" Diane frowned, huffing loudly.

"Go to school, little girl. I don't ask you where you go, do I?" she rolled her eyes and sighed.

"I didn't ask where you were, did I?" Diane walked off sucking her teeth, cutting her eyes over at her mother.

"That stupid, child. Raymond! Get down here," she yawned, covering her mouth ever so slightly.

"What?!" he came dragging himself down the narrow staircase.

"Don't yell at me, boy! Get your shoes out of this living room. How many times have I told you to take your stinky shoes upstairs? This is not your filthy bedroom."

"I was coming to get them," he stomped towards the living room, grimacing the entire time.

"You kids just don't listen to anything I say anymore. One day I won't be here for you not to listen to," she exhaled, with one eyebrow going down.

Suddenly, the telephone rang and Jessica reluctantly answered it.

"Yeah," she picked up the receiver, plopping down on the sofa.

"Jess, is that you? It's Sean."

"What do you want?" she sat back, clearing her throat almost immediately.

"I just wanted to make sure you made it home safely, and the kids got off to school all right."

"The kids are being rude to me as usual. Why aren't you here? I can't control them when they get like this," she rolled her eyes and twirled the cord of the phone with one finger.

"Where were you, Jess? We all waited up until two o'clock this morning," he whispered with a scratchy voice.

"I told you before I left that I wouldn't be back until late. I'm off today, remember," she sighed and blew her lips together.

"Don't make that sound on the phone with me. I'm not annoying you. Where were you?"

"Out! Why do I have to answer to you? I have a life outside of this house," she shook her head.

"Your job is to be a good wife and mother, too. Why can't you do that?"

"I have to go. Is that all?" she rolled her eyes again and again.

"I'll be home early today. Please be home," he gulped.

"I can't promise that. Maureen is coming over in a few hours."

"Maureen is single, Jess. She can afford to hang out all hours of the night. You have a family that worries about you. Can't you show us some consideration?"

"Good-bye, Sean. If you don't hang up now, I'm going to hang up on you."

"You wouldn't," he exhaled slowly.

"Bye!" she slammed the receiver down, breaking a nail in the process.

Maureen wasn't coming over but someone else was.

Sean didn't know how to handle his wife. She had changed since getting that new job. Jessica wasn't the same, and it was definitely hurting the family. He turned to his best friend, Jonathan Matthews, his boss, for help.

"I don't know what to do, Jon. I've tried talking to her. The kids have sat down and talked to her, but she's determined to live the way she wants. I want her to give up that job but she won't. What can I do to get my wife back?"

"Why did you tell her not to pay any bills with her paychecks?" he tilted his head slightly with one eyebrow raised.

"I wanted her to have something of her own. All of our lives we've worked hard to provide for our family. Once I got this position, it afforded us the freedom to have just one worker. I figured if she had a job of her own and money of her own, it would make up for all of the sacrifices she made for me and our children over the years. I didn't care about myself. I'll work until the day I die, but I worried about her. I wanted her to have some nice things. That's where my mind was," Sean sighed deeply, lowering his head to the desk in front of him.

"Don't worry about it. I have a feeling everything is going to be all right. Just go home tonight and try talking to her again. Pour out your heart. Take her some flowers. Take some candy. Have you tried that?"

"I haven't, I must confess, but it sounds good. I think I will pick up some candy and flowers on the way in tonight," Sean lifted his head slightly.

"Good. There you go. Hey, I'm taking Beatrice out for dinner tonight. Do you want to come along?"

"A double date," Sean grinned.

"Sure. Why not?"

"All right. What place do you have in mind?"

"Charlie's. Have you ever been there? It's over on Branch and Sycamore," Jonathan walked towards the door.

"No. I can honestly say I've never been there. Charlie's it is. Where is it, again? We'll meet you and Bea there," Sean smiled.

As this plot thickened, another was brewing across town in a more wealthy neighbor. A retire couple of forty-three years was settling into their easy chairs to watch a good movie when the unexpected happened.

"What is it, Harrison? Are you ill?" Myrna stood immediately, reaching out to him.

"I'm having an affair and she's divorced. I will be leaving this house on Saturday to live with her," he swallowed slowly, allowing the saliva to glide lifelessly down his parched throat.

"You're having an affair," Myrna's face arched and caved in as the blood drained away in buckets and she stood there looking at him cross-eyed holding the remote control, stiff as the mighty oak.

"I can't do this another day, Myrna. I need a lot more, and you're not the one to give it to me now. I'm sorry," he exhaled, grabbing his coat from the nearby sofa.

"You're having an affair and you're leaving me this Saturday."

"Yes," he nodded, clearing his throat just a little.

"Saturday is Stephanie's 6th wedding anniversary with Marlon. We're taking them out. Don't you remember?" she regained some of the color in her face and soon afterwards dropped the remote control, which seemed to weigh two tons, onto her easy chair below.

"I thought that would be the best time to tell the family," he shrugged his shoulders with a feeble, raspy tone.

"At her 6th wedding anniversary! You are some piece of work, Mr. Crane. You want to hurt our little girl like this by announcing something that will completely shock the entire family. Why? Why are you leaving me?" Myrna gazed into his deep blue eyes and let out the longest moan ever performed in the history of the world.

"She's better in bed. She does things. All we do is stay cooped up in this house. I want to live a little. I'm 54 years old. You're 50. Why can't we travel and do things? We have the money and time now. Whenever I suggest some place to go, you shoot it down. I can't die before I've lived, Myrna."

"What are you talking about? We just came back from visiting your sister in Las Vegas. You gambled the entire time. I said nothing," she clutched her chest and heaved heavily, as her hand moved gracefully up and down in a somewhat hypnotic rhythm.

"I've said all I needed to say. I think I better go now," he started for the front door.

"What on earth are you doing, Harrison Philip Crane?! You will disrupt everything by leaving. Our family and friends will know all of this. How can you embarrass this family by doing something so tawdry and vile. I will never forgive you. You will be cursed if you go through with this, Harrison," she followed closely behind, speaking quickly and sharply.

"I love you, Myrna, but not like I used to. It's over now. I've found someone else. I want us to end this peacefully and graciously. Can we?" he placed his hand on the door knob and turned it slightly, looking directly into her tear-filled eyes.

"I will not go peacefully into that good night, Mr. Crane! You want to leave me for some trollop. I'll give you the opportunity to pay good money for that privilege. I'll take you for every cent you have. When I'm done with you, all she'll have left is a fifty-four year old gigolo!"

"I'll see you on Saturday at the restaurant. I hope you will be more open-minded and civil by then," he opened the door and sighed.

"Get out! Run to your whore! I hope she enjoys you now because I'm about to unleash a punishment you won't soon forget," she pushed him out and slammed the door shut.

Meanwhile, back at the Patrick residence, things were dicey as Felicia took every opportunity she could to hoard money and other necessities away in the event she got a chance to leave Dennis.

"What are you doing in there?" Dennis pounded on the bathroom door and grabbed the knob, turning it over and over again.

"I'm using the bathroom. Can you wait a minute?"

"I don't hear any water running," he leaned in, placing his right ear firmly to the door.

"That's because I'm on the toilet. Will you give me some privacy, please?" she eked out the words with pounds of sweat running down her forehead, across her face and back.

"Open the door, Felicia. I want to see you on the toilet," he continued leaning in and listening through the closed door.

"I'm using the bathroom, Dennis. You've never been this suspicious before. Why now?" her tone was high-pitched and fading in and out.

"Open the door or I'm breaking it down," he backed away slowly.

"All right," she flushed the toilet and quickly turned on the water.

"Open the door!" he huffed, forming two huge fists.

"What is all the fuss about?" she flung the door open just as he started to run towards it.

"Dennis!" she screamed, sweat pouring from her face.

"You weren't using the bathroom," he stormed inside, looking around.

"What else would I be in there doing, Dennis?" she cut her eyes at him and pushed out the words through her tightly clinched teeth.

"Don't lie to me, Felicia. I know you too well. What are you planning?" he walked back out.

"I'm going downstairs to eat. Are you coming?" she bit down on her bottom lip, hard.

"You're up to something, Felicia, and if I find out what it is, you're dead. We're all dead," he grabbed her arm and peered into her eyes.

"I don't want to die, Dennis," she pulled away, huffing slightly.

"Good. Don't give me a reason to kill you," he pointed towards the stairs.

Back at the Henderson household, Jessica was busy entertaining her male companion. Of course Sean was still at work thinking about the surprise dinner plans he had made with Jonathan.

"You have got to be a little more understanding, Jess," a voice echoed from the shower.

"I am understanding. I listen to my husband. He doesn't listen to me," she sighed and fell across the unmade bed with out-stretched arms above her head.

"You have got to be more giving. He may begin to suspect you're cheating."

"Sean's too naïve, my dear. He'll never suspect that in a million years," she laughed.

"Don't underestimate your husband. He's smarter than you believe," Jonathan Matthews emerged from the bathroom wrapped in a fluffy white towel.

"I thank you so very much for hiring Sean. He talks about you all the time," she reached out for him.

"Does he?"

"He does. He thinks you're the best friend he's ever had," she grinned, grabbing the towel and ripping it from around his body.

"Does he?" Jonathan smiled, leaning in to kiss her.

"I say he's right. Giving him that job has been the best thing for everyone involved," she wrapped her arms around his neck and pulled him down on top of her.

The news of her husband's abandonment sent shockwaves throughout the Crane family. Myrna immediately got on the telephone and called her son, Noah, who was a television news reporter and on assignment in California covering the abrupt wildfires that had enveloped the southern part of the state.

"I need to speak with my son, Noah Crane," Myrna gripped the receiver and winced.

"This is Noah. How can I help you?" he finally answered.

"Noah! It's your mother," she gulped, letting out a huge sigh of relief.

"Mother, what is it?"

"It's your father. He's left me for another woman."

"What?"

"Your father has left me. He walked out of this house not twenty minutes ago. I know he's on his way to that tramp's home," she grunted and gripped the receiver even tighter.

"What are you talking about, Mother? Father would never walk out on you," he frowned, trying to come to terms with what his mother was actually saying.

"When are you due in, son?" she wiped her eyes slowly.

"Friday night. That's if everything moves on time."

"I can't believe what your father has done, Noah. He left me, his wife of forty-three years, for some floozy. I know that slut is with him right now."

"Mother. Try not to think about it. I'll get an earlier flight if I can," he glanced at his watch and then caught sight of a passing field producer anxiously trying to set up camera shots for the next segment.

"I'm sorry to call you at work. Please forgive me," she lowered her head and whispered.

"It's all right, Mother. I would've been more upset if you said nothing at all."

"Call me the moment you arrive. I'll be at the airport to pick you up."

"You don't have to do that. Marlon and Stephanie will be there."

"I see. Well call me anyway. I want to know that you made it in safely."

"I'll call. And you get some rest. We'll straighten everything out once the family comes together," he cleared his throat.

"Thank you, son. Good-bye."

Like clockwork, Noah called his sister, Stephanie, when he was off the air, to tell her about the shocking developments that had just taken place within the family. Stephanie was the oldest of the two children and naturally she was consulted by many members of the immediate and extended families before major decisions were made because she was the oldest and sometimes the most experienced.

"You're joking, Noah," Stephanie's lower jaw dropped as she eased into a nearby chair.

"No. Mother just called me. I'm surprised she hasn't called you."

"You know me and mother aren't exactly close," she shook a little and swallowed partly.

"Whatever differences you and mother may have must be put aside now. She needs the both of us."

"What about father? He needs us too. We just can't turn our backs on him."

"Look at what he's done to mother. It's his fault," Noah frowned and growled into the receiver.

"You're only hearing one side, Noah. We have to hear from the both of them."

"Why would father cheat like that? Why?"

"I don't know, but we must be fair to both our parents," Stephanie nodded.

Sean arrived home after work and found Jessica lounging around, reading the Victoria Secret catalog.

"Hi," he entered and walked directly into the living room area.

"Hello," she glanced up and rolled her eyes, letting out a strong sigh.

"I have a surprise for you," he sat beside her, ignoring the noise.

"What? Jewelry?" she dropped the magazine and held out her hand smiling from ear to ear.

"No. I don't have any jewelry, Jess. But I do have two tickets to a movie and afterwards, dinner at a place called Charlie's," he pulled the tickets from his pocket.

"Two tickets to the movies. Are you serious?" she started to laugh.

"What's so funny?! I'm trying to reach out and do something nice for the both of us. Why can't you just meet me half way?" he stood and huffed, hunching his back and making two fists.

"A movie, Sean. My tastes have grown. I don't go to the movies anymore. I go out to fabulous restaurants and bars. Movies are for teen-agers and losers. You take the kids to the movies. I'm staying home," she picked up the magazine and started looking through it once again.

"You're not even going to try, are you? Not even try," he exhaled, peering at her and losing some of the redness in his face.

"I have nothing more to say about this ridiculous subject. Take the children and have a good time. I'll stay here and make a nice dinner for one," she never bothered to raise her head.

"I will take the kids out to the movies tonight. They need to let off some stress," Sean stomped by her and up the stairs.

"Loser," she shook her head and laid back on the sofa, continuously thumbing through the magazine.

A few days later, Felicia decided it was time to go. Dennis had hinted that he purchased new bullets and dug some grave sites in the nearby woods. He was becoming unglued as he traveled back and forth between Vanessa and Felicia.

"I'll be back soon," he grabbed his coat, gloves and car keys.

"I'm going out to the store to pick up some things," she glanced at an empty pot on the stove.

"What things?" he frowned, tilting his head slightly to the left and leaning in towards her.

"For dinner tonight. I'm making spaghetti," she opened a cabinet door and pulled the box of noodles down.

"That sounds great. I'm sure to have an appetite later," he grinned, smacking her on the butt.

"Don't do that, Dennis. You know how much I hate it," she moved away and flinched.

"Stop being so uptight. This arrangement is working out great. I bought you a new ring yesterday. Where is it? Why haven't you worn it," he slipped his left arm into the coat's sleeve.

"I haven't found the right thing to wear with it," she glanced at him, exhaling quickly.

"That ring was bought for wearing. I want it on your finger tonight. Do you understand?" he walked towards her grabbing the left arm tightly and firmly, cutting off the circulation.

"Dennis! You're hurting me," she yanked and pulled with all of her might.

"Be still!" he raised his right, clinched fist.

"What do you want from me?" she swallowed slowly, allowing her body to fall limp.

"Put the ring on. Have it on by the time I get from Vanessa's. Is that clear?" he finally released her arm, allowing the warm blood to pulsate through the air-starved veins again.

"Yes," she fell to the floor, letting out a high-pitched moan, with an ever-so-slightly hint of growl.

"Don't give me a reason, Felicia. I love you too much. Put the new ring on and make me happy," he fastened the coat, ramming the tightly stitched buttons into each slot.

"I'll have it on," she sniffed hard, wiping one side of her face over and over again.

"Get off the floor, baby," he reached down to her, opening up his huge hand, palms up.

"Thank you," she grabbed his hand, shaking and choking on the only two words she hated saying to him the most.

"Things can be good if you just accept what's happening a little each day. I will continue to provide for you and Vanessa. All I ask is that you give this arrangement a chance to work. Can you, baby?" he peered at her, with his thick, dark eyebrows slowly digging deeply into his forehead as the ridges on his face became contorted.

"I will try to accept this a little better," she eked out the words, watching his dark pupils pierce straight through her and clean out the other side.

"I'll be back soon," he suddenly smiled and kissed her on the forehead.

"Dennis," she called out before placing her hand on her neck and wiping it downward.

"What is it, sweetheart?" he turned, gripping his gloves harder and harder.

"Would you actually kill me and Tara?" she breathed in and out, faster and faster, waiting to hear his response.

"I would actually take my gun and shoot you in the head, first, and then Tara. I would shoot myself after I've written a note to the world," his tone was almost whispering.

"What kind of note?"

"Just go and get the dinner for tonight. I'll be home soon," he walked deliberately out of the kitchen and Felicia could hear the front door open and slam shut behind him.

Jessica Henderson was still living high on the hog. Hanging out at tawdry bars almost every night and coming back home whenever she pleased. Still, this woman found the time to go to work and pile more and more money up into her bank account. Loving Sean continued paying the bills, alone, and tolerating his wife's abusive behavior towards him and the kids. Whenever he couldn't take it anymore, he would turn to his trusted friend, Jonathan Matthews. Sean went to college with Jonathan years earlier and the two hung out all hours together and got into trouble many times. Jonathan's family had the money plus influence, and they would be the people who bailed the renegade boys out of jail on misdemeanor charges constantly. Sean couldn't say enough about his best pal, Jon. The guy he would give his life for in a moments notice. Little did he know, this best friend of his was helping himself to a lot more than a good friendship.

"Are you sure he's gone for the entire weekend?" Jonathan whispered, closing the door of his den slightly.

"He took the kids to his mother's house. I had to talk him into it," Jessica leaned back on the sofa grinning from ear to ear.

"What are you wearing?" he reached down and grabbed his manhood before squeezing it.

"A two piece from Victoria's Secret," she slowly licked her lips and insidiously twirled the cord of the receiver around one freshly manicured finger.

"That sounds nice," he cleared his throat and sat up straight.

"When can you come over? I have the wine chilling and the dinner on the stove," she sat up and uncoiled her finger.

"Beatrice is bugging me about taking my kids out tonight. I was going to take them to a movie and have a quick dinner some place," he sighed.

"A movie and quick dinner. That sounds great. Why don't I get dressed and meet you and your kids at the movie theater."

"You wouldn't mind," he frowned.

"Of course not. Tell me where you're going and I'll meet you there," she grabbed a pen and paper from the coffee table and started to write.

CHAPTER TWO

Yes. Felicia ran and ran that same night Dennis admitted he would actually kill her and Tara. She ran like never before, hoping and praying to get away. She ran throughout the house grabbing all of her stashed money and important papers. She grabbed her daughter and just ran. Jumping into the car and driving away as fast as she could. Away from the very house she helped to make a home so many years earlier. Away from the life that had become all so familiar to her. Away from the good people and neighborhood she called hers. Away from the family who loved her. Where would she go? What would she do? Who could she become? What to do with Tara? The questions raced, as her pulse moved in tamdum. Dennis would be angry. He would be furious, and nothing on earth would be able stop him from coming after her and that child. But she threw all of those fears out the window, as the car turned onto the nearest highway and never once saw a breaking pattern for steering its way back home. The entire experienece was likened to being "out of body" by Felicia. Things were just happening. The car was speeding away, Tara was in the backseat crying and screaming, her pulse was racing, the questions were building, the fear-factor was rising, the thoughts of death were looming. But still she ran and ran and ran. All of that went out the window too, as her car kept moving in one direction only- out of his reach. Out of his grasp. Out of his piercing gaze. Out of his forboding stare. She ran and ran. What would happen next? That dominant question finally peeped its huge head around the corner of her mind, and just sat there waiting and waiting and waiting. Always patiently waiting for things to die down, so it could stand and be noticed. Always waiting, like a pregnant woman sitting in the doctor's office waiting on news of her baby. Just sitting right there, patiently waiting. How could this be? How could my life have been reduced to this mess? What has this man done to me? The questions kept coming, like the many stab wounds inflicted whenever Dennis would visit Vanessa. But that one question just sat there patiently waiting for her mind to dispense with all of the "fluff" before she could deal with it. What would happen next? It just sat there waiting for that special moment when all of the drama was over. When all of the fright had subsided. It patiently sat there awaiting its turn to be thoroughly vetted. Dennis returned home. He finally rolled back over and sat his big butt on the side of Vanessa's bed smiling and laughing at all of the fun he had just had. Allowing his seed to aimlessly fill two nearby condoms, discarded after frequent use. Yes. He had had his fun and now it was time to return home and fulfill his "husbandly duties" for Felicia. He kissed her goodnight. He stood there, plain as day, on the front porch, with the lights blazing and cars passing by. He stood there and tongue-kissed that Vanessa woman goodnight and then walked off to his car, like a snake moving slowly after gobbling down its kill and scurrying away. Yes. He actually tongue-kissed her and scurried away, heading for home. Those same crusty lips and tongue he used to French kiss Vanessa with, he used on Felicia. He was heading for a house with the front lights on and the stove full of hot foods to eat. There was, in fact, an appetite. A big one at that. He was hungry. He wanted that homemade spaghetti Felicia had said she would cook. His mouth watered as he thought of it. Turning onto the nearby parkway, he reached over to make a quick call on his cell phone.

He didn't care about the law, which plainly stated that no one could drive and talk on any device at the same time. What law could contain this man? What authority figure could give this man advice to follow? This man did what he wanted. This man ruled his home with an iron fist. This man threatened to kill his wife and kid if they ever left him. This man wasn't a man at all. Yes. He returned home. He drove to his home. The home he had built with Felicia so many years earlier. The only home where he ever received genuine happiness with his wife. The home where, earlier, he rested his head at night after saying prayers with, then, his three year old daughter and loving, adoring wife, Felicia. This was the home he believed he was returning to, but that home had went away long ago. What home was he returning to now? What home was this? What home would be waiting for him? He didn't really know or care. Yes. He returned. He came back. He returned to his home to find not a welcoming light on the front porch. He returned to find not a kitchen busting with activity and a stove hot from cooking all evening. No. He returned to find a forboding front porch and a squeaky door, which opened slowly to reveal a cold, empty and forgotten home. A home that would cry out for tender affection, if it could talk. A home that painfully wept in agony over the tremendous sadness within its stucco walls. This is the home he returned to. This is the home that greeted him. Like a depressed bride not quite ready for the ailse. Like a sports player, whose leg or arm is severely ailing, this is the home that stood right there prominently, dark, lonely and melancholy. Yes. It stood there with its squeaky door and ice cold-to-the touch walls. But, nevertheless, it greeted him as he entered and stood silently in the foyer, looking around. He knew. He knew in his heart when he opened that door. He already knew. The tension was rising. She was planning something. I knew she was planning something. I should've been more vigilant. I thought I had scared her enough. I thought she was under my control. He knew the moment he entered that gloomy place, that had lost its real happiness so long ago, that she was gone. Tara was gone. The path they traveled had been different and growing further apart for a long time now. This was the situation that presented itself to Dennis. But he stood there, thinking about all he could've done to scare her more. She actually done it. She actually left. I can't believe it. He stood there, as the brandnew grandfather clock, which cost at least $2500.00 chimed. It announced to the world another hour of misery had passed for this family. It announced to the world that another 60 minutes had passed for these pitiful people. It didn't have to be like this. It didn't have to come to this. Why? Why couldn't she just accept my new life? Why couldn't she just accept the gifts and be quiet, still, understanding? Why couldn't she just endure? The questions kept coming as the cold air enveloped the home. The front door still wide open as Dennis stood there, unable to believe that Felicia was really gone. After all of the threats and harsh treatment, she left anyway. Nothing more could be accomplished by talking. It was time to act. The time had come to end everything for everyone. She pushed me to this point. She is making me go after her and Tara. She has caused this unhappinessness to fall upon our household. I have to take care of her. I have to show her that I'm in control. She can't just walk out and leave me like this. Who does she think she is? I told her never to leave.

But did she listen? I have to fix this broken situation. I have to make things right again.

I have to go after her and prove what I said some time ago. Dennis was beyond furious. Words couldn't describe his feelings. Felicia had defied him and left the house for good. There was no appeasing him, as the anger and resentment built up. He continued standing there allowing his thoughts to collect. The cold air pouring in and the grandfather clock ticking away. The rustling of the dead leaves outside and the occasional passing car. All of these things went totally unnoticed by him as he stood there, motionless, allowing his thoughts of killing Felicia and Tara to mount. *Where did she go? What did she take? I knew she was around here doing things. I knew she was up to something.* He finally moved again, for the first time, since entering the house.

The same night Jessica met Jonathan and his children at the movies was the very night everything came to a head. Sean had decided to take his mother and children out that same night. After a day at the mall, they went to a place called Lacey's for a hamburger and fries. Not ten minutes later, Jessica, Jonathan and his kids walked in. Because of where Sean and his family were sitting, they could see everyone who entered and left the restaurant. As they ate, Raymond asked to go to the restroom. On his way, he noticed the front door open and he distinctly heard his mother's laugh. He immediately turned and she was coming through the door with Jonathan and his two kids. The whole group was laughing and talking about the movie they had just seen. He quickly made his way back to the table unnoticed. By the time he reached the table, Sean had already seen the couple and children enter the establishment. They were seated and menus were brought over. Sean walked over and confronted his wife and best friend. Before long, management was brought over to help manage the situation. Jessica had been caught. The most ironic thing about all of this was the fact that Lacey's was one of Jonathan's kids favorite places to eat and that's why they all went there in the first place. The ecstatic crew had passed three other restaurants before reaching Lacey's. Jessica told Sean that she wanted to leave him for Jonathan. She also told him that she wanted to take the kids with her. Sean vowed that he would never relinquish the children to her under any circumstances. She insisted on them choosing who they wanted to live with indefinitely. Diane, fifteen, loved her mother very, very much despite the fact she didn't care for her debauched lifestyle. Raymond, seventeen, loved his father and wanted to stay with him. Jessica abruptly told Diane that she could never have any contact with her father if she wanted to be with her. She also told Raymond that she wanted nothing to do with him if he wanted to stay with his father. Diane hugged and kissed her father for the last time, crying and sobbing on his broad chest.

Raymond peered at his mother and raised his right fist towards her face. The two decided together to bring the courts into the situation. Sean promptly resigned from his job at the marketing agency where Jonathan was his boss. Beatrice, Jonathan's wife of twenty-two years, was told of the distasteful incident, and she quietly divorced Jonathan. Sean was hurt and despondent for many days after the altercation at Lacey's. How could his wife cheat with his best friend? How could Jonathan do this to him? They had been through so much together. The time and attention they put into their relationship over the years meant absolutely nothing to Jonathan. He was just selfish, arrogant and heartlesss.

Sean's mother, Deborah, despised Jessica anyway. This situation just made her even more insensed. Mrs. Henderson even looked into having her killed. She went as far as to meet with a hitman and pay him half of the money before she became weak and scared. The hitman told her that there was no refund. She told him to keep what was paid and forget about Jessica. That was the only time Jessica ever came close to being murdered for all the wrong she had done to her family.

The dinner that was to be given for Stephanie and Marlon's 6th wedding anniversary was immediately cancelled. Harrison insisted on bringing Gail, his mistress, there. Myrna was very angry and told Stephanie that she would make a spectacle of herself and totally ruin the occasion if her father dared to show up with that woman. A few days afterwards, Noah went to his father's new apartment to finally speak to him one on one.

"Father. Why? You're suppose to be this devout Roman Catholic, who follows the church doctrines. What are you doing?"

"Don't you dare bring the church into this. My relationship with God is my own. You have no right to question that. Now, I love your mother very much, Noah, but not like that anymore," he lost some of the redness in his face and sighed, lowering his head.

"Do you truly understand what you've done to her and this family, Father?" he exhaled with one eyebrow digging into his forehead.

"I realize that my actions have damaged this family to some extent, but I have to be happy. I'm fifty-four years old, son. I'm not ready to pack it in and just wait to die. I've worked hard all of my life. With your mother's help, we put you and your sister through school; and now it's our time to live. I just want to live with someone else."

"How is that even possible? Mother still loves you," he shook his head frowning.

"You don't understand any of this, and I'm not even sure I do sometimes. But I love Gail. We go places and do things. We have fun. I live when I'm with her. Believe me, son, if this situation could be done without hurting you or the rest of the family, I would do it. The last thing I want to do is hurt anyone, but I won't be denied happiness because of my grown children," he nodded and pointed his finger directly at Noah.

"You are some piece of work, Father. You're actually playing the victim in all of this. Stick to the culprit; the victim doesn't suit you," Noah grabbed his coat and left.

Felicia kept moving. From cheap motel to cheap motel, stopping only to use the restroom or eat at some dive way out in the boondocks. Always off the beaten path, behind the cut, obscure, backdoor, never using the phone to contact relatives. Learning how to depend on herself to survive the cold nights and an exasperated, crying child. Running and hiding, hoping that old or frail waitress doesn't notice the black woman with the small child who needed a coloring sheet to keep quiet and not draw unnecessary attention.

"Is that all, Miss?" the waitress looked over the horn-shaped rim of her glasses.

"Yes," Felicia smiled, always turning slightly away.

"She's such a cutie pie. Those bright ribbons and bows all done up pretty-like," the waitress walked away smiling.

"Tara, are you all right, baby?"

"I want to go home, Mommy," she pushed her plate to the side and laid her head down on top of the table.

"I know what we can do later on," Felicia sat up straight and clasped her hands together.

"What?" she moaned, looking up at her mother.

"We are going to play the Highway Game," she nodded and folded her arms.

"The Highway Game. What's that?"

"Well, my dad used to play it with me whenever we went on a trip to visit my grandmother."

"What is it?" Tara sat up and exhaled slowly.

"You try to remember how many signs you see along the road as you're traveling."

"There are lots of signs. You can't catch them all," she frowned.

"Yes. But the trick is to catch all the signs that have places that start with the first letter of your first name," Felicia smiled.

"That's stupid," Tara sighed.

"I bet you can't catch all the places that start with T."

"I can. That's easy," she cut a smile and leaned back.

"Well, I would always win when I was little. My dad would always lose."

"I'm ready," Tara folded her arms and smiled too.

Myrna Elizabeth Crane wasn't taking the separation of her and her husband, Harrison, well. She had devoted many years to him and the marriage. A house wife is what she was. Taking care of their two kids. Making sure dinner was always on the table and the worries of bills never affected the family. Once Harrison made the money, it was placed into a special account, which she drew off of every single month. Harrison never encouraged her to work, but she would volunteer at the kids' school from time to time. Myrna gave of herself in other ways too. Whenever a member of the extended family was ill, she would travel to them and stay until the ailment was gone. She was the best when it came to comforting others, but now she was in dire straights and needed to be consoled.

"Oh, Myrna, baby. How are you?" Deloris Simms, a good friend, sat next to her.

"I'm not well, dear. Harrison has his new place with that slut. I know who she is. That Gail Sheehy Bates," she grunted, making two fists and stomping one foot against the floor, hard.

"Don't become so worked up. This Gail woman isn't worth it."

"You're right. She's definitely not worth it. I know where she lives, too. She has a sleazy apartment outside of Harrison's place. He is so stupid, Deloris. She's a commoner. A woman far, far beneath you and I of course," Myrna raised her nose and head up high.

"Of course she would be. The tramps always are. These types of men care absolutely nothing about the status of the whores they collude with in the bedroom. It's the wives that have social status and class," Deloris rolled her eyes and leaned back grunting.

"I never knew Harrison felt so badly about things. I've worked all of my life to make things better for him and our family. Always cutting corners and making ends meet when he was in college, and we struggled terribly to get by in those earlier years. When our Stephanie came along, we scraped, but managed. I did that. On the little we had, I made it stretch and work. How can he just trade me in now? When all of the hard work is over and done with, this Gail person just walks in and takes over. That's not fair. Where was she when I had to go to bed hungry in order for Harrison and the kids' to eat something? Where was she when our heat was going to be cut off, and I had to negotiate a payment arrangement with the gas company so that me and my family wouldn't freeze to death in our little apartment? Where was she, Deloris?! Where was this Gail Sheehy Bates woman then?!" Myrna dug her manicured nails deep into the plush arm of the leather sofa and held on tightly, with clinched, perfectly set white teeth and bald-up manicured toes.

"You're about to pop, Myrna. I'll get you some water," Deloris hurried into the kitchen.

The Crane children were lining up and taking sides. Noah didn't believe his father had the right to demand anything from the family. He saw him as the wrongdoer and the total aggressor in this entire saga. Stephanie, on the other hand, totally acknowledged that her father was wrong, but stopped short of blaming him to the point of total exile from the entire family. She still loved her father and hoped to repair the damage between the two of them, eventually. This issue caused huge problems between the two siblings, who were quite close before this whole episode happened. It even came to a point where they couldn't even be in the same room together without yelling and screaming at each other over this very situation. Marlon, Stephanie's husband, was often used to keep the peace between the two of them. Harrison Crane had caused great division and pain within his family. Yet, he insisted on having Gail around him, and he never once apologized to anyone for his blatant behavior, wherever she was concerned.

"I better stay here tonight," Gail slumped down on the sofa.

"You are going with me. Stephanie has agreed to be nice this evening. You're with me," he smiled, leaning over before kissing her on the lips.

"Your wife would scream if she could see you kissing me," Gail grinned.

"You have nothing to worry about. Myrna is completely harmless. It's going to take her some more time to get over the shock of us not being an item anymore. It's just you and me, baby," he nodded.

"Are you sure you want me there tonight? I could stay home and balance my checkbook," she bit her bottom lip and exhaled.

"I have a great idea. Why don't we go and show our faces and then sneak out and see a movie," he laughed.

"A movie. I haven't been to the movies in years. Are you sure?" she stood.

"Positive. There's a new one out that everyone is raving about."

"What's the name of it?" she looked at him with a slight tilt of the head.

"I can't remember," he snickered.

"You're too much, Harrison," she burst out laughing.

Dennis brought Vanessa Wright, his mistress, back to his home. That wretched home, which sat melancholy and full of dead men's bones. He told her that she was welcomed to anything she wanted. He opened up the squeaky front door and gave her free reign. Like a kid in the candy store, Vanessa headed straight for the posh master bedroom and Felicia's huge walk-in closet. This wicked woman, who had slept with Dennis on many, many occasions, found herself in the very household and on the outskirts of the closet of one of the most fashionable people in the entire area. Mrs. Felicia Patrick was always known for her clothing, and her exquisite tastes in choosing just the right outfits and fashions for each season. This was the one thing Vanessa could never do in a million years. This woman, with little education and style, has found herself about to rummage through the closet of the lady who set the standard for woman all around the neighborhood and beyond. It was Felicia who turned many heads at Dennis' countless million dollar dinner parties. It was Felicia who made men wish they weren't married. It was always Felicia's face and body men saw in their minds eye, as they laid across their soft beds and blissfully masturbated in the quiet of any still night. It was Felicia who, at one time, had nothing but respect for only one man. But on this terrible day in October, a bitter stranger, an imposter, a true derelict, a sleazy, desperate, unfortunate woman finds the good fortunate to be standing outside the walk-in closet of Mrs. Felicia Patrick. Dennis of course cared nothing about the clothing or priceless jewelry that laid helplessly across the many tables and chairs throughout the closet. His focus was always on Felicia and making her pay the ultimate price for leaving him. He spared no expense in trying to locate his wife. This so-called man even hired the same private investigator Felicia used to spy on him. He sent his menions out with one set of instructions. They knew what to do. They were fully briefed on what the boss wanted. These men and one woman had their orders and it was time to get Felicia back to Dennis. Back to a man bent on murder. A man bent on revenge and nothing less. He continued making love to Vanessa as she slept in Felicia's bed and wore her clothing. There was no shame here. There was no regret or dissatisfaction with the arrangement. She was getting the best end of this deal. Keep her man happy and enjoy the "stuff" he allowed her to have. What whore wouldn't enjoy this gig? Before long, Dennis grew tired of Vanessa and started sleeping with another woman. Did Vanessa care? Of course she did, but not for the reasons you may think. There was no love there. The relationship was strictly sex. She agreed to leave the house and take a few of Felicia's things with her. Dennis gave her a certain time to be out, and she was. Soon enough, Gracie took her place in keeping Dennis extra warm at night. Gracie Moore had a home of her own. She was only looking for companionship from Dennis. But did she know Dennis was married and actively pursuing his wife and daughter? Yes. She knew, and didn't care. She, too, slept in Felicia's bed and wore a few of her dresses and jewelry. This meant nothing to Dennis Lamont Patrick III. He spent all of his free time assisting the investigators in tracking down his wife and kid. Whenever a detective or investigator got close, he would quickly fly out to see for himself. But just as they closed in, Felicia would move on and disappear again. Blending into the tapestry of mankind. Moving stealthily. Knowing when to hover and when to move at top speed. Always one step ahead.

Not caring about physical appearance but life itself. It was almost like some divine intervention guided her, and it was leading her somewhere special. Leading her to some place- a conclusion. A place of rest.

Things weren't going well with Sean and Jessica. By this time, Jessica and Jonathan were living together. While the divorce between Jessica and Sean was in progress, the courts in fact stepped in to decide the custody of the two children. The court awarded custody of Raymond to his father and it gave visitation rights to Jessica. Of course she never intended to use them. The court also ruled on Diane. They gave custody of her to Sean as well, but because Diane begged the judge to allow her to go with her mother, the court allowed it. Custody was then changed, with Sean's consent, and Diane went to live with Jessica and Jonathan. Sean had visitation rights. Of course Jessica was against this emphatically, but there was nothing she could do. This arrangement created many more problems. Whenever Sean would go to Jessica's to pick Diane up, she would seldom be there, and when she was there, he had to coerce her to get into the car and leave with him. Despite everything, Sean wanted to keep the peace and make the terrible situation work. He never spoke to Jonathan again. Whenever he went to their new home, he would ring the door bell and then stand off to the side. If Jonathan answered, he would causally walk back to his car and get in. If Jessica answered, he would walk a short distance away from the door to wait on Diane to come out. This happened almost every weekend. Eventually, Sean gave up, and allowed Diane to stay with Jessica and Jonathan on weekends, too. She never called him, but he would call regularly and leave tons of messages on the answering machine for her. Diane was being pressured not to return any of his phone calls and to pursue other interests that would take her mind off of her distraught father. Jessica hated Sean with a passion, and wanted him dead. During many of their altercations, she would actually threaten to take his life. This brought up more negative feelings in Sean's mother, Deborah, who actually paid a hitman money to "off" Jessica.

"It's all right, Mother," Sean entered her home and rubbed his temples.

"She shouldn't treat you like this. You've been good to that woman," she closed the door and shook her head.

"How was your day?" he walked into the kitchen, heading straight for the refrigerator.

"I did the usual. Watched the soaps, and spoke to Ruby Carmichael," she sighed.

"Why don't you come over tonight? I've got a new movie from Video Outlets Inc."

"You rented a movie. Why? This is a week night," she frowned.

"Let's live dangerously," he smiled.

"Oh Sean," she grinned and touched his shoulder.

Myrna invites Harrison over to the family home to talk. She explains to him that she needs closure. He agrees to come and see her in person. After arriving, the two start to speak.

"I'm here. What is it you need to move on, Myrna?" he sighed.

"I love you, Harrison. What more is there I need to hold on to you?" she looked into his strong blue eyes with her voice becoming weak.

"There is nothing you can do, sweetheart. It's over. I'm in love with Gail."

"Why Harrison? What did I do that was so terrible? Tell me. I'll fix it. I'll become whatever it is you want," she gulped, clasping her hands tightly together.

"There is nothing you can do. What's done is done. We must move on in our own separate directions. This isn't healthy, Myrna. We've got to let each other go," he nodded, looking towards the floor.

"You're willing to just let go like that. Why? What can I do? I know there's something I can do. Just tell me, Harrison," the tears began to well-up within her eyes.

"There is nothing left to do. What do you want from me, Myrna?" he sighed again.

"Your love and affection. Your attention. Your understanding. I want what any other wife of forty-three years would want. I want to be able to live out these years with the man that I married."

"Stop this, Myrna. You're not making this easy for any of us. I never wanted to hurt you. I'm not in love with you anymore. That's all," he exhaled and started for the front door.

"I will allow you to have her. You want Gail. You can have her on the side. Just come home to me. Is that all right?" she broke down completely, allowing the ocean of tears to flow as her voice became hushed.

"You would allow me to have Gail on the side. That's your solution," he stopped and turned.

"Yes. I don't care anymore. I'm willing to live with your new lifestyle. All I know is that I love you Harrison Philip Crane. Nothing on earth can stop that. I've devoted too many years to just walk away. You can have Ms. Gail Sheehy Bates. I won't stand in your way. Just keep her away from me, please," she wiped her face and sobbed.

"Guess who I saw at the movies the other night?" he smiled.

"What?" she frowned, wiping her eyes.

"Billy Montgomery. You remember Billy, don't you?" he cleared his throat.

"Harrison. What are you going to do?" she became weak in the knees.

"Billy asked about you, Myrna. I told him we were separated, and I believe he's interested," he eked out the words and then became very quiet, still.

"Are you trying to fix me up with Billy Montgomery? Harrison. How could you? I need some air," she stumbled backwards, knocking over a $3,000.00 vase.

"Myrna," he reached out for her.

She ran over to the patio door and tried to open it, but the latch wouldn't allow her to free herself from the confinds of the prison like home. The latch wouldn't let go. It wouldn't yeild to her constant pressures to release itself. Harrison raced over to her to help. Once he was within striking distance, she turned and slapped his face, hard. The two of them standing there, eyeball to eyeball. Neither one flinching. Neither one moving an inch. Their eyes locked. His with hers. Theirs. Both people just standing there. It was almost like God himself came down and made them be still and just examine one another. Neither one could move. Their eyes locked, and the gaze so powerful it could move a mountain. Peering into each others eyes revealed a lot. The many years of sacrifice. The hard times and the good. Before the children. Before college. Before this Gail woman. Before life became so complicated. Yes. Those years, so long ago. When a dark-haired, bow-legged boy of 23 met an awkward, little blond-haired girl of 19. This is what they saw in each other. The many years of being together. Shivering in the cold months and buring up in the summer time, before being able to afford that air-conditioner. Eating peanut butter and jelly sandwiches five days a week in order to pay the rent. Going to Goodwill to get clothes to save money. Shopping at discount stores and cutting out a thousand coupons on a regular bases. This is what they saw gazing into each other's eyes. No kids, no Gail, no car, no expensive home and no bank accounts full of extra money. The years were difficult but manageable. The years brought joy, too. This is what they saw standing there, unable to move. Locked in each other's eyes. Stephanie's birth. The night she was conceived. Harrison's first real paying job after college, and a celebration that led to Stephanie being born. Noah's conception night. Harrison's first promotion and raise. The celebration that led to him being born. These are the moments, the precious moments that truly mattered. These are the moments that made a difference. There was no Gail involved. There was no fancy, high-paying job or bank accounts. Those were the Crane family's best years. The years of sacrifice. The years of coming home exhausted but hopeful, falling asleep in front of the television set. Reading bedtime stories to children even though his bed was screaming out for an occupant. Those years were the ones that truly counted.

There was no Gail or outside influence then. It was family and work. Family and work. These were the scenes that played over and over between them. These were the images they saw standing there, with one another, unable to move. Locked in each other's eyes.

One thing you learn about people is that they will disappoint you from time to time. There will be hurt feelings and crushed hearts. Some will hurt you on purpose and others will do it unintentionally. Either way, you get hurt. Once everything is said and done, all that matters is if you have the courage and fortitude to get right back up and keep on going- always pushing ahead, despite the pain and anguish. Many people are simply jealous and they act out of fear and frustartion because of not being like you or having the things you have. This, unfortunately, happens all to often among imperfect human beings. But the key point is always whether or not you have the courage and fortitude to get right back up and keep on going forward. Felicia Patrick had that kind of drive, and she kept advancing forward, despite the threats and abuse. Always pushing ahead and moving from one place to another to stay out of the grasp of Dennis and his money-hungry henchmen. Felicia's parents died in a car accident when she was only twelve. As a result, she went to live with her not so mild-tempered aunt. This was her father's oldest sister, who by the way, helped to raise him so many years earlier. Aunt Rhonda Oliver didn't play, and when she hadn't heard from Felicia in a reasonable amount of time and Dennis kept giving her the run around, she wised up and went straight to the police. They all showed up on Dennis' front porch demanding answers.

"Mr. Patrick, we just want to know where your wife is?" Officer Tilman leaned his head slightly before pulling out a small pen and tablet from his holster belt.

"I told you, Officer, she's not here. My wife left weeks ago. I can't tell you when exactly, because I don't have a clue," he walked over to the bar and opened a brandnew bottle of scotch.

"You can't recall when your wife disappeared. That's not possible. When did you notice she wasn't here?" Officer Gamble shook his head and sucked his teeth.

"My wife goes on trips all the time. She may be away for two days or even five. Who knows? I come home from work and she's gone. You try to figure it out," he poured a little of the liquor into a shot glass.

"This doesn't make any sense, Mr. Patrick. Your wife just takes the kid and leaves. She leaves no note or forwarding address. All of this doesn't add up, sir," Officer Tilman looked around the huge living room and exhaled.

"You can believe what you want. I have proof that I'm trying to find my wife, sirs," he sat the glass down and motioned to leave the room by pointing to the door.

"Where are you going?" Officer Tilman sighed.

"To my office. I want to bring you the proof I'm speaking about," he grinned.

"Are you sure you haven't harmed your wife in any way, sir? Tell us now," Officer Gamble frowned.

"I wouldn't touch a hair on my wife's head. My God, she has my daughter," Dennis fain distraught.

"All right, Mr. Patrick. What kind of proof do you have?"

"Allow me to go to my office, please," he pointed again.

"Go with him, Tilman," Gamble casually strolled around the living room.

"Let's go, sir," Tilman and Dennis walked off.

"You don't believe him, do you?" Rhonda finally spoke up.

"We have nothing to say he's lying, Ms. Oliver. As far as we know, Mrs. Patrick has taken the child on a trip. Nothing seems out of place," he glanced around the room again.

"My niece would never just leave like this. She would contact me."

"Has your niece ever left to go on trips like this before? Is Mr. Patrick correct?"

"She has gone on overnight trips. Those I know about because she would always call. This is not like her, Officer Gamble," she bit her bottom lip and swallowed hard.

"I know you're concerned, but there is nothing we can do. We can only hope that Mrs. Patrick returns within a reasonable amount of time," he folded his arms and shook his head.

"He's done something with her. I know he has," Rhonda's eyes started to well up with tears.

"I wouldn't go that far at this point, Ms. Oliver. She could be on some kind of vacation. The daughter is gone, too. Mr. Patrick wouldn't hurt his own child, would he?"

"I never trusted him. Even when Felicia brought him to my home so many years ago, I was against any marriage. But Felicia did what she wanted, and this girl wanted Dennis Lamont Patrick III. He promised her the world, you know. He promised her so much over the years. All he really brought was trouble."

"Mr. Patrick owns his own archetecture firm, correct?"

"Yes. He has his own business. What does that have to do with anything?" she frowned.

"I was just curious. I heard of Patrick Industries. He must have his hand in all kinds of things," Officer Gamble nodded.

"Yes. He's always had a head for figures," she paused.

"I have the list, Gamble," Tillman emerged from the hallway and back inside of the living room.

"What list?"

"These are people Mr. Patrick has looking for his wife right now. He called a few people, and I spoke with them. It all looks legitimate," he cut his eyes over at Rhonda.

"Will that be all, gentlemen and lady," Dennis walked into the living room with Gracie by his side.

"Who are you?" Rhonda suddenly gasped and clutched her chest.

"My name is Gracie Moore. I am Mr. Patrick's houseguest. Nothing more," she smiled.

"Why is this woman staying in my niece's home? Felicia would never allow this person to live here," Rhonda looked directly at Officers Tillman and Gamble.

"Where do you live, Ms. Moore?"

"Officer Tillman, here is my address," she walked to a coffee table and wrote her information down on a blank slip of paper.

"Why are you taking in houseguests? You don't need the money," Rhonda huffed, peereeing straight at Dennis.

"What I do in my own home is my business, Ms. Oliver," he grinned, walking back over to the bar.

"You are such a cad. I knew you were no good when Felicia first brought you to my home. I should've thrown you out the door then," she shook her head.

"Now, now, Aunt Rhonda. You had no power to do such a thing. Felicia would never have allowed it. You loved her so much that you were just too afraid to disappoint her. Throwing me out would've alienated our dear Felicia, and you weren't about to do that, were you?" he picked up his shot glass, still filled with fresh scotch.

"You think you're so smart, don't you? I hated you then and I should've thrown you out. It was my mistake not to act on my feelings, but what you're doing now will bring you down soon enough," she deliberately walked to the front door and turned towards the two officers.

"Give us a call when your wife returns, Mr. Patrick. This case isn't closed," Officer Gamble looked directly at him.

"Of course it isn't, Officers. Thanks for stopping by," he raised his glass and smiled.

"Here is my information. Check it out?" Gracie gave the slip of paper to Officer Tillman.

"If you have a house of your own, why are you here?" Officer Gamble frowned, slightly tilting his head in Gracie's general direction.

"My home is being painted. My superintendent's number is on the paper as well. Call him," she cleared her throat and walked toward Dennis.

"Come on, Ms. Oliver. There is nothing more to do here," Officer Gamble exited the house looking at Rhonda.

"I won't let this go, Dennis. Felicia will be found," she glanced back and grunted loudly.

"Have a good day folks," Officer Tillman left and closed the door behind him.

"That old lady is going to be a problem," he threw the glass up against a nearby wall.

"You handled everything well. The cops were thoroughly convinced. You even convinced me that you had nothing to do with her disappearance," Gracie smiled.

"What are you saying?" he frowned and grabbed her arm, firmly.

"I was just congratulating you on getting out of going to jail today," she grinned, pulling away from his vice grip.

"I didn't kill my wife, Gracie. At least not yet anyway," he grumbled and made a fist.

CHAPTER THREE

Diane felt very guilty about not taking any of her father's telephone calls. She felt so sorry that she had hurt him so badly. One day she just went to her room and cried for over twenty minutes. By the time her mother and Jonathan arrived home, the frustration was gone. The guilt had subsided. The pain was a little less. Jessica didn't even want Sean's name mention in her home and definitely not in her presence. What would make this woman hate a good man like Sean so much? Especially since it was her actions that led to the divorce proceedings and the severely broken relations with her other child, Raymond.

"There were some more messages left on the machine by that man," Jonathan entered the kitchen and grunted.

"Did you erase them?" Jessica pulled the seasoned chicken breasts from the refrigerator.

"As usual, I did. Hey, Beatrice is remarrying. We've got to discuss what's going to happen to my children."

"Why can't they stay with her and Robert?"

"She doesn't want to be bothered with them anymore. I simply can't see how a mother could just turn her back on her own children like that. For a man no less. They want to come and live here with us. We do have the two spare bedrooms," he nodded.

"I don't have a problem with it, Jonathan. Our door is always open for your children. You know that," she walked towards him and they kissed.

"You are so good to me. How in the world did I make it all of this time without you in my life?" he smiled.

"I don't know, but you won't be without me ever again, baby," they kissed again.

Felicia was now in resting mode. She had stashed her money wisely and knew how to budget and spend thriftily. She rented a room under the name of Joanna Cole. But things were getting hot. One of Dennis' henchmen was right on her trail and he wasn't letting up. Actually he was the best of the group. This was the same man she had hired to spy on Dennis for her. But Dennis didn't know this.

"What do you want me to do about that, Tara?" Felicia moaned.

"I want to go home. I want to see daddy," her face bald-up and little tears streamed down her swollen cheeks.

"You know we can't go back to that house. Things aren't good there."

"What about Aunt Rhonda? Can we see her?" she sobbed.

"Aunt Rhonda is very busy right now. Maybe one day we'll get the chance to call her," Felicia knelt down and smiled with teary-eyes.

"Mommy, why are you crying?" Tara reached over and wiped her face with the back of her little left hand.

"Because this isn't the life I wanted for you or myself. But I promise you that things will get better. I promise that you will make new friends and have a brand new school with good teachers. You will have everything you deserve. I promise," she hugged her.

"I love you, Mommy."

"I love you, too, baby."

Investigator Charmers was literally on her heels. He had visited many of the restaurants Felicia and Tara had been in earlier. He spoke to everyone in every establishment. But then he came across the famous eatery where the waitress had commented on the ribbons and bows in Tara's hair. He spoke to everyone in that particular restaurant except the woman who actually waited on them. She happened to be off from work that day. But this didn't deter the eager investigator. He was going to track her down, too. Nothing was going to stop him from finding Felicia and turning her in to Dennis for the finder's fee and bonus.

"I know that waitress is off today. Your manager just told me," Investigator Charmers sat at the end of the semi-vacant counter and cuped his right hand against his mouth slightly.

"Yeah. She'll be in tomorrow. Come back then," Leala swallowed hard.

"I can't come back tomorrow. I'll be in another town by then. Give me her address," he pulled out a $100.00 bill and slid it towards her.

"I can't possibly tell you where she lives. You could be a serial killer," Leala frowned, with one eye on the money.

"All right. Why don't I pull out another $100.00 dollars. I'll give you $200.00 if you tell me her address," he whispered.

"She's a good friend of mine. I couldn't possibly do that, sir," Leala's throat became dry and her palms were becoming wet.

"All right. I'll add another $200.00 dollars to this. I really need that address," he sighed.

"I can't," her left leg started trembling and shaking.

"Thank you for your time," he stood and placed his hand over all of the one hundred dollars bills lying on top of the counter.

"Some things aren't worth selling, sir," her left leg shook one final time before she finally walked away.

Noah had heard of the secret dinner party his sister had thrown, and he also found out that his wayward father and Gail were there too. He hurried to her home to confront her over this travesty in his mind against their beloved mother.

"Noah, it's no big deal. It was a simple get together. Why are you acting like the two of them were here to get married?" Stephanie shook her head.

"How can you joke about this that way? You invited Father and his mistress to your house for a dinner party. Am I the only one in the room that sees something wrong with that picture?" he clenched his teeth as his eyebrows dug deeply into his forehead.

"You're getting way too worked up over this, baby brother. Father was here with Gail. Yes. Marlon and I allowed it because Father asked me to do it for Gail," she sighed.

"He asked you to throw a dinner party, here, for Gail. Why did you do it? You should've told him no," he huffed, making two fists.

"Stop it, Noah! You're acting too strangely now. This isn't funny," she sat down.

"I'm acting strangely. Stephanie. You threw a dinner party for Father's mistress. How can you say I'm acting strangely?"

"Father asked me to give the party and I did. Hey, this is my home. I can do what I want in my home. Why don't you find yourself a wife and then you can tell her what she can and can not do in your home. That's what I want, Noah!" Stephanie grunted, rolling her eyes at him.

"My love life is not the discussion here. You turned your back on Mother. How could you?" he shook his head with contorted features in his face.

"Don't look at me like that. I didn't do anything wrongly here. Father asked me to do something for him. I did it. Why can't you just accept that our parents' marriage just may be over. There is no neat little box you can wrap everything up in, little brother. Father is happy. Have you actually seen him lately? He's smiling and laughing. How many times has he smiled or laughed when he was with Mother? You can count it on your fingers. He's really happy with Gail. She brings something out in him. I can't explain it, Noah, but it's special. I hope you find a love like that someday," she nodded and exhaled.

"You truly disgust me, Stephanie. I don't know quite what to say after hearing that crap. But I do know what I didn't hear from you, and I guess that, alone, was more telling than anything else. It was your natural concern for the welfare of our poor mother, whose at home right now crying her red eyes out over what Father has done to this family. That's what I didn't hear from you, big sister," he turned and headed for the front door.

"Noah," she called out and stood.

"There is nothing more to say. You've taken your side and I've taken mine," he turned and nodded.

"You have to grow up, little brother. Relationships are not perfect and neither are the people in them," Stephanie sighed.

"Yes. But no one, here, is looking for perfection, big sister, just loyalty," he stormed out, slamming the door behind himself.

Myrna Crane was beside herself with grief. It would appear Harrison was still bent on being with Gail, and there was nothing she could do that would change his mind. It's like this mysterious woman had some kind of spell over him. He wouldn't even entertain the idea of returning to Myrna. The mere thought of them being together in a sexual way sent Myrna insane. She couldn't eat or sleep. Her days and nights ran together. Breaking expensive objects Harrison had bought for her was a hollow victory. Why would he just walk out on the family and leave her to pick up all of the broken pieces? This wasn't fair. What about the enormous sacrifices she had made as a devoted wife and caring mother? All of the missed opportunities to fulfill dreams and wants she craved over the countless years. This entire situation made her absolutely sick. Before long, Myrna found herself driving down the street. How did I get here? I was just in my living room pacing the floor and throwing things. What's happening here? She just kept driving, but it was like she wasn't driving. The car seemed to move all by itself. Making sharp left and right turns on queue. Stopping at red lights and moving quickly through green lights. Nothing out of the ordinary. She was the passenger, sitting back watching her body take control and drive this massive black, detailed town car. Where was her body taking her? She was trapped within her own mind looking out onto the rest of the world. The air was cold, crisp and bitter. The streets were busy at some points and desolate at others. Vacant. Still. Quiet.

The car never hesitated. It kept moving forward. But where was it going? Myrna had no idea where this car was taking her. Suddenly it stopped and the engine went absolutely silent. Looking around, the neighborhood was familiar. Myrna had been here before.

She had followed Gail to this very apartment. It was Gail's home. But why was she here? Why did the car bring her here? What was the reason? There were just so many questions. Myrna leaned over the front seat passenger side and looked up through the window at the third floor of the apartment building. She could see that the lights on the far side were on. But was Harrison Crane inside of this place willingly giving apart of himself to her. That terrible woman who stole her husband. That woman who has just moved in and taken Myrna's place. That woman who had no rights to anything within the Crane family. Yes. That's the woman who lived here and was possibly getting the thick, nine and a half inches of Harrison's manhood that belonged strictly to Myrna. This whore, this slut, this woman lived here in this building on this day in this part of town. A seedy part of town at that. Myrna remembers this part of town. She grew up in a part of town like this. This place brought back horrible memories for her. It would seem appropriate that Gail would live here. Everything that hurts Myrna lives or lived here years ago. Maybe not this particular place but a place just like it. Why was Myrna here? Why?

"I bet she's in there with him," she sobbed, bellowing out huge moans and grunts while throwing her head across the steering wheel.

There was no consoling her. She leaned over once more, with a face filled with tears, to look up at those lights. Those infamous, white lights, which signaled that the whore was at home and she was probably with Harrison. Myrna got out of the car immediately. She deliberately got out of the car and grabbed her purse. What am I doing here? Why did this car bring me here? You were wrong car. You were wrong to bring me here. I don't belong here. There's too much pain and sorrow here. Why did you bring me here, car? She wanted to get back in, but her legs and feet wanted to move on to the apartment door's main entrance. "No. No. I have to leave. I have to leave." Her feet and legs wouldn't obey. They kept moving towards the front door of the apartment building. Please stop. Please stop. She wanted her legs and feet to just listen and obey, but they didn't. They kept moving and advancing even faster towards that front entrance door. She couldn't stop it. It just happened. The glass door revealed everything that was in the small, cold lobby area. But the door was locked. There was no way to get inside without buzzing an apartment. This was what she needed. I can leave now! I can leave now because I can't get in. I have to leave this awful place. I must leave. But as soon as she had convinced herself to leave, a kind woman was exiting her apartment and coming down the stairs.

"Oh, God, please give me the strength to leave," Myrna whispered to herself.

Of course she didn't leave. Reaching out, she grabbed the handle of the door as the woman exited the building and walked right past her. She now had complete access.

Sean loved his wife, still, and would do whatever it was that she wanted. Whenever Jessica called with demands about what Diane needed, he would go out of his way to get it. He took a new job with a rival company to Jonathan's. He reported to work on time and worked his way up from Asst. Marketing Manager to Marketing Manager in a relatively short period of time. His work was masterful. He and his team turned out products that made their competition sweat bullets. Jonathan was feeling the heat. His bosses were leaning on him as to why he allowed Sean to slip through his hands. They charged him with getting Sean back. His job depended on it.

"What are you doing here?" Raymond opened the front door and saw Jonathan standing there wide-eyed and pale.

"Is your dad home, kid?" he sniffed.

"He's in bed."

"I need to speak with him. Will you get him?"

"Get away from my house, you punk!" Raymond slammed the door in his face.

"Who was that?" Sean came running down the stairs.

"It's Jonathan. He wanted you, and I told him to get lost," Raymond smiled, popping his collar and pimping away from the front door.

"Good job, son," Sean yawned and scratched himself before turning to go back to bed.

Soon, there was another knock on the door.

"Dad, I bet it's him again," Raymond sighed, shaking his head.

"Leave it to me this time," Sean came all the way down the stairs and walked to the front door.

"What do you want, Jonathan?!" he snatched the door open and gritted his teeth.

"I just wanted to talk. That's all," he gulped, stumbling backward a few steps.

"Talk about what?! About my wife, and how we're having problems? How I can get my marriage back on track?! Do you have any more of your sage advice while you're screwing Jessica?"

"I guess I deserved that. But this is strictly business. Nothing more. I promise. Can I come in, please?" he looked over Sean's shoulder, rubbing his hands together.

"No, you can't come into my home. What do you want? Talk fast, I'm cold."

"You remember Mrs. Stevenson and Mr. McGregor, right?"

"Yeah, so what?"

"They want you to come back to the firm," he looked straight into Sean's eyes.

"Are you crazy? There's no way I'm going back," Sean bellowed, making a fist.

"They are willing to triple your salary and give you traveling expenses anywhere you need to go on company business."

"Tell them no. I will stay right where I am."

"Sean, man, listen. This is a chance of a lifetime. They will triple your salary. They are giving you travel expenses. Everyone else has to pay for their own travel. That's a good deal," Jonathan rubbed his hands together again.

"I have nothing against Mrs. Stevenson or Mr. McGregor. My problem is with you."

"I know I hurt you, man. I did something that should never have happened. But your coming back is important to everyone. We all want you to return."

"As long as you're there, I will never return. You go back and tell them that. What you did to me Jonathan is beyond horrible. You took something that was extremely sacred to me and you violated it. Our friendship is over indefinitely. I wish you well. Now, get away from my home," Sean closed the door in his face and turned the porch light off.

Felicia wanted to call Aunt Rhonda and speak with her for a few minutes. She knew there was a slight chance Dennis had her phone bugged, but she wanted to hear a comforting voice after all of this time of running and hiding.

"Hi," Felicia broke down in tears, standing in the semi-lit phone booth.

"Oh baby," Rhonda gasped, falling to the kitchen floor and trembling violently.

"Don't pass out on me now. I'm calling from a phone booth. I don't want to use my cell phone," Felicia laughed slightly through the tears and cracking voice.

"Oh baby. Where are you? I'll come right now."

"I can't say. I'm just phoning to tell you that I'm all right. Tara is here. She wants to speak to you. Hold on," she gave the receiver to Tara.

"Hi Aunt Rhonda," she smiled.

"Hello baby. How are you?"

"I'm fine. I'm coloring and making lots of pictures. I made some for you," she coughed.

"You sound sick. Are you catching a cold?"

"Just a little one. Mommy said she would get me some medicine."

"Put your mother back on the phone. It's was good to talk with you."

"You too," she handed the receiver to Felicia.

"What are you doing, girl? Tara is sick. Do you need money or something else?"

"I know she's sick. I'm going straight to a store as soon as we get off the telephone. I have enough money, too. There is so much I need to tell you about Dennis and me, Aunt Rhonda. You were so right all those years ago. I can't speak too much now," she glanced down at a sleepy Tara.

"I understand. Call me when you can. Take care. I love you, baby," Rhonda's face contorted and the tears rushed down her cheeks like a torrent of water on a rainy, cold, windy and miserable day.

Myrna ended up standing in the small, cold foyer of the building of Gail Sheehy Bates. She knew where the apartment was. All she had to do was climb the stairs and knock on the door. How troubling this was? To be standing outside looking in. Trying to clear some mental space in her mind. Why am I here? My legs and feet did this. They brought me here. That car brought me here. I should walk right out of that door now. I should. I should, but I can't. My feet won't let me. They want me to climb those stairs and see this Gail woman. They are taking control of me. My feet have taken over. What am I doing here? She climbed the stairs slowly, gripping the paint chipped, loose railing with every step upwards. The distinct clopping of her seven hundred dollar boot heels against the cold, dirty, stain-filled concrete stairs announced, boldly, that company was arriving. There was no denying that Myrna was going to meet with Gail this night. Her legs and feet kept moving forward. They kept climbing those rugged stairs. Climbing until they reached the top landing. She could smell the odor of food cooking in an oven. Some kind of roasting meat. It could be chicken or roast beef. It enveloped the top floor thoroughly. Maybe there is a private dinner party for the two of them happening inside. Maybe they are dancing to some soft, slow music, as the meat finishes cooking. Maybe they're kissing right now. Who knows what's going on behind the closed door of apartment 302. This woman has usurped her life. This Gail woman has entered and completely taken over.

Jonathan returned home to tell his lover, Jessica, what had happened at work that day. He also told her about visiting Sean.

"You went to ask him to take his old job back," she exhaled, rolling her eyes.

"Yes. If he doesn't take that position back, I'm out of a job," Jonathan fidgeted and paced the floor, lighting up a cigarette and coughing a few times.

"You're a fool. Did you actually believe he would take that job to save yours? I knew you were stupid but not this stupid," Jessica shook her head and sat, crossing her paper-thin legs at the ankles.

"What am I going to do now, baby? We can't afford this big house if I lose my job at the firm," he gulped, turning as white as a brand new sheet from the clothes line after it's been bleached and dried in the pure sunlight.

"Your parents have money, don't they? We can borrow some of that from them until you get back on your feet, right?"

"My parents aren't well-off anymore. They lost most of their money in the Enron scandals. Between my dad's gambling and my mom's shopping, they have nothing left practically. We can't depend on them for help."

"So, what are we suppose to do until you find another good paying job? I'm not moving into some shack in the seedy part of town either," Jessica bellowed, jumping to her feet.

"We can make things work using your paychecks, and the saved money you have tucked away in that bank account," he grinned.

"Are you crazy, Jonathan? Do you honestly believe that I'm going to use my savings on you? Get a clue. I'm out of here," she pushed past him and headed for the stairs.

"You can't just walk out on me like this. I've been there for you," he frowned.

"Yes. But you had money then. You had a good paying job. Now, you're just broke. I will not go down with you, my dear," she walks up the first few stairs, stops and turns.

"I'll convince them to let me keep my job, and when they do, you're no longer welcomed here. Sean was right. You are a backstabber," he huffed, watching her turn around slowly.

"They won't give you your job back, idiot. You know that as well as I do. They all blame you for allowing Sean to get away in the first place. Your job will be Sean's, if he wants it. We both know that, now don't we?" she shook her head again and continued up the stairs towards the master bedroom to pack and vacate the premises.

Myrna stands outside of Gail's apartment twitching and fidgeting, mumbling the entire time. This is so crazy. What am I even doing here? This no good woman doesn't deserve my presence today. I will leave this awful place. Yes. I will leave. She started to turn, but her legs and feet wouldn't move. They stayed planted right there in front of Gail's door. Like concrete slabs, they couldn't even spare an inch in movement. Myrna tried to move her body, but there was no use. She then raised her left hand and clamly knocked on the door three times. After that, she lowered her hand and exhaled quietly. Three quick hits. Not very loud hits but distinguishable. Gail grabbed the knob and flung the door open in a hurry. There she was. There she was, finally. This woman who had stolen Harrison away. Here she stands in all of her false glory. There is nothing special about her. She has hair and teeth just like me. She wears dresses just like me. She's about as tall as I am. What's so special that Harrison would leave me for her? I can't figure this out, but there she stands. There, the home wrecker stands. The smell of roasting meat isn't coming from this apartment. She wouldn't be able to cook anything. All she's good at is sleeping with my husband. This woman stands here before me looking like a regular person I would see in a store, but in reality, she's a disgusting, old hag, bent on stealing my husband away. There is nothing I have to say to this woman. She stands here looking into my face and frowning. Could it be that she has no idea who I am? Could that possibly be? This can't be the case. I know Harrison has told her about me. I know he has shown her my picture. She must know who I am. She has come into my life and disrupted everything I hold dear, and, yet, she has no idea what I even look like. This is amazing. How could Harrison not tell this harlot that I am his wife? How could he not show this

Jezebel a picture of me and tell her to her face that this is the woman you've replaced in my life? Could my Harrison have been that much of a coward earlier on? Could he have been that much of a snake? Why wouldn't he tell her about me? But here she stands. This woman named Gail Bates.

"Can I help you?" Gail cleared her throat and tilted her head to the right slightly, pulling her silk gown together.

"You have no idea who I am, do you?" Myrna frowned, trembling and shaking her head over and over again.

"I'm sorry, Miss. Should I know you? Are you new to the building? How can I assist you?"

"How can you not know who I am. You're sleeping with Harrison," Myrna gasped, clutching her chest and swallowing repeatedly.

"You can't be the wife, are you?" Gails eye's opened wide and the blood drained completely from her face.

"I am Myrna Elizabeth Crane. You have been sleeping with my husband, Harrison."

"I see. Would you like to come in?" Gail reluctantly stood to the side.

"Yes, considering the circustances," Myrna entered slowly, looking around.

"You're extremely hurt, and I do understand that. Would you like a cup of decaf coffee? I away have a small cup before turning in," Gail closed the cheap, hollow door, rubbing her hands together anxiously.

"Ms. Bates, you can't begin to know what I feel. What you've done is unimaginable."

"You can't just blame me for this, Mrs. Crane. Your husband is a willing participant as well. He was lacking something at home that apparently drove him into my arms," she gulped, moving stealthily away from the front door and towards the kitchen.

"How dare you say that to me! You have no right. My relationship with Harrison is our business. You intruder!" Myrna's eyes followed her closely as she growled.

"I can sympathize, Mrs. Crane, but there is nothing I can do to help you?"

"There is something you can do, Ms. Bates. I want you to leave Harrison alone."

"You want me to give up the best thing I've ever known. I simply can't do that," she shook her head, grinning as she picked up the hot coffee pot and hastily poured one cup.

"Do you love my husband?" Myrna's face suddenly contorted, the tears rolled down.

"I do love Harrison. The relationship we have is very special. I wouldn't ever expect you to understand."

"How can you have a special relationship with my husband? You haven't known him for as long as I have. You weren't the one staying up all hours of the night when he battled various addictions like drug abuse and alcohol dependency. You have no idea what we went through as a couple- as a family. There are things you have absolutely no knowledge of," Myrna exhaled, gripping her purse, hard, and swallowing vigorously in one huge gulp.

"Maybe I was out of line with that response, but you must come to terms with the fact that your husband belongs to me now, because there was a serious problem somewhere within your marriage."

"Again, you don't have the right to speak about my affairs with Harrison like this. Keep personal thoughts to yourself." Myrna, huffing, chest heaving and face still contorted.

"Would you like that cup of coffee now?"

"I am totally disgusted with this entire affair business, Ms. Bates."

"What do you want then? There is no way I'm leaving Harrison. He loves me and I love him. It's a connection between us that you could never understand. I listen to him. I hear him when he speaks. It's not just sex. Some people may believe that, but it's not true. My love for Harrison Philip Crane goes deeper than you may imagine. Please, just allow us to be happy, Mrs. Crane. He'll give you whatever it is you want or need to get over this sad incident. I'll see to it, personally. Just tell me what you want, and I'll make sure it's given to you, willingly, within the divorce proceedings. My heart aches for you to be well too," Gail nodded, placing her hands inside of the pockets of the silk robe she was wearing.

"How do you even have the nerve to stand there and say those things to me? That was a nice speech, Gail, but I wouldn't worry too much about your heart. Apparently, you never had one to begin with," Myrna's chest heaved as she clutched her purse even harder.

"I'm not going to entertain you anymore, Mrs. Crane. I've said what I needed to say and you've done the same. The point has been made to you. Harrison is getting a divorce. He wants to be with me. I want to be with him. It's as simple as that."

"Nothing is ever that simple in matter such as this, Gail Sheehy Bates. This whole life that you've created with my husband is a mirage. It's not real. It will crumble and fail," Myrna finally wiped her face.

"I believe this conversation and visit are over. Will you please leave my home?" Gail pointed to the door.

"I think I would like that cup of decaf coffee now," Myrna sniffed, clearing her throat too.

"What?"

"Yes. You offered me a cup of decaf coffee, didn't you?"

"But you didn't want any of my coffee, Mrs. Crane. That's the impression I got."

"I never said that I didn't want any coffee. Besides, I have more things to discuss."

"There is nothing more to say about this matter. Me and Harrison will be together. You will just have to get over it and go on with the rest of your own life," Gail nods.

"Can I have that cup of coffee now?" Myrna smiled through the free flowing tears.

"Have coffee at your own home, Mrs. Crane," Gail pointed to the door once again.

"You're a terrible hostess, girl. You offer me coffee and then change your mind. What on earth are you doing?" Myrna shook her head and sighed.

"I think you should go now, Mrs. Crane. I'll tell my Harrison that we talked today."

"I don't need you to tell Harrison anything, Gail," she immediately turned her back to her while reaching into the purse and pulling out a kitchen knife, discreetly placing it beside the purse in her hands.

"I think you should leave my home, Mrs. Crane," Gail walked towards Myrna and grabbed her arm, hard.

"You are such a rude woman, Ms. Bates. Hasn't anyone taught you not to grabbed people in this manner?" Myrna immediately pulled away and lifted her head up high.

"Hey lady! I've been very accommodating about all of this, but now I want you out of here," Gail grabbed her arm once again, making a fist with the other hand.

"Fine," Myrna gripped the skinny, piercing knife's handle, hard, and plunged it directly into Gail's gut, twisting and turning it several times, slowly, like maneuvering the knob on a radio or old wind up toy.

"What have you done to me?" Gail whispered raspingly, with wide-eyes and a hanging, bloody tongue, before falling dead to the floor, blood gushing from her mouth and gaping wound.

"That's what happens when you grab people unexpectedly, Ms. Bates. This is such a mess now. I must be going, Gail. It was not a very pleasant visit, however. Good-bye," Myrna smiled, with wide eyes of her very own, and a robotic, blank stare while leaving.

Felicia had to take little Tara to the hospital. The coughing produced blood and she was terrified that something very serious was wrong with her daughter. While at the hospital, she phoned her aunt again.

"Aunt Rhonda," she wiped her face.

"What is it, Felicia? Where are you, girl?!" Rhonda jumped out of bed, scrambling for the light switch.

"I'm at the hospital. Tara became ill. I had to tell the doctors what was happening."

"Where is Dennis? Did they call him?"

"Not that I know of. The police are on the way to speak with me," she sniffed.

"You have got to tell me what's happening, Felicia? I need to know," Rhonda trembled, squeezing the receiver tightly and closing her eyes momentarily.

"I ran from Dennis. He is cheating on me. It's with some woman from work. I don't know who she is," she took her finger and dabbed just under her eyes to catch and wipe away a few of the falling tears.

"I think I met her," Rhonda gulped, exhaling and loosing the mighty grip she had on the receiver.

"What do you mean? How? Where?" Felicia swallowed hard and became perfectly quiet and still.

"I went to your house a few days ago, with the police, and I saw Dennis there with this woman. She says that she is a house guest, but I know you wouldn't allow such a trashy woman to stay in your home."

"I don't care anymore, Aunt Rhonda. Dennis has threatened to kill both me and Tara if I ever took her and ran from him. He is searching for me now. I know he is," she nodded, looking over her shoulder.

"He is. He has private investigators after you day and night, baby. Dennis is a creep. I knew he would be a disaster eventually. Your entire relationship with this ignorant man had catastrophe written all over it."

"You're so right, Aunt Rhonda, but it wasn't like this at first. He was gentle and kind earlier on. I just don't know what happened. What did he do? What did I do? How could I have been a better wife to him? I just don't know what to believe or think. This man has completely turned me around."

"I will come out there and bring you back here to my house. Where are you, baby?"

"In Washington, D.C. I'm at Howard University Hospital."

"In Washington, D.C.! How did you get all the way out there?" Rhonda gasped, grabbing her chest and exhaling quickly.

"I drove. I just got in my car and drove. There is nothing like a good drive to clear the mind. After so many hours of just driving and stopping at local dives to eat, I ended up here."

"You stay put. I'm on my way," Rhonda nodded.

"Dennis will know where I am. I used a credit card to pay for services here," she lowered her head and paused.

"You just stay right there and wait for me. I know where that hospital is."

CHAPTER FOUR

Raymond returned home from school and found his mother had moved back into the house. He was stunned. Diane was in the kitchen cooking and Jessica was on the telephone talking to a friend. He couldn't believe his eyes. Sean was upstairs in the shower. Raymond immediately ran to the bathroom and flung the door wide open.

"Dad!" he pulled the shower curtain back.

"Raymond! What are you doing?" he quickly covered his private parts with the partially lathered Coast soap rag.

"What are Mom and Diane doing here? You let them back into this house. How could you? After everything they did," he huffed, stomping out of the bathroom and straight into his father's bedroom.

"You don't understand, son," he turned off the water and grabbed a robe.

"Why did you let them back in here? They humiliated you," he gasped, staring at his dad, with his hands in the air, palms up.

"Your mother says that she's sorry for everything that happened. Diane apologizes, too. We must forgive and forget."

"She openly slept with your best friend from years ago with no hesitation or feeling for how it would affect you or this family, and you're just going to let that go," his eyebrows digging deeply into his forehead, nose flaring, with squinting eyes, and shrugging his shoulders growling; his back hunched up in the air and his hands in a claw formation.

"Son! I know you're upset, but this is my choice. I've forgiven your mother and sister for walking out on us. This will be a loving family again. She has left Jonathan for good."

"Why did she leave him, Dad? Is it because she doesn't love him anymore or something else?"

"She says that she misses me and you. Diane misses us, too. We can be a family again. I want your mother and sister back here and that's final. You will be obedient to her. She is still your mother," he swallowed partially and nodded, standing totally erect, with his hands extended towards Raymond in the bedroom's doorway.

"I can't believe you're doing this. Letting them back in here is a big mistake. After what they did to us, Dad, you're just going to forgive them and let them come right back into this house to live. Why? This makes no sense at all to me," Raymond became teary-eyed, shaking his head and allowing his body to fall limp, suddenly.

"I know you're hurting very much, son, but things will get better for us. We'll be a family again. Your mother has promised to change her ways and I believe her. Just give them a chance. Can you do that for me, at least?"

"I can't. What you're doing is crazy, and I want nothing to do with it," he pushed past his dad and went straight to his bedroom.

"Where are you going, Raymond?" Sean sighed, following closely behind and reaching out for him.

"I'm going over to Sam's tonight," he threw a few clothes into a plain, white sack and wiped his face with his forearm, sniffing over and over again, shaking his head, with loud grunts from time to time.

"This is insane. You're not going over Sam's house now. You live here," Sean blocked the bedroom doorway and huffed, folding his arms and standing perfectly straight and still.

"Let me out of here, Dad. I'm not staying in this place with you and them," he exhaled quickly, pacing the floor, staring directly into his father's eyes.

"You can't just run from this. We're a family, Raymond. I want to bring all of us together again. We can get over this as a family. Work with me, son, please," Sean sighed, still blocking the doorway with his broad upper body.

"There is no way I'm staying in this house with you or them. Let me out. Let me out!" Raymond stepped into his face.

"Don't scream at me. I'm still your father," Sean raised his right hand to Raymond's face, and pushed him back.

"Don't touch me!" he charged at Sean and hit him square, knocking him backwards and out of the doorway's tight entrance.

"Why are you acting this way, Raymond. I thought you wanted them to come back. This is what you told me you wanted. They're back," Sean bounced back and looked at his son, who was preparing to charge again.

"Let me out of here! This was suppose to be our home. Mom gave up her right to live here. She shouldn't have any say in what happens here, but she does. You allowed her back in," Raymond shook his head over and over again and huffed.

"If you want to leave, I'll let you. Just call when you reach Sam's, all right?" Sean stood to the side and lowered his head.

"I'm not doing anything," he grabbed his white sack, packed to the brim with clothes, and ran out of the room and down the stairs.

"Where are you going, boy?" Jessica stood in front of the door.

"You better get out of my way before I hurt you, lady," he dropped the bag and raised his fists, waving them back and forth in her face.

"If you want to hit me, go ahead. And the moment you do, I'm pressing charges," she stepped into his face and pointed her finger, poking him in his chest very hard.

"What?" he frowned, moving back and breathing heavily.

"So. I poked you a little. What are you going to do about it? Hit me," she grinned, folding her arms and sucking her teeth.

He cocked his right hand back and let it fly. He puched her so hard that she turned totally around in a complete circle twice before dropping to her knees and then the floor. After that, he ran from the house and down the block as fast as his legs would carry him, with the white sack thrown haphazardly across his left shoulder.

A neighbor of Gail's found her body in the apartment and called the police. It wasn't long before the evidence led investigators right back to Myrna, who was found in her own home clinging to the murder weapon and ranting about Harrison and the kids. She was promptly and gingerly taken to police headquarters. Noah and Stephanie were contacted, along with Harrison. Noah showed up first with the family attorney, Mr. Thomas Cobb.

"You didn't say anything, did you?" Mr. Cobb entered the investigation room where Myrna was being held.

"Hello. Are you here for the party. I'm giving my little son, Noah, a birthday party today. He's turning nine," she snickered loudly, covering her mouth slightly.

"Mother. What's wrong with you?" Noah exhaled, taking her hand.

"Hi, sir, are you here for the party, too? I must ask my husband if you can come. Harrison is very particular about how many people are in the house at one time," she sighed, blinking quickly and fidgeting.

"Mother, it's me, Noah."

"My son is named Noah. He's nine years old today. Oh, I almost forgot to get the cake. I must run out and get the cake. We can't have a birthday celebration without a cake. You all wait here. I'll be back soon," she stood.

"Mrs. Crane, you're not going anywhere," a detective frowned, grabbing her arm and forcing her back into the hard, black chair.

"You don't have to man-handle her, Officer. She's very sick. Can't you tell that?" Noah pushed the detectives hand off of his mother and stood in front of him with clinched fists.

"Calm down, Mr. Crane. We don't need you arrested, too," Mr. Cobb grabbed and pulled him away from the detective, shaking his head and grimacing.

"You boys shouldn't fight like this. I'm sure my Harrison will allow everyone to come to the party. But I must get the cake, and pick Noah up from school. What time is it? Oh, my. I'm late. They leave children outside by the curb when parents don't make it on time. My poor baby. I must get to his school," she stood up again, biting at her nails and looking all around trembling and shaking.

"Mother. I picked the cake up before coming here, and little Noah's being pick up by Harrison. Remember, you wanted Harrison to keep him out until everything was ready. The cake is in the car. I'll go out and get it in a minute, all right. I need you to sit down a few minutes more," Noah smiled, helping her down into the chair very slowly.

"You bought the cake already. Good. Oh, bless your heart, young man, but did you know what kind to get? My Noah is very particular about what he eats," she rubbed her hands together and stared into his eyes.

"I know what he likes. You wrote me a note. Just sit still and relax, all right," he nodded, gently taking her hand and smiling.

"Let's cut to the chase, Officers. You know my client isn't going to run. Look at her. Just allow her to post bail so we can get out of here," Mr. Cobb sighed, opening his briefcase.

"That's for a judge to decide, Counselor," Detective Hawkins grinned.

Rhonda eventually made it to Washington, D.C. She had been here before. Strolling on the National Mall so many years earlier at Dr. Martin Luther King Jr.'s famous 'I Have a Dream' speech. She had many fond memories of this beautiful city, tucked away neatly like a thick winter coat in the blazing heat of the summertime. With all of its rich heritage and colorful townspeople, it stands out as one of the world's most visited and cherished. The neighborhoods bustle with activity every single night. From Columbia Heights to Ridge Road, there is nothing but fun and hoopla to go around. The cab dropped her off about a block from the hospital, somewhere on Florida Ave. The police and ambulance were blocking Georgia Ave. There was something going on, and Rhonda was curious.

"What's happening?" she leaned forward and tapped three times on the plexiglas.

" I have no idea, lady. It could be a car accident. We do have those from time to time," he grinned, looking back at her.

"Well, I know where the hospital is. Let me out here. I'll walk the rest of the way," she reached into her purse and pulled out a twenty dollar bill.

"Thanks," he extended his hand.

"Keep the change. It was an eventful ride," she smiled, getting out and slamming the door shut.

The cars were really gridlocked. Whatever the problem was had affected cars in all directions. From Florida, and U St, things were at a total standstill. Rhonda walked up the block towards Georgia Ave. She could see the lights from the ambulance blazing and the police cars all around. She couldn't help but allow her mind wonder to her niece who was inside of Howard waiting to see her and finally go home.

"You can't come this way, Ma'am," an officer stopped her as she walked through the oceans of gawking spectators and near the corners of Georgia Ave and Florida Ave.

"What has happened? I had to walk here from my cab a block away," she frowned, peeping around him slightly.

"There was a multiple shooting a few minutes ago. That's all I know," he raised his right hand and signaled for her to back up.

"How am I suppose to get to the hospital? My niece is waiting on me," she sighed, looking all around and shaking her head.

"There are some back streets that will take you behind this section of street and put you right at the hospital's entrance," he pointed back the way she walked.

"Fine. At least tell me if the person(s) shot is/are all right?"

"I can't disclose that information, Ma'am. I'm going to have to ask you to move back now," he nodded, stepping closer to her.

"All right, all right. No need to get forceful," she turned, walking back the way she came.

Rhonda wasn't sure if Felicia would answer her cell phone, but she called anyway to say that she was trying to get to the hospital.

"Hello," a husky, deep, and slow voice was immediately heard.

"Hi," Rhonda frowned, stopping dead in her tracks.

"Who is this?"

"Who is this?" she gripped her cell phone and swallowed hard, dropping her purse.

"I am Officer Taylor. Who am I speaking with?"

"Rhonda Oliver. I am the aunt of Felicia Patrick," she exhaled, feeling the blood literally drain from her body.

"Where are you, Ms. Oliver?"

"I'm trying to get to Howard Hospital to see my niece. The entire street on Georgia is blocked off," she nodded.

"Go back to the scene if you're not there. I will send an officer out to meet you," he cleared his throat.

"What has happened?! Did Dennis show up?! Where is he?! What has he done?! Where is Felicia?!" she panicked, shaking and screaming into the cell phone.

A police officer did manage to track down where Rhonda was standing. She was unable to move. A horrible feeling enveloped her totally. What had Dennis done? She heard what Felicia told her. Dennis would stop at nothing to find her and Tara to get revenge on them for having the courage to finally leave him. What was she going to find? Where was Felicia? My God. What was happening? Rhonda could hardly walk as the officer helped her move one step at a time. The dreded walk. The dreded walk all of us have had to take. That walk to the conclusion. The finish line. To have your fears finally revealed to you. That person can't really be gone away from here. That person can't really be dead. It's not feasible. It's not right. It's not acceptable. I was just speaking with her. She was just here. Those questions race through your mind. Why did this happen? Where is this person taking me? Why is he taking me to meet the fear I'm dreading? I can't handle this. Why is he leading me to a conclusion I'm not ready for? Why? This police officer is wrong to do this to me. He is dead wrong to be taking me to this conclusion. I don't want to go, but I have no choice. I have to know. I must know what has become of Felicia. My God. What has Dennis done to her? What has he done to their family? This coward of a man. This person who is less than a man. Why didn't I throw him out of my house so many years earlier? Why didn't I say 'no' to Felicia and watch her hurt for a little while. Why didn't I choose to look out for her best interest? It's my fault. This conclusion, this finality, this ending that I'm being forced to see and hear is all my doing. I wouldn't be in Washington, D.C. if I had thrown Dennis out of my house so many years earlier. I would be at home enjoying Felicia and her decent, upstanding husband. This is my doing. I hate myself for the conclusion this officer is taking me to face. My God. What do I do next? Help me.

The two police officers walked up to the front door of Sam Murphy's home and knocked three times. There was no answer at first, but then, a small woman opened the front door.

"Hi, Ma'am. We're looking for a Raymond Henderson. He told his parents that he would be staying here," Officer Phillips flipped through some notes.

"Ms. Murphy. I'm sorry but Raymond isn't here. I haven't seen him all day. Wait a minute. Let me ask my son, Sam. You gentleman may come in," she stood to the side.

"Thank you, Ms. Murphy," they both entered, looking around and rubbing their hands together briskly.

"It's really cold out there, isn't it?" she smiled, walking towards the stairs.

"Yes. Old Man Winter is upon us, again," Officer Bradford grinned, shutting the door.

"Sam! Sam!" she called up the stairs, looking squarely in that direction.

"Yeah, Mom," he answered, running part of the way down.

"The police are here. They're looking for Raymond. Have you seen him today?"

"No. What's happening?" he walked the remainder of the way down the stairs and stood in the living room area, exhaling slowly, with one eye-brow up and the other digging into his forehead.

"We're looking for Raymond, Sam. His dad told us that he was staying here. You haven't seen or heard from him, correct?" Officer Phillips looked into his eyes, rubbing his chin and shifting his head to one side, just a little.

"I haven't seen or heard from Raymond today. Sorry," he shook his head, turning completely around to go back up the spiral staircase.

"If you hear from him, please contact us right away. This is my direct number. I'm Officer Phillips and this is Officer Bradford. We're at the Third District Station," he handed Ms. Murphy a little, paper card, filled to the brim with his personal information.

"We will call if we hear from him. Is everything all right, Officers?" she frowned subtly, walking back towards the front door and opening it slightly.

"That's nothing for you to worry about, Ma'am. But thank you for your time," Officer Bradford smiled, as they both left the house, entering the cold, relentless air, yet again.

"Samuel Timothy Murphy. You're not lying to us, are you? Have you seen Raymond?" his mother immediately shut the door behind the two officers and peered at him, folding her arms and taking quick, sharp breaths.

"No. I haven't seen him. What's going on?" he placed his right foot on the first step, heading back to his secluded bedroom.

"I don't know. I'll call his father and see if there's anything I can do," she walked off into the kitchen and Sam headed back to his bedroom.

The merciful judge had granted Myrna bail, but she was under the direct care of her son. Stephanie decided she wanted nothing to do with her mother after finding out that Gail had been murdered by her. Noah was livid. He just couldn't understand how his only sister would be so cold and unfeeling towards their mother. He hated her for taking the mistresses side in all of this. He also blamed his father for everything happening in the first place. Harrison rushed over to the family home, which Myrna would retain in any divorce proceedings.

"How could she just kill Gail like that? What was she thinking?" Harrison sobbed, looking into Stephanie's eyes.

"Mother was jealous of what you two had. It's that simple," she grunted, shaking her head and rubbing his back gently.

"I can't believe what I'm hearing. Mother is sick. She still thinks we're kids, and at some elementary school waiting to be picked up for a birthday party. Clearly she didn't know what she was doing," Noah hopped to his feet in strong defense of his ailing mom.

"Your mother was simply jealous, just like Stephanie said. She didn't want me to be with Gail. She hated her. What she did was wrong. It was totally senseless. The law will make her pay for it, too," Harrison wiped his face and sniffed.

"You actually want your own wife to go to jail over this. In my business of television, I've seen and heard things that I just couldn't believe, but this, here, today, takes the cake. What mother did was snap. She couldn't take the humiliation and pain. She couldn't take being forgotten and treated like yesterday's newspaper. Father, it was your responsibility to make her feel special. This woman took care of you and this entire family for many, many years, without any complaints. Why didn't you take care of her needs? She was crying out for your love and affections. But where were you? Out with that Gail person, giving all of your time and attention to her. You drove mother to this terrible fate. I don't blame her for killing Gail Sheehy Bates. It was you, Father, that drove her to it," Noah huffed, forming two fists and inching close to him with every deep, penetrating breath.

"You can't blame me for this! I told your mother I would give her anything she wanted in the divorce proceedings," he raised his head up high, grunting.

"Things! Things! She never wanted things. She wanted you, us, the family to be together. Didn't you hear her cries? Didn't you see her pain? Didn't you know what your wife was feeling? Stop making excuses for what you failed or chose not to recognize. This is all your fault. Every bit of it," he growled, huffing and spitting out the words.

"How can you blame our father for this tragedy? It was our mother who took that kitchen knife over to Gail's. It was our mother, who had the perfectly good sense to get into a car and drive, that went over to Gail's and deliberately rammed that same kitchen knife into her gut. She is the guilty person here. Mother is the blame for all of this," Stephanie stood and placed her hands on her hips, rocking from side to side and waving her right index finger occasionally.

"You two are some piece of work. I never knew I could feel nothing but total shame and hatred for members of my own family. This is something I abhor. I think you both should leave while mother continues to rest," Noah went to the door and opened it.

"Gladly," Stephanie took her distraught father by the arm and they both stormed out.

Dennis had in fact known that Felicia and Tara were in Washington, D.C., from one of his excellent, highly paid detectives, who had been monitoring the use of her many credit cards; and like an innocent fluttering moth to a bright, dancing flame, he got to D.C. as fast as modern transportation would allow him. He carried his special gun. You know. That same special gun he promised to use on Felicia, Tara and himself. He carried that same gun to Washington, D.C., determined to carry out his promise. He also knew where Howard University Hospital was. His family had lived in good old Washington, D.C. before moving west. This man was thoroughly familiar with all of the local, traditional landmarks, including that famous hospital. His wife and child were tucked away inside of H.U.H. and nothing was going to prohibit him from carrying out the plan to kill his entire immediate family. But there was a problem. A huge one. He had to get Felicia and Tara out of the hospital and onto the public streets below, so he hired an older woman who agreed to act like her Aunt Rhonda, on the telephone, for a small fee of five thousand dollars. The greedy woman called Felicia's cell phone number and unfortunately, she answered. No one knows why she answered, but she evidently did. What was going through her mind? Didn't she know that it could've been Dennis on the other end? Well, he had to have known where she was anyway, by her using that credit card for Tara's emergency medical treatments. There was no more hiding or running. She would make her stand right here in Washington, D.C.- the nation's capital. It was this great city that would host the final battle of Mr. and Mrs. Dennis Lamont Patrick III. The deceitful, crafty woman, sounding so much like Rhonda, was able to get Felicia to leave the comforts and protection of the hospital and venture out into the parking lot.

Before long, she saw him. She came face to face with him. The man she had married so many years earlier. The man who had promised to love and cherish her above all other women. The man who had told her that he would move mountains, heaven and earth, oceans, the universe, to make her happy. Yes. This was the same man she now saw as her enemy. Her nemises, her killer. There was nothing in his eyes but hatred. She could feel his tention from a mile away. She could feel his anger and bitterness. She could feel his ugliness. She could feel his desperation in wanting to get his hands on her and Tara. She could feel the barrel of his gun, poking directly into her back as he moved her along quietly through the parked cars.

"Why?" she cried out.

"Not too loudly, baby," he grabbed her left arm firmly, looking around.

"Where's Tara?"

"She's having tests done, Dennis. Our daughter is very sick," she exhaled.

"Well, baby. It looks like it's just going to be you and me then," he guided her back to his rented car and placed her in the passenger seat, before slamming the door shut and hurrying around to the driver's side.

"You don't have to kill me. I won't tell anyone," she lowered her head.

"It didn't have to be this way, Felicia. I told you not to leave me, didn't I?" tears formed in his eyes.

"You don't have to kill me or yourself, Dennis. Tara needs us both," she nodded, turning towards him.

"She doesn't need me. I'm nothing compared to you. She doesn't even like me. She's afraid of me," he shook his head, voice cracking and fading in and out.

"That's not true. Who told you that? It's simply not true," she whispered, pausing between breaths.

"This gun will end all of our suffering, Felicia. We won't have this pain or anguish anymore, baby. I'm just sad that Tara can't come with us," he gripped the handle of the gun, which was pointed directly at Felicia.

"Where is your letter, Dennis?" she swallowed, sniffing a few times.

"Letter," he frowned, allowing his grip to loosen a little on the gun's handle.

"You said that you would write a letter to the world before you died explaining why you killed everyone. I would like to read it before you take my life," she cleared her throat.

"I didn't have time to write it. I was too busy trying to find you," he wiped his face with his left hand while the other continued holding the gun on her.

"Do you want me to write it?" she nodded, quivering a little.

"We don't need it. Tara will tell everyone why I did this to us. She will be our legacy to this world. She will be our memorial. She will tell the people how much I loved her and you," he smiled, cocking the gun and swallowing.

"Don't move!" a police officer was seen pointing his gun at the driver side window.

"Put the gun down!" another officer had his gun aimed at the other side of the car.

"What did you do, Felicia? What did you do?!" he pulled the trigger, and it didn't fire.

Felicia immediately opened the car door on her side and jumped out, scurrying away as fast as her legs would carry her.

"Come back here! Come back! Come back! Come back!"

He raised the gun and fired again; this time, it worked. The bullet flew out of its dark, metal chamber and hit a parked car two spaces over. The two officers then opened fired into the rental car, and Dennis Lamont Patrick III was killed instantly. Felicia was finally reunited with her aunt. Rhonda cried and cried upon hearing the story of how the situation unfolded. When asked why she left the hospital in the first place, Felicia answered: " I knew the woman on the other end of that telephone wasn't my Aunt Rhonda. I've known my aunt for many years, and that woman, although she tried, was not very convincing. But I knew that if I didn't confront Dennis here, today, I would be running for the rest of my life. Something had to give. It was going to be him or me, so I called the police to Tara's room after the phone call; and we hatched the plan that I would go out and pull Dennis from the shadows. It worked. He gravitated straight towards me, and the police were able to surround him without his knowing. Now that everything is over, I wish to put Dennis and this entire episode behind me. I have a daughter to raise." But Felicia's troubles weren't over yet. It would seem Dennis planned for every contingency. A few days earlier, he went to see his lawyer about changing his will. He had the will redone, making Gracie Moore, his female houseguest/lover, sole beneficiary upon his death. He was determined to get Felicia one way or the other. Whether in death or in life, he wanted her to pay for leaving him. Felicia tried to fight the new will with the old one, but it was no use. Dennis was judged to be in sound mind when he made the changes and everything, including the townhouse and cars, went to Gracie Moore.

The courts did award Felicia five million dollars in damages, however, for the pain and suffering she endured with Dennis. She decided to use this money as a stepping stone to a better life. After starting a new, successful line of clothing, she ventured out into real estate, hiring a core group of people that was loyal to her, first, and then others. Today, Ms. Felicia Oliver Patrick owns thirty-six high end clothing and shoe stores along the east coast, and she has just started three modeling agencies in Los Angeles and two in sunny Miami. There are future locations set for Orlando, San Diego, New York City and even Washington, D.C. At its height, Dennis's one company was worth about nine million total. After a year or so, Felicia's businesses and real estate holdings combined were worth a whopping one hundred fifty-two million. Oh and, by the way, Aunt Rhonda was labeled the President of Personnel for all locations.

The Lawrence family lived in the suberbs and enjoyed the white picket fence, two children and nice income from the father, as the sole financial provider. Carol Lawrence couldn't help but feel that her husband of eighteen years was cheating on her. From the time Wayne arrived home from his job to the time he went to bed, she hounded him about where he was during the lunch hours, when she just decided to call and check up on him. Carol stayed up at night going through his cell phone numbers and personal papers, trying to find any evidence to satisfy this obsession she was feeling about the unfaithfulness of her husband. Wayne grew tired of the questions and constant explaining that nothing was happening. He found himself turning away from Carol emotionally. This would be a problem if left unchecked. Neither of them realized, at the time, what was happening.

"I called," Carol slumped down in the chair and raised her right fist in the air.

"I was probably at lunch when you phoned. What is all of this about now?" he sighed, lowering his head and placing his face into his hands.

"I just want to know who the woman is you're sleeping with. Just tell me, and I'll stop questioning you," she stood.

"I'm not having an affair, Carol. I love you way too much to step outside of our marriage with anyone. Why can't you just accept that and leave me alone about this issue?"

"I can't believe you're not fooling around on me. We haven't have sex in three weeks. You're getting it from somewhere," she folded her arms and shook her head.

"I love you and only you. There is no one else."

"You used to bring me flowers and candy. That doesn't happen anymore."

"That's because you wear me out with that constant questioning. If I bring home flowers or candy, you'll probably worry me to death about who else I brought candy and flowers for. I'm not going through that battle with you. No way," he exhaled, looking up slightly.

"You don't do any of the things you used to do. I know you're seeing someone else, Wayne. Just tell me who she is and I'll stop asking."

"I'm going out to get some air. I'll be back soon," he grabbed his coat and ran from the house.

Raymond went over to his grandmother's home and Sean showed up there with the police.

"Why did you hit your mother?"

"She wouldn't get out of my way," he huffed, pacing the living room floor.

"Mrs. Henderson wants to press charges. You'll have to come with us, Raymond," Officer Bradford reached for his handcuffs and unlocked them.

"My wife won't press charges if Raymond comes home with me right now," Sean was on his cell phone speaking with Jessica, who was recovering at home in bed.

"What are you going to do, Raymond?" Sean peered at him, holding the cell phone up.

"I'm not going back to that house, ever," he turned around and placed his hands behind his back.

Officer Bradford put the handcuffs on him immediately.

"I can't believe you're allowing your own flesh and blood to be locked-up for striking that tawdry woman. What kind of son did I raise?" Deborah gasped, clutching her chest and falling backwards a little.

"Raymond hit his mother. I've given him the chance to end all of this. You saw the choice he just made," Sean pointed.

"Look at what Jessica has done. She has torn your family apart. You have that woman living in your house again. This is unbelievable. I fought for you, Sean. I am on your side, but this is not right. Raymond is your son. Protect him now. He needs you on his side, not hers," Deborah stepped into his face.

"This is my family, Mom. I want my son to come back home. If he doesn't, he goes to jail to cool off a little. That's the decision we have made."

"Are you insane to be speaking to me about Jessica and a decision you have made with her? I am your mother, and I know what's been happening in this family. Who has been your rock and stability? Who has been you pillor? This boy is your son. He looks up to you. Allowing him to be lock-up is wrong, Sean. Let him stay here with me. There is no harm in that," Deborah extended her hands.

"Take him away," Sean looked at Officer Bradford.

"I have no son," Deborah turned her back on him.

"I want my family back, Mom. I don't care what that takes, but I want everyone back. Things will be the way they were," he placed one arm into his coat.

"Well, I have news for you, child. Things will never be the same again. And regardless of how many times you wish it, Jessica will never again be faithful in that distasteful shame of a marriage. I have seen the real woman she is, and so have you. The sad part, of course, is that you haven't accepted it, and will be doomed to more disappoint in the future. Now, get out of my house," she deliberately walked to the front door and flung it open, wide.

"Good evening, Mrs. Henderson," Officers Bradford and Phillips left with Raymond in handcuffs.

"Good-bye, Mom," Sean left as well.

"Go!" she slammed the door shut after he stepped out.

Myrna Elizabeth Crane pleaded not guilty to first degree murder by reason of insanity. Her lawyers fought for her. Every day of the trial, Harrison and Stephanie, along with her family of course, sat behind the prosecution team. Noah sat behind the defense team. The lawyers, on both sides, battled hard, but in the end, she was found not guilty by reason of insanity and sentenced to three years in a psychiatric institute. Before she was sent away to start serving that three year sentence in the institution, she humbly asked to speak with Harrison, one final time. Surprisingly, he agreed.

"You got away with murder, Myrna. It's as simple as that," he swallowed, refusing to sit anywhere in her presence.

"Why won't you sit down, Harrison? I just wanted to talk," she sat perfectly still.

"You should be going to jail, not some cushy institution up state. How much did Noah have to bribe the judge with? This is crazy," he choked, hard, shaking his head.

"Even now, you hate the sight of me, don't you? Even now you can't stand to be around me," she suddenly crossed her legs at the ankles.

"What you did was horrible. I had to plan Gail's funeral. She had no other family," his eyes became teary, and he moaned.

"Would you plan mine, Harrison? If I killed myself, would you plan my funeral?"

"I wouldn't. I couldn't. I would allow Noah to do it. He would do the best job possible," he wiped his eyes and sniffed.

"How many years did I give to you, Harrison? How many years, total, did I sacrifice to you, as your wife?"

"Don't you dare try to use your years of marriage to me as a justification of what happened to Gail. You murdered her in cold blood and managed to get out of it somehow. It would seem her life meant very little to this judge," he shook his head and one tear rolled down his left cheek.

"You stand there and you cry for that horrible woman, even now. You cry for her, as she lays in that grave rotting and stinking. You cry for her and not your own wife. She never gave you the years of sacrifice I did. How could you?" she huffed, standing and walking towards him.

"Gail understood me, Myrna. She understood the things I wanted for myself and us. She listened to me. She was always there when I needed to talk or laugh or cry. That lady was a good friend as well as lover. Nothing you say right now will ever dampen that feeling of closeness I will always have for her. You may have gotten away with murder, but you will never get me back. I hate you," he snarled, stepping into her face and grunting.

"This is not about you, Harrison. It was all about me. For once, I did something that I felt benefited me," she smiled, lifting her head up high.

"Are you confessing to murder?"

"Gail was dying, Harrison. She had cancer."

"What are you talking about?!"

"It's amazing she never told you," Myrna walked back to her chair, sitting slowly.

"What are you talking about? Gail didn't have cancer. She would've told me something that important."

"I saw the medication in her home while I was there. She was taking lots of pills, and I would assume some kind of radiation treatment."

"You're lying. I would know if she had cancer and was taking drugs. I would know. She would've told me," he frowned, stumbling backwards.

"I saw the pills. I know she was sick."

"You're just saying this to upset me," he gulped, his chest moving up and down quickly.

"Why do you look so worried? She's dead and gone now. You can relax. After all, while I was there, we discussed her cancer treatments. But only briefly."

"You never told any of this to the police. Why didn't you?"

"I didn't want to besmirch the whore's name any further. She was going to leave you anyway, Harrison. One way or the other," she nodded.

"Why should I believe you?"

"I'm the only one who saw her, for the last time, alive."

"Why tell me this now, Myrna? What do you gain by telling me this now?" he lowered his head, finally allowing all of the tears to come rushing down his red, irritated cheeks.

"Do you remember the day we met?" she stared at a blank white wall, with one eyebrow moving towards her blondish-gray curly hairline.

"What does that have to do with anything?" he raised his head, an inch at a time.

"Do you remember the building I was coming out of when we met?" she sat, leaning back and exhaling subtly.

"I don't remember a stupid building, Myrna," he shook his head.

"You should. I was coming out of the Performance Arts Academy. You even commented on it," she chuckled, folding her arms and running her tongue across her top lip slowly.

"Oh, yes. You wanted to become an actress," he paused sharply, eyes wide open, drying his entire face with both hands, grimacing, allowing his jowls to sag, hitting the floor.

"Just think about that as you remember my 'reaction' following Gail's untimely death. I always told you that I could win an academy award if given the chance. Too bad I wasn't nominated. Have a good life, Harrison," she stood, walked over to the door and knocked two times, loudly. An orderly immediately arrived to take her away. Harrison committed suicide three days later. He was found hanging limply from the rafters of his apartment, with a two page letter addressed to Gail sitting nearby.

CHAPTER FIVE

Raymond was released from the police station and went back to his grandmother's house to live. Sean allowed this reluctantly. He told his mother that Raymond could stay there with her but only if he checked in with him on a regular basis and his grades stayed up. Everyone agreed. Jessica wasn't too upset that her son didn't want to live in the same house with her. This allowed more free time at home to mess around, still, behind Sean's back. Diane wasn't a problem for her mother by this point. Although feeling guilty about how she treated her dad in the past, she quickly learned the unsavory ways of her crafty mother and started dating males twice her own age. Sean would come home from work and find a thirty year old man sitting in his living room. Diane always apologized and promised she would never do it anymore, but sure enough, it happened again and again and again and again. Jessica always defended her daughter's right to see boys and told Sean on many occasions that she would leave the house and live elsewhere if he didn't stop being so overly strict on Diane. Sean gave in, as usual, and allowed Diane to date openly. The males could come to the house, but Sean had to meet them all first. That was his rule. Of course, when did Jessica or Diane ever follow any of Sean's many rules? Still determined to bring his family together, Sean never allowed any of this to deter him from trying to get his family back.

"Where's Bruce?" Jessica looked at Diane and folded her arms.

"He came by earlier but dad told him to leave," she rolled her eyes and sucked her teeth, huffing as her father walked by.

"Why did you tell Bruce to leave, Sean? I actually liked him. He had potential," she grinned, licking her lips on the sly.

"He wasn't dressed appropriately. I sent him back home to put on something that represented a decent young man," he nodded, picking up the newspaper.

"You shouldn't have sent him home, Sean. Diane wanted to see him then. You're always doing too much," she sighed, shaking her head and grunting loudly.

"I only did what any father would do. He wasn't dressed correctly, so I told him to leave, change his clothing, and then come back. That's it."

"He better come back, Dad. I like Bruce a lot," Diane placed her hands on her hips and rocked slowly, her cheeks turning beet red.

"Don't worry. He'll be back," Sean sat and opened the paper, grabbing a cigarette from its case on the end table.

Bruce never returned, and both females gave Sean the silent treatment for a solid week.

When Wayne Lawrence finally returned from getting that air he wanted, Carol was sitting in front of the computer again. Wayne noticed that every time they had an argument or disagreement, Carol would run to the computer. He was curious.

"Why are you always on that computer? Who are you talking to?" he walked up behind her and leaned over, his sweet breath caressing the back of her neck.

"Nobody. I'm just in the chat room having fun. Where did you just come from? Seeing your whore," she hit the stop button, powering down the machine and standing.

"There you go again. I am not having an affair, Carol. Why can't you just accept that and move on?" he turned around and headed for the kitchen.

"I didn't cook any dinner. The kids ate hotdogs and I had a small salad. You'll have to make due with what's in a can," she grinned.

"I've been working in that filthy garage all day long. The least you could do is have a hot meal prepared for me. Why not?" he groaned, rubbing his stomach as it growled.

"Tell me what I want to know, and I'll stop nagging you. It's that simple," she huffed, placing her hands on her hips.

"That's it! I'm going out to get some food. I'll be back when I come back," he stomped to the front door, opening it widely.

"Wait, Wayne. Wait, baby!" she followed, grabbing handfuls of her long night dress dragging the carpet.

"What?!" he turned, half way out the door.

"Just tell me her name and all of this ends," she nodded.

"Bye!" he walked out, slamming the door shut behind him.

While Carol and Wayne were clearly hitting a rough patch in their 18 year relationship, Michael and Judith Parker were definitely having their cakes and eating them to. Both spouses were cheating on one another. Their children, ages 10 and 12 were much too young to take a side and fight over who they wanted to live with should a divorce ensue.

Little Henry, 12, loved his mom and dad; he tried to make their lives comfortable by staying out of trouble and not fighting his younger brother, Stanley, age 10, too much. The atmosphere inside the home was very rocky and with both mom and dad finding the beds of strangers more appealing than their own, it was only a matter of time before the emotional pain and anguish of this entire awkward situation truly reared its ugly head.

"Henry has soccer practice tonight. Are you going to pick him up from school and take him?" Judith placed the ice cold juice into his lunchbox, closing the lid immediately.

"I have a meeting late this afternoon. I won't get done until around seven or eight o'clock. You're going to have to pick him up yourself," Michael grunted, pouring hot coffee into a mug and moving quickly towards the toaster.

"I just picked Stanley up from his club meeting yesterday. I was truly inconvenienced. You must pick Henry up and take him to practice tonight. It's only fair," she sighed, shaking her head and tapping on the solid, oak table with one finger.

"I have an important meeting, Judith, and that has to come first today. It's a major account with the firm. Call your mother. Ask her to pick Henry up from school."

"I can't ask my mother," Judith gasped, pushing her coffee cup away and leaning forward.

"Why not? She loves spending time with our kids. Call her. I have to go. Bye," he grabbed his leather briefcase, coffee mug and semi-burnt toast, running from the house.

"I'll pick you up, Henry. You won't be late for practice, I promise," Judith shuffled from the kitchen and up the stairs.

The Grahams were your facade of the American family. There was a husband, wife and two kids. The only thing that wasn't typical about the Graham family was the fact that Tobias, the father, was not only cheating on his loving wife with a mistress he had known since college, but his two children were also on a friendly bases with this woman, too. They would all go different places and do exciting things together, as a "family". Cheryl Hampton was her name. This woman who would think of Lucy, Tobias's wife, as an extension of him. She was more than happy to play the role of second fiddle to Lucy. She saw it as an honor to follow in the footsteps of a woman who could do so many amazing things, according to Tobias. The Graham's relationship had everything a person could ever ask for or want, but selfish Tobias always wanted a little bit more. He wanted what he had before being married to Lucy Eleanor McCain. Cheryl was his number one person to call when he felt horny. Cheryl was his back-up sex whenever a date didn't want to put out, or he just felt like being pleasured all of a sudden. She was always the first one he called. Cheryl also got something from this twisted relationship. She was never, ever pressured into a permanent commitment, and she could be a mother vicariously through his children. She enjoyed the gifts and money Tobias would give to her quite frequently. The two children would even shop for her, secretly, for her birthday! To Cheryl Hampton, all of this spelled out a very good relationship to be in. She had a secure, well-off man that wanted nothing but sex from her, and two loving children who wanted nothing but her free time. That wasn't easy to give up. There was nothing shocking about this insane situation to her. Tobias certainly enjoyed having both Lucy and Cheryl sexually, sometimes on the same night! His kids were another issue.

Tobias introduced the children to Cheryl when they were ages 14 and 16. Clearly, they could make a distinction between right and wrong. They chose not to tell their mother about Cheryl and helped their father to keep the affair with Cheryl a secret even longer.

"Are we going over to Cheryl's tonight for dinner?" Jake looked at his father.

"Not too loudly. Your mother is upstairs. But yeah. Cheryl is making homemade pizza for the football game," he smiled, folding his arms and leaning back on the sink.

"I love her homemade pizza. All of those toppings. Hers is even better than Sam's Pizza," Lori grinned, rubbing her stomach a few times.

"What's better than Sam's Pizza?" Lucy came walking into the kitchen carrying an arm full of clothing.

"Nothing. I have homework," Lori ran off to the downstairs den.

"So do I," Jake followed, glancing at his dad and laughing.

"So. How was your day?" she dropped the clothes in the middle of the floor and reached over to kiss him.

"It was great. I closed two accounts and opened up a third. I believe a raise is in the wind," he hugged her tightly, as they kissed.

"I always knew you could do it. This family is so grateful to have you here taking care of us the way that you do. Thank you, honey," Lucy smiled, looking into his eyes, near tears herself.

"Hey. You're still going out to that book club thing this evening, right?"

"Yes. Do you want to come along?" she reached down and grabbed his butt.

"All right now. You're going to make me take you upstairs," he reached down and grabbed her butt.

"Take me, baby," she growled, falling into his arms even more.

"Oh yes," he squeezed her butt again, solidly, with one hand, and caressed one of her breast with the other.

"I think we better get up to our bedroom and do this thing before the kids become wise to what's happening," she grabbed his left hand, pressed solidly against her behind, as they both raced from the kitchen and up the stairs quietly.

Jessica continued her naughty, naughty ways outside of the home. Sean never saw her cheating on him, so he didn't really bother investigating or jumping to any conclusions about the scornful matter. She was still withholding sex, to a large degree, which he tried earnestly, over and over again, to get her to relinquish. One day, he asked Diane to spend the night out, so he could prepare a special meal, and get to some good, old-fashioned loving with his still wife, Jessica. He prepared the fancy dinner, with all of the trimmings, and decorating the king-sized bed, drenching it in fresh, blood red rose pedals. He even brought the most expensive champagne he could find. The mood had been set. The food, piping hot and the music playing softly in the back ground. He left his home to surprise his wife, by picking her up from work that very day. He would tell her to leave her car at the job and ride back with him to the house. Everything was set. He called her place of employment and was abruptly told that she was getting off in a few minutes. He raced downtown to her office building and sat a few spaces down from the main entrance across the street, waiting for her to emerge and go to her car. Not ten minutes after he arrived, he saw Jonathan Matthews pull up in front of her building and park his car in a handicapped parking space. His car was definitely a step way down from what Sean could remember. Through the grapevine, Sean found out that he was in fact fired for insubordination at the firm. In reality, it was the removal of an arrogant "fool" that let one of the company's best marketing people scurry off to the brutal competition. That alone warranted termination, and he was hit with it, squarely. Just then, as he saw Jessica run from the office building with a newspaper over head, it started to rain. First, a very light drizzle. But then it became harder and harder. Sean saw her jump into Jonathan's car and then he sped away. He immediately gave chase. While making a large U-turn in the middle of the street, he almost cause a major traffic accident. But allowing Jonathan and Jessica to get out of his sight, however, was not an option. He managed to stay one car length behind the two of them. The rain had started pouring, by this time, and it was harder to make out what car belonged to whom. The road was slick and the glare of taillights started to blend together. But before long, he noticed the blue, four door SUV pull into a motel, off the beaten path. A filthy, stinking motel that reeked with the undesirables of the neighborhood all around it. A very long way from what Jessica was used to back at home. Sean watched the two of them running into Room 107. Yes. That distasteful, uncharacteristic room. It would hold the woman he loved for so many years. That room would be the room that drove a stake through the heart of one man, while bringing pleasure to another. That room was there, open, vacant, free, available, trustworthy, how could it be? How could it spread its doors wide open and accept this woman that he loves from the depths of his heart? Why, Room 107?? Why would you allow her inside of you to commit the most sinister sin of them all! To let her come inside of your four walls to commit adultery is not right; it's not holy; it's not helpful; it's not loving. This deceitful man, Jonathan, and this room share a distasteful bond. They both have much to account for. They both have my tear-stained heart on their consciences. But I'm sure Jonathan Matthews has no conscience to speak of. He hasn't even apologized for hurting me so badly the way that he has. But this motel room has opened up, widely, to receive someone that I hold most precious to me. That terrible room, fill with vile and disgust. It has hosted the infidelity of my wife and former best friend. It has allowed sin to be practiced within its pale, white walls.

It has stood silent and said nothing to the adulterers that roll around on the soft bed, between the sheets within it. They lie there kissing and fondling one another, but this room says nothing. It stands quiet, unashamed and undeterred to be resolute in doing absolutely nothing, simply because, it can't. It's just a room. Sean stepped from his idling car. Bewildered and stunned, he crossed the crumbling half-paved street to go to Room 107. The rain beat down on him like a drummer hitting a bongo drum at top speed. The relentlessness of the rain made him cringe, as the cold chill of the evening enveloped everything. He took one lonely, miserable step at a time, inching forward towards that infamous Room 107. The room on the far, far end of the long line of trashy, welcoming motel rooms, which have received many other people just like his wife and Jonathan. This pathetic, useless and complicated space called itself a room. It held my beautiful wife, my other half, my life's partner, and she was with another man. A man with no substance and no feeling. Yes. A man short on everything of importance to humankind. He had my wife of twenty-two years in this God-forsaken room, and they were enjoying the delectable fruits of one another. This was my reality. This was it, right here. It was standing directly in front of me. I could choose to see this situation for what it was, or walk away and pretend that none of this ever happened to me, greeting Jessica, when she returned home, with a hot meal and warm bath. Maybe they're in there talking about leaving one another for good. It could be that Jessica was saying her final good-byes to him. What if I break the door down and charge in expecting one thing and get another? Maybe I'm being a little hasty here in what I'm actually seeing. Sean stepped gingerly to Room 107's door and leaned his head over quietly, pressing his right ear firmly against the discolored, green door. He could hear the distinct moans and groans of a woman being satisfied. This wasn't what he needed to hear tonight. The complete realization that Jessica was really cheating on him with Jonathan again was about to present itself to him, for the first time, in all of its splendid glory. He crept to the window, which extended seven feet across from the front door. The crooked blinds and paper-thin curtains were old and dilapidated. They allowed outsiders to simply look into any one of the rooms with ease. He stood there, unable to move an inch. He just stood there peering inside of this infamous room, completely flabbergasted. There she was. The mother of his two children. This woman he had promised to love and cherish. There she was. This woman he had promised to take care of and put first in his life. There she was. This woman who had shared his bed for many, many years. This woman was on her back, legs wide open, and receiving Jonathan wholeheartedly. There she was allowing her private parts to be violate with another man's excited organ. There she was enjoying the rhythmic flow of Jonathan moving up and down, like a rowboat straddling the waves of the sea. It was horrible, it was terrible, it was horrendous, it was happening right before his eyes. Sean stood there. He simply stood there looking in. They never noticed him of course. But he stood there watching and being filled with the most indescribable pain imaginable. His wife and former best friend enjoying one another's bodies, in perfect harmony. They eventually exploded into each others arms, letting out a huge groan of pure, unadulterated pleasure.

But Sean stood there watching it all. Not much later, he turned and went back to his car. Shuffling along and moving at a snail's pace. The destructive winds and rain were kicking into high gear; he could no longer hold back the pain and emotion of what he had just witnessed. He started to wail. People passing by him on foot and car paid little to no attention to a grown man, with a wet face, in the rain, but the tears flowed; they ran; they poured out in buckets. The sounds of whimpers and groans and trembling, and grief filled him up completely, as he walked across that crumbling, half-paved road. He cried as he opened that car door. He cried as he got back inside of his car and started it up. He cried as he shifted the car into drive mode and took off down the block. This situation was definitely a turning point for Sean, and the final result of this little visit, to an off the beaten path motel and infamous Room 107 by Sean, would play itself out much later at the house.

Michel Parker never had an important meeting to go to, job related, in the afternoon, that would extend into the evening. He simply didn't want to pick his son up from school and take him to soccer practice because this was his afternnon with Monica. This woman, Monica Stevens, was his lover, his mistress, his good time on the side. Michael did everything he could to make her happy. Even though she would treat him like dirt, he would keep coming back for more. The relationship even reached physical abuse. She would hit and punch all the time when she didn't get her way. Eventually, he would give in and she would take whatever it was that she wanted. Michael never had time for his family, but he found time to spend with Monica and her bratty nephews. This was a relationship that was sure to end up on skid row central. Judith, on the other hand, had a male lover that truly loved her. Even though he was married but had no kids, nothing stopped him from providing her with all of the latest jewelry and clothing that she wanted. He was always there to take her to the most expensive restaurants and weekend getaways at posh, exclusive hotels out-of-town of course. William Holton believed in spending time and money on his mistress. The kids were always in the middle. Henry knew that his father stayed away from home a lot but he really didn't know why. One day, he actually witnessed his dad kissing Monica outside of the family home. She was dropping him off after a blissful night of pleasure. Gazing from his bedroom window, he saw his father lean over and give her a quick peck on the lips. Nothing long and tongue-swallowing. Just a simply kiss. He was disturbed about the situation but never said a word to anyone. His mother was far more discreet with hers. She never allowed William to bring her home. She would always drive her car to different places, just in case she had to leave in an emergency. The women are always thinking ahead, it would seem.

"We have to stop here. Henry's practice is almost over," Judith climbed off of William's weakening manhood, after a delightful burst of pleasure.

"That was great, baby," he exhaled, wiping his face and sniffing.

"Next time, we'll find a nice little motel nearby," she quickly put her clothes on and scurried back to her minivan to wait for Henry and his friends.

Carol Lawrence turned back to that computer every chance she got, and drove her husband absolutely crazy with the constant naggings of his infidelity. Little did she know that she was cultivating a special relationship with a certain individual online that would lead to a tragedy that no one would ever recover from.

"What's your name again?" she blushed, typing in the words and leaning back in the black, swivel office-like chair.

"I'm sitting with my left hand down my pants and thinking of you, baby," he typed, grinning from ear to ear and running his tongue across his top front teeth.

"I should stop typing messages to you," she swallowed hard, waiting for his response.

"So why don't you?" he replied, smiling.

"What's your name?" she typed again.

"Hand-in-pants," he said, exhaling slowly.

"Stop being nasty," she laughed.

"I see that you're laughing by your sign at the end of your sentence," he nodded.

"My husband is out again. He left to meet someone. I don't know who she is. I'm seriously thinking about a divorce."

"Your husband is a total fool, Carol. Why would he want to mess with someone else when he has you at home waiting?" he shook his head.

"I agree. I still have my looks, and I can cook my pants off. Any man would be happy to have me," she cleared her throat and folded her arms.

"Where do you live? I'll fly there and take you out to dinner. A nice dinner."

"What? I couldn't have you to do that," she frowned, before biting her bottom lip.

"You can. Just tell me where you live, and I'll come out there. We'll have fun."

"Oh, all right. But I have two children. What about them?"

"What are their names? I'd love to meet them as well. We all can go out together, like a family. I don't mind if you don't."

"I'll have to think about taking the kids with us. But my son is Jason, and my daughter is Susan. Jason's 16 years old, and Susan is 12 years old."

"I want to meet them, too. Where do you live? Stop being coy," he swallowed, leaning forward a bit.

"I'll just type everything in to you on the one-on-one privacy board. When can you come out here?" her bottom lip trembled, as she literally salivated with the thoughts of meeting this mysterious man with the sexy chat fingers.

"I can come out next Friday. I have some time off from my job. How's that?"

"Great. I'll be waiting," she switched to the one-on-one chat room and gave him her address, phone number and places to go for fun in the city.

Wayne returned home from work and for the first time wasn't hit with a torrent of questions about where he had been and who he was with. It was like Carol had found a different hobby now. Instead of dwelling on why she wasn't questioning him, he just kept quiet and enjoyed the moment. And boy did it feel so good. For the first time, he really enjoyed being inside of his own home after work. She had even cooked dinner- his favorite! Not one peep about another woman or anything of the kind uttered from her lips. This was heaven. Of course Wayne had never cheated on his wife, Carol, and he was convinced that she had realized that and decided to be rational, finally. Boy, was he wrong.

Tobias and his kids saw Lucy off to her book club meeting and then prepared themselves for Cheryl's house. They all allowed their mother/spouse to continue doing her regular thing on Moday nights at the book club while they all ran over to Cheryl's for dinner and Monday Night Football on her seventy-five inch television screen. It was amazing how Lucy never suspected a single thing. She never saw the deceitfulness in her own children. She never witnessed the conniving, selfish and greedy nature of her own husband. At this particular book club meeting that evening, the group of five women and four men were discussing a brand new book by a semi-new author called T. J. Gray. It was all about the many different ways families live with infidelity today. This one book showed the group how each family dealt with the horrible situation they found themselves in. Many of the skeptical people, there, simply couldn't believe the situations written about. Some were impossible to imagine. But they were real. The young author truly believed that there was a reality behind every situation people deemed as ficticious and not remotely possible. As Mrs. Lucy McCain Graham, herself, was about to realize and come face-to-face with in a matter of hours.

CHAPTER SIX

Sean drove all the way back home almost by remote control it would seem. Making turns and stopping at red lights. He didn't miss a beat, even though his mind was clearly back at that cheap motel with Jessica and Jonathan. He stumbled from his small car, almost forgetting to take his keys from the ignition. After slamming the door shut, he shuffled up to the front door and opened it. The smell of food warming in the oven greeted him. The soft music from their favorite record was still playing over and over again in rote. He walked into the house and closed the door behind him. He looked around, inside of the foyer area, at all of the warm, soft lighting and decorations he tried to put up to impress Jessica. As a frightened animal would suddenly lash out at a predator, when backed into a corner with no escape, Sean completely lost it for the very first time in his life. He ran into the living room and tore the DVD player from the wall, ending the music, silencing it, cutting it off at its knees. Dead. The recessed lighting was immediately knocked out, as he grabbed the nearest stick and broke out each bulb and socket, with every ounce of force he could muster up. The picture perfect house started to look like it had been viciously burglarized by the very best of criminals. Huffing and puffing, he tore off his expensive coat and scarf, ripping a few buttons in the process, and turned towards the smell of the dinner he had so patiently and lovingly prepared. Storming into the kitchen, he grabbed the handle on the over's door and flung it wide open, almost breaking the hinges on the oven door itself. Taking the mouth-watering roast beef and potatoes out and slamming the entire pot against a nearby wall, created a huge hole and food everywhere. He then picked up the various pots on top of the stove, which held the scrumptious side dishes, and threw them all against another wall. Grabbing the refrigerator door, he opened it wildly and took hold of that one bottle of Champaign, which cost so much, and threw it straight out of the backdoor's huge glass window. The sound of breaking glass could be heard for miles around. He stomped into the dinning room area, where he had carefully arranged all of the plates and expensive silverware. He snatched a handful of the freshly ironed, white, spick and span table cloth up, and ripped it off of the solid oak table with one powerful thrust. The items all hit the floor with one unified and tremendous clashing. After doing all of this, he groaned savagely as he made his way out of the dining room and up the stairs to the cozy, well-decorated bedroom. He took the entire bedspread, holding all of those fine red rose pedals and dragged it downstairs and out into the muddy backyard. With the rain coming down in sheets and the winds blowing at what seemed like top speeds, he dumped the whole thing into the huge garbage can and slammed the lid shut. Totally soaked and exhausted, he stumbled back into the house and upstairs to the bedroom. He grabbed a suitcase from the closet and started to throw all of Jessica's clothing into it. Nothing was folded or treated kindly. It was rammed, with full force, into the suitcase and left to rot for all he cared. He went into the bathroom and grabbed all of her toiletries and other female items. Getting a trash bag from the laundry room, which was on the second floor level, he packed as much of her things as he possibly could. He dragged everything down the staircase to the front door and sat on one step waiting. He sat right there, staring at the front door. He sat there huffing and puffing, hurt, alone, scared, exhausted, humiliated, frustrated, and most of all bewildered.

He never thought that he would see his wife in a compromising position like that in his life. There was no turning back now. Jessica had made a total fool out of him for the very last time. He wanted to keep his family together, but there was no way Jessica was going to change her evil ways and be the woman, the wife, the mother, the best friend she was so many years earlier. His wise mother, Deborah, had been right all along. She saw right through Jessica's machinations and desperately wanted him to see through them as well. But it took a sleazy motel and Room 107 on a stormy, miserable night to finally convince Sean that the relationship couldn't be saved. She had left him long ago.

Thomas and Claudine Felder were the typical upper middle-class power couple of the suburbs. They had some money, status around town, nice house and two great cars, friends coming out of the wazoo and, most of all, they both had lots of extra time on their hands after a hard day's work. They married when in their mid-twenties and claimed to have never look back with regrets. There were no children produced because Claudine was barren. But children weren't what Thomas wanted anyway. He enjoyed being free to worry about only two people in his life, and they were himself and Claudine, to a certain extent. Claudine Felder did want children, however, but because of her unfortunate condition, she put off the nagging thought of not being able to conceive continuously, filling her life, instead, with expensive material "things" and a little extra-curricular activity, with a fellow colleague, whenever hubby wasn't around. Thomas, likewise, did the same. The women he ran around with were immaterial to him. They already knew, up front, that he was only after their sex, and that his bread and butter was always at home waiting on him. The family house on Peacock Dr. had become a traditional rest stop of sorts. Simply a place to sit down and have a cup of coffee and danish in the mornings before work, and some hot microwave dinners at night before bedtime. Occasionally, there would be a home cooked meal Claudine would make, and then she would invite the extended family over to enjoy some of it as well. But all and all, there was no quality time between the two of them. There was no movie night or snuggle night. There was nothing there that would bond these two together for another fourteen years.

""What time will you be home tonight?" Claudine poured some coffee into a cup, opening the newspaper.

"Around eleven. Why?" Thomas walked into the kitchen fixing his tie, looking skyward.

"I have some important shopping to do after work. I won't be home until around ten-thirty or eleven myself. Do you want me to pick something up, or will you have a microwave dinner as usual?" she looked over the rim of her glasses, placing the paper down on the table.

"I'll pick something up, Claudine. Don't worry. Oh, Joshua is coming over tomorrow to pick me up for basketball with some of the other guys from work. I'll be getting up very early in the morning," he cleared his throat, opening the refrigerator and looking inside.

"Really? How early are you leaving out?"

"Around seven or seven-thirty. It's Saturday," he frowned, turning towards her.

"I just thought we could finally go out and pick up your coat tomorrow morning. I told you Monday that I had some free time this Saturday morning to do that," she sighed.

"We can still go out and get that coat. I'll be back by ten or eleven at the latest. We can still go, baby," he grabbed an apple, kissed her on the cheek, and headed out the front door.

"Whatever," she mumbled, shaking her head and sighing just short of a full two seconds.

Sean continued sitting there, on that last step, waiting for Jessica to return home. The house was a complete mess. The sounds of the falling rain and blowing winds penetrated the kitchen area through the open backdoor and broken window. The warm, enveloping smell of savory foods waffling in the air earlier was replaced with the cold, damp smell of a woodsy kind. Broken pieces of glass and plastics littered the polished oak floors from room to room. Nothing matter to Sean. He felt ashamed and abused by his wife. He felt used and abandoned. He felt alone and full of pain.

The moment of truth had arrived for him, and it was standing there, right there, in front of him, so boldly and so conspicuously. Jessica had to go. She had to leave this house. She had to take her things and go, because if she didn't, he'd kill her just as sure as his name was Sean Anthony Henderson. She had to take her wretched, used, unclean, immoral body to someone else for love and attention. She could not crawl back into their sacred bed after what he witnessed this night, at a sleazy motel, in Room 107. She could not come and kiss him on the cheek and claim everything would be fine in the morning. This was a situation that needed to be resolved. It needed closure. It needed to be put to rest once and for all. Sean wanted his family unit back, that's it. He wanted the wife he'd married so many years ago. He wanted the children he bounced on his knees and took to school every single day. He wanted the strong family bond that he had growing up with a wonderful father and loving mother. Yes. That's what he wanted. He didn't want to divorce his wife of twenty-two years. He wanted to love her and take care of her forever. He wanted to be her morning sun and moonlit night. He wanted to be her before and after, always. But, alas, that cannot be. For Jessica has damaged any hope of reconciliation. She has driven the sharp, two-edged sword into any hopes of getting back together as a family. With that one senseless act, she has placed a picture in Sean's mind that will last him the rest of his natural days. She has managed to do something not even the most ardent critic of their marriage could ever do with words. She has allowed herself to be seen actually engaging in the act of infidelity itself. That takes on a special meaning for the abused spouse. To see your mate loving someone else. Giving a part of herself to another man so willingly and so full of vigor, is disgusting. It's vile, it's outrageous, it's indecent.

How I long for the days of the past. The days of coming home to small children and a house filled with love. Back then, there were no signs of unfaithfulness. Back then, the love was strong enough to withstand all of the fiery troubles that hit us. Back then, we could move mountains with one huge push. Working together and moving towards the same goals. Our attitudes were ones of defiance towards a world that didn't want to know us and tried to shape us into something we weren't. That's what we were. Now, that's over. Time has passed us by, and you have changed. You've become some creature from another planet. We no longer see things the same way. Moving in one direction doesn't suit you at all. You rather move in your own direction and leave me out in the cold to wonder alone, aimlessly, alone, thinking about why and how to get you to come back. What has happened to us? My Jessica has damaged everything between us. I sit on this one step waiting. I sit here, waiting, to tell her, finally, that it's over. I will take no more.

The book club meeting let out early, this particular evening, due to an emergency for the conductor. Lucy didn't mind. Dorothy Silver was a very good friend of Lucy's, and they attended the book club meetings together. Since the session ended so abruptly, Dorothy suggested that they have dinner at her place. But she needed to stop by the neighborhood grocery store to pick up a few items first. Lucy agreed, and they took off for the market.

"What did you think about that book this month, Lucy?" Dorothy asked, as they met up in the parking lot, after parking their cars.

"I thought it was all right," she sighed, dropping her keys into the left pocket of her coat.

"Really? I thought it was fascinating. Can you believe those situations actually happen everyday? The things people go through are amazing," Dorothy shook her head, gasping.

"I simply don't believe all of those things happen everyday, Dot. Take the example of the naive woman whose husband and children were seeing the "kind" mistress. Come on, now. Will a woman's children actually turn on her like that? Would the children actually keep a secret of that magnitude from their own loving mother? The mistress going places and doing things with them. The adoring children buying her things for her birthday- even holidays, too. I find that a little hard to swallow in the realm of reality," she grinned, grabbing a nearby shopping cart as they entered the store together.

"I guess you're right. But that particular character did have your name, Lucy McCain. It would seem the author had you in mind when he wrote it. How coincidental is that?" Dorothy joked, laughing as they walked along.

"Don't say that, Dot. I must admit. It did make me cringe at first, but it's only a book, right? I do applaud the author for trying anyway," she nodded, taking some Blue Cheese salad dressing from a shelf, placing it into the cart.

"Hey, Lucy. Isn't that Jake and Lori down there?" Dorothy pointed, whispering and leaning towards her.

"Where?" Lucy turned, sharply focusing in on the area in question.

"Over there. In aisle two," she pointed again, turning her head to the side slightly, frowning a little.

"Yes. That is Jake. The girl doesn't look like Lori. What is Jake doing here? Where's Tobias?" she scratched her head.

"Well, if your family is here, you might as well go on home with them and have dinner," Dorothy nodded.

"I don't see why we can't still have dinner. I assure you that the football game won't be a pressing issue for me at home. By the time I get back, they will all be asleep or on the way. But I should go and see Tobias at least," Lucy started down aisle two.

By this time, Jake and the mystery girl had left the aisle and wondered off somewhere else. Lucy kept looking around, walking throughout the store. She finally found Tobias standing in the frozen foods aisle with a tall, blonde woman, with short hair, rubbing up against him constantly. She was totally dumbfounded. Could this really be her Tobias standing here, in front of her, allowing another woman to rub on him in this way? She then turned her back on the two of them, who were half-way down the aisle giggling while choosing ice-cream, and rubbed her own eyes again and again. Am I losing my mind in this store tonight? Is something wrong with me, God? I didn't just see my own husband, of twelve years, standing in this very aisle with some trashy woman rubbing against him. Did I really see what I thought I saw, God? Maybe I'm sick or something. I have been a little achy lately. I can't be that ill. I know what I just saw. I saw Tobias and some woman standing, there, in this very aisle. Where's my Jake? It had to be Tobias with her, because Jake is here. She suddenly turned back around, and the two of them were long gone. She exhaled and walked down that same aisle and stopped, at the very spot, where she saw the woman groping a more than willing Tobias. Oddly, she could still smell a tiny whiff of Tobias's aftershave. It was faint but noticeable. She could never forget that smell. That beautiful smell that greeted her in the mornings and welcomed her in the evenings, with a kiss. That smell was her husband and no other man. Lucy gingerly walked to the end of that same aisle and surveyed all of the lines leading to the busy cashiers. One long line at a time she examined carefully. And then, suddenly, there they all were. Tobias, the woman, and Jake. The three of them laughing and playing around like normal. The woman actually reached over and kissed Jake on the cheek, rubbing his head and nodding. Tobias placed the items, in their basket, on the conveyer belt and smiled from ear to ear as the two of them continued the playing around. Lucy was at a total lost for words.

There was nothing she could do but stand right there and watch her world come crashing down. She simply stood there, watching, and not making as much as a poop sound. She watched as Tobias paid for the items and packed the things into a plastic bag. The three of them then headed out of the store. The woman's arm around Tobias's waist and Jake leading the crew. Just at that moment, Dorothy approached her.

"I finished the shopping for tonight's dinner. Did you see Jake?" she asked, glancing at her and the cart.

"I just saw Tobias," she eked out the words.

"Lucy, girl. You look like you just saw a ghost. What happened?" Dorothy took her hands.

"Tobias was here with another woman, and that's not the worst of it," she gasped, trying to breathe through the heaviness that sat, squarely, on her chest.

"What?" Dorothy's eyes grew wider, her voice raising a few pitches, her psalms becoming sweaty, and her lips quivering.

"Jake knows that woman. He let her kiss him," she lowered her head.

"You're lying. Oh, my God. It's T.J. Gray's book, Lucy," Dorothy's words faded, as they both started to cry and management ran over to be of assistance.

Sean sat on that bottom step waiting for Jessica to arrive and enter the house. The quiet was deafening, chilling, cold. But soon, stirrings were amiss. The sound of keys grew louder and louder. The footsteps also became more apparent. They stopped right in front of the door.

The jingling was heard as Jessica stuck the bottom lock key into the slot and turned it. The front door opened effortlessly.

"What in God's name happened in this house, Sean?" she entered, looking around, gasping.

"You get your things, Jessica, and go. I want the divorce to go through as planned. This relationship is over," he stood, totally spent from the evening's events.

"What have you done? Look at you? What is all of this about?" she closed the front door and stepped into the chaos all over the polished floors.

"I saw you, tonight, with Jonathan. The very man who not only stabbed me in the back by sleeping with you in the first place, but didn't even have the decency to apologize to me for what he did. I went to your job and followed the two of you out to some sleazy motel and Room 107.

I looked through the window and saw you, on your back, with your legs wide open receiving Jonathan willingly. I saw it all, my dear, so there is no need to deny it."

"I wasn't going to. What started off as a private meeting to tell Jonathan that the affair was definitely over turned into one final romp in the sack. That's what you saw, Sean. I told Jonathan that it was over. I had decided to give us another chance."

"You have the tongue of the angels, my girl. The sweet tongue of a goddess. But I'm done being your fool. I've packed your things. They are by the door. Go back to your lover and allow him to provide for you. I want the divorce, and that's final," he spat at her, frowning his face and shaking his head.

"I deserve to be scorned for what I did. Sleeping with Jonathan was wrong. But we have a bond, Sean. We've been together for many years. You can't be willing to just let all of that go. I still love you, baby," she reached out to him.

"Stay away from me, Jessica. Do you know what I did for us today? Of course you don't. So allow me to tell you. I went out and bought your favorite meal. I cooked it. I bought red rose pedals and put them all over our bed. I bought the most expensive Champaign I could find and chilled it. I had our favorite song playing on the DVD system. All of this I did for us, today, but what I got in return was a picture of you with your legs straight up in the air having sex with one of my former friends. There are no amount of apologies that can cover over this great, hurtful sin. I want the divorce, and you will not get a dime from me. I will hire the best attorneys possible to fight you every step of the way. I'll even file to get full custody of Diane, too."

"You wouldn't dare!" she huffed, making two fists and exhaling slowly.

"Oh yes I would. And that job you're so proud of. That company you work for does its marketing with my firm. I'm sure I can convince your boss to fire you to get some free advertising work kicked his way, on my dime of course. I will see you penniless and out on the streets for what you have done to me and this family. The blinds have finally been lifted. I see you for what you really are," he coughed and staggered a little.

"You won't have the chance to do all of those things, Sean," she reached into her purse and pulled out a small pistol.

"A gun. What are you going to do with that?" he grinned.

"I'm going to shoot you, in the heart, and claim self-defense. The place is a mess anyway. I'll just tell the police that you snapped and attacked me. You found out that I wanted to leave you again, for Jonathan, and you simply attacked me. I really had to defend myself, Officers. He was going to kill me if I didn't shoot him," she lifted the gun towards Sean, smiling the entire time.

"No one will believe it, Jessica," he sniffed and wiped his nose.

"Why not? It's the perfect plan. You've done most of the work for me," she glanced around the room.

"Before you shoot, take a look behind you," he pointed.

"You're not going to fool me with shenanigans. Now, it's time to die, Sean. I should've put you out of your misery a very long time ago. This way, I'll get everything you own and have my hunk, Jonathan, still," she grinned, lowering the gun a little.

"You didn't plan to leave him at all, did you?"

"No. I must admit. I'm addicted to his sex. It's better than ours ever was. He's gentle, and he takes his time with me, making sure that I have my moments of pleasure, first, before he just explodes, turns over, and falls asleep. I enjoy my private time with him. He's all you never were. But, if it's any consolation, I did care for you, however the love was gone years ago. Enough talk. Time to go bye-bye, Sean," she raised the gun again, aiming it directly at his chest.

Knock, Knock, Knock, Knock ....

"Who's that?!" she looked directly at Sean

"The police," he fell to the floor.

"You called the police here. When? How?" her eyes opened wide, jaw dropping.

"I wasn't sure if I could see you tonight without killing you, so I took the precaution of calling the police to facilitate our separation," he looked at the door again.

"Open this door!" an officer pounded, hard.

Jessica quickly put the gun back into her purse and ran to the front door, opening it immediately.

"Oh, gentlemen. I'm so glad you're here. My husband just tried to kill me," she gasped, rubbing her neck.

"Are you all right, Mr. Henderson?" Officer Collins entered with Officer Speck.

"I'm fine. I just want this woman out of my house. Oh, and she has a gun in that purse of hers. I bet it isn't even registered," he was helped to his feet by Officer Collins.

"Do you have an unregistered gun, Mrs. Henderson?" Officer Speck peered at her.

"I do have a gun for protection. It's crazy out here. Us women need protection," she gulped, clutching her purse tightly.

"She turned the gun on me, gentlemen. She said that she was going to shoot me and make it look like I attacked her. She had no idea that I phoned you all, earlier, to be here when she arrived."

"You snake, Sean. You disgusting snake. You'll get yours! You'll get it good!" she huffed, as Officer Collins took out his handcuffs.

"Give me the purse, Mrs. Henderson?" Officer Speck looked into her eyes.

"He's lying," she quickly reached into her purse and pulled the gun out, firing at Sean. Fortunately, she missed, and the bullet hit a nearby wall.

The two officers tackled Jessica, to the floor, arresting her on the spot.

"I hate you, Sean! I hate you! I hope you die! I hope you die! Take your hands off of me! Ahh! Ouch! You're hurting me! Take those things off of me! Take your hands off of me! I hate you, Sean! I hate you!" she yelled, they dragged her out kicking and screaming.

Raymond and his grandmother, Deborah, arrived at the home immediately after being notified of what happened. Sean eventually recovered and repaired his home. He went to court and filed for full custody of Diane and received it. Although he was responsible for her, she kept running away from him and joining gangs of prostitutes. Sean would find himself prowling the streets at night trying to locate his daughter on many occasions. One day, Diane simply disappeared. The police had given up all hope in finding her, but Sean never did. He put up posters of her and ran ads every chance he could, but there was no luck. It was like she dropped off the face of the planet. Raymond went on to graduate from high school and enter college. Whenever he came home on break, he would stay up at night prowling the streets with his dad on the off chance they might catch a glimpse of Diane or see someone who might just know where she was. Jessica became pregnant with Jonathan's baby, and he, of course, claimed no responsibility for it. Jessica did lose her job, at the company, where she worked, and eventually went on welfare. The government found her some cheap housing, which she hated staying in. Jonathan deserted her soon after his child was born. Whenever she applied for child support, he would always use his clever attorneys to block all of her attempts to get money from him. Only when she was truly desperate, did she go to Sean, who also refused to assist her every time. Not being able to support herself or the child, she gave it up for adoption and soon went into a deep depression. Sean never remarried. He eventually opened up his own marketing company. Raymond vowed to work with his dad, and when he finally graduated from college, Sean changed the name of the business to "Henderson and Son". They never looked back.

CHAPTER SEVEN

Henry went to the local park one day and failed to return home. The babysitter, who was at the house taking care of Stanley, became worried and called the police when he didn't come back around seven o'clock. She had allowed him to walk the one and a half blocks all the time to the small, public park to play with the other neighborhood boys. There was no trace of him anywhere. She immediately called his parents, who were busy with their lovers at the time, to come home and speak with the police. Michael dropped Monica off at her house and sped home as fast as his car would carry him, and Judith left William at the restaurant. The two anxious parents didn't miss a beat heading home to find out what had happened to their oldest son. All the way, they each prayed that he had just wondered off and would be found shortly. They each asked God to watch over their child as the cold night's air began to really set in. Michael made it home first.

"What happened, Brenda?" he plowed through the front door, ignoring the police officers.

"Mr. Parker. I waited for Henry to return. You know he goes to that park alone all the time. There was nothing different about today. But around seven, he hadn't been home, and it wasn't like him not to be home before seven o'clock."

"What time does he normally come home after playing at the park?" he took off his coat and gloves.

"I would say around 6:30 p.m. at the latest. I just thought he may have been running late, so I gave him an extra thirty minutes. At around seven, I called the police, and then I called you and Mrs. Parker," she nodded, wiping her eyes.

"You didn't get suspicious when he didn't come home around 6:30 p.m.? Why didn't you call the police then?" he paced the floor, making a fist.

"Mr. Parker, the babysitter simply thought that the child was running late. She wanted to give him a few extra minutes to get here. That's not unusual, sir," Officer White cleared his throat.

"I'm so very sorry, Mr. Parker. If I had it to do all over again, I would call the police immediately. Please forgive me for waiting," she lowered her head.

"What's happening, here? Where's Henry, Brenda?" Judith ran into the house, slamming the door shut behind herself.

"Mrs. Parker. My name is Officer White and this is Officer Betts. We are the first on the scene. Do you have any idea where your son could be? Does he have any friends that live nearby? Does he go to any stores or video arcades in the area?" Officer Betts took out his pad and pencil.

"What's this? The Inquisition. You should be out there trying to find our son," Michael huffed, rolling up his sleeves and gritting his teeth.

"We're doing everything possible, Mr. Parker. Just relax and tell us when you saw Henry last," Officer White folded his arms.

"I've called in a description of your son to headquarters. They will put an A.P.B. out on him. Believe me. There is nothing to worry about," Officer Betts went back to writing in his pad.

Suddenly, Judith's cell phone rang.

"Yes," she answered.

The voice garbled out a few things and then stopped.

"I can't talk now, Betsy," she looked away, hanging up immediately.

"Who's Betsy?" Michael frowned, easing into a chair.

"She's someone I know from aerobics class," she nodded, placing the cell phone on vibrate.

"What happens now," Brenda looked at the two officers.

"We will continue to look for Henry on the streets. You call all of his friends. Make sure he didn't go over to someone's house."

"Is that it?" Michael rolled his eyes, shaking his head.

"That's all we can do for now, sir. We'll find your son, but acting immediately is the sure way to get him back home safe and sound," Officer White exhaled, looking around the room.

The magic day had finally come. Carol Lawrence was all giddy with anticipation over meeting the mystery man. He had promised to show up and take her and the children out for a nice dinner. After all, Carol was thinking about asking Wayne for a divorce. That morning, Susan complained bitterly about having an upset stomach and headache. She allowed her to stay home from school. Jason also wanted to stay home, but his mother flatly objected and sent him on. Wayne got up as usual and, for the first time in years, had a hot breakfast waiting. He couldn't believe it. Carol was in a very good mood, and all of that talk about mistresses had dissipated. This made him even more loving towards her, in wanting to please her. He even regain much of his sexual urges back. But Carol didn't want to waste a roll in the hey with her inept, brutish husband.

She wanted that mysterious man, on the other end of her computer, to come and sweep her off of her feet, taking her away and loving her until the cows came home. This is what she desperately wanted. Wayne went to his job, managing a 15 car service station/garage. With all of the stress and other pressures at work, Carol easing up at home made him ten times more efficient. More work was accomplished, and his supervisors noticed. Bonus talk was in the air, and it was well-deserved. At around 10:20 a.m. that morning, the door bell rang. Carol, caught up in the daily humdrum of a housewife, put down her cleaning items and answered. A tall, light-skinned man with short brown hair and green eyes stood on the welcome mat smiling.

"Can I help you?" she looked at him, frowning.

"Are you Carol Lawrence?" he asked, leaning forward slightly.

"I am. You're not the mystery man from the internet, are you?" she gasped, clutching her chest, cheeks turning bright red, like cherry flavored lollipops.

"I am. Hello," he smiled, blushing himself.

"I wasn't expecting you until much later."

"Well, can I come in or what? It's cold out here," he grinned.

"Oh, yes. Come on in," opening the door wider, she touched up her hair.

"This is a wonderful neighborhood you live in. Very quiet and peaceful," he entered, looking around, rubbing his hands together.

"We've lived here for over ten years. I was right in the middle of cleaning the bathroom. I'm sorry you caught me like this. Please, take your coat off and sit down," she closed the door and scurried up the stairs, into the master bedroom, to change.

"You have a nice home," he nodded, picking up a framed picture from the coffee table.

"Thank you," she replied from the top of the stairs.

"Nice indeed," he whispered, reaching into his coat's very deep pockets, pulling out some rope and duct tape.

With her breath stuck in her throat, and the room spinning across the edges of her eyes, Lucy trembled. Dorothy had taken her from that infamous supermarket to her home to recover from what she saw. She sat on Dorothy's sofa, frozen solid. Could it be that the author of that book peered curiously into Lucy McCain Graham's life and wrote about it?

Could it be that a husband of twelve years would stoop so low as to bed a mistress and actually have his own children as accomplices? This was so outrageous. It couldn't be explained. Nothing like this ever happens in real life. That couldn't be Tobias standing there, in that store, with another woman. He wouldn't do that to me. We have a past. We share a history together. We grew up in the same town and got together right after college. He has always been faithful to me. I've never had a reason to doubt him. He has always given me a reason to love and cherish him. This is a strange feeling for me. I've never been in this place before. Where am I? What has happened to my life? I want the Lucy McCain Graham that left her home this evening, for a simple book club meeting, to come roaring back soon. I want her life. I want her dreams and her aspirations. Where have they scurried off to? Where have they gone? Why am I being left with this shell of an existence? Who is this I find myself being? Who is this woman that has been cheated on for God only knows how long? Who is this person that feels this type of pain and anguish? I don't know her. Why is she here? Where is the real Lucy McCain Graham? I sit here, at a friend's house, afraid to move. Afraid to say a word. Afraid to even blink. Hoping and wishing and praying that my life will be what it was, and I can gladly go back home to what I left a few hours ago. What has happened to me? I sit here, on a friend's sofa, thinking about my life and what I must do. This "thing" has presented itself before me now. This "thing" has come down and chosen to make a basket case, a guinea pig, a trial balloon, a scapegoat out of me. This "thing" has corrupted my family to test my will somehow. How can I fight back? What can I do? Tobias is my world. He is the reason I get up in the mornings. He and my children. My children. My beloved children. My sneaky, deplorable children. My son, Jake, and daughter, Lori. How could they betray me like this? I've done so much for them, and that's what I get in return. Who stayed up with Jake all night long when he contracted the chicken pox? Certainly not Tobias. Lazy, selfish Tobias. I see that now, so clearly. Who ran back and forth to the pharmacy when Lori was terribly ill from the flu bug last year? It wasn't her father, again; it was me. Always me. I performed those tasks, duties, responsibilities, chores, whatever you may call them, because that was my job as their mother. Who makes sure that the bills are paid on time, and dinner is on the table every night? I have done so much, for my entire family over the years, and this is how they all repay me. They bring this woman, this fraud, this substitute into our circle and allow her to take my place. They happily shove me aside, and bring her in to enjoy the best parts of their lives. The fun parts, the agreeable parts, the magnificent parts. I cringe at the thought of them buying her gifts and making sure that she's happy on her birthday and holidays. I remember when they all forgot my birthday. I actually had to remind them. It would seem they didn't forget hers. This mystery woman, this woman of little taste and intelligence. What type of woman would do what she has done? What makes a mistress anyway? She is a pariah, an outcast, a home wrecker, a witch, a whore, a disgusting piece of trash, completely worthy of having her fingernails pulled from her bony, little hands one at a time, extra slowly. This person calls herself a woman. She walks into someone else's life and takes over. She comes in and simply makes herself right at home. She never gives thought to the hurt or pain she has caused. She never cares what happens to the poor wife involved. This woman just plops down, like dung falling from the anus of a well-fed elephant.

Yes. She's the scum of the earth, right along with my Tobias. He's not immune from my heated scorn, hot with anger. He has allowed this young harlot to walk into our lives so freely. He has given her a free pass to be with our children. He has allowed her the chance to operate with no restrictions. Well, maybe one. That she not tell me that she exists. That restriction is one I'm sure she has no problem adhering to. I am going to be sick. What has Tobias done to me, to us, to this family? What has my children done to me, their mother? I saw her kiss Jake. That's my boy, my son, my own flesh and blood. I saw her put her grimy, boney hands all over my boy, and I watched him like it. Her touch was like a soothing bath after a hard day's work. It was like a cold glass of water on a hot day. It was enticing and gracious. There was no shying away or anger, evil eyes or disgust. There wasn't a hint of contempt or even bewilderment. It was simply all right with him. My own child would do this to me. I guess that author was right. Things like this really do happen to people like me.

"Come on to the table, Lucy, and have some dinner," Dorothy pulled the chair out.

"You didn't see it, Dot. There they were, standing there, feeling up on one another. She, having free reign to just grope him right there in the frozen foods aisle. I am so humiliated," Lucy lowered her head.

"This isn't your fault, girl. Tobias has to answer for his actions now. You've seen this. God has revealed this to you. The next move is yours," she sat next to her on the sofa.

"What do you mean?" Lucy turned towards her, sobbing.

"You can do one of two things now, Lucy. This entire situation has presented the chance for you to confront your family, directly, about what you saw and get full explanations. Perhaps, clarifications. The flip side would be that you take this situation and bury it deep down in the crevices of your mind and attempt to forget about what you saw tonight. But I warn you, sincerely, the latter will lead to more hurt and pain later on. I should know, girl. John, my husband of 43 years, cheated on me for eight of those years. I knew he was out running around with someone else, but I chose to turn a blind eye to everything. The coming home all hours of the night, accepting his terrible excuses. I never knew if he thought I believed them all, but he never gave her up. The buying of gifts when it wasn't my birthday or a special day between us. Even on holidays, he would buy things he knew I wouldn't like. All for her, I surmised. When he died three years ago, I found out, in the will, that he had left her half of his estate. He had inherited some property, up in Maine, from his parents the year before. Anyway, since we didn't have any children, he figured he would provide for the both of us- me and the mistress. Of course I fought that every step of the way, but he was deemed of sound mind, when the will was changed, so she got half of everything he inherited. I felt so cheap and violated. It was like he cheated on me one final time from the grave itself. How could he give this tramp our things? She had no rights. But then I thought about his state of mind when the will was changed.

John had always been a kind soul. He wanted everyone to have, or no one would have. That was a part of his personality. That's what I fell in love with so many years ago. So after the initial anger had worn off, and I had the opportunity to just be still with my thoughts and with John's memory, I finally understood. I didn't agree, of course, but I understood why he did it. I still keep his picture by my bedside. I still love him after everything he's done to me. But there are times when I wish I had confronted him about her. What if I had laid my cards down on the table and told him to choose? Me or her? I've always been afraid of the choice he might've made. I know he loved us both, in his own special way, but telling him that I knew about his mistress would've been good for me, too. Do you understand, Lucy?"

"Yes. Thanks Dot," they hugged.

Henry had simply vanished. There was no way of knowing if he was dead or alive. Michael and Judith Parker panicked. They immediately started offering rewards for the safe return of their oldest son. The chief of police established a special task force to try and locate the boy. Michael knew the mayor very well. Henry's case was given top priority by the police department. The little blonde haired, blue-eyed kid was on every television station, across the city, by 9:00 p.m. that night. But, still, no Henry. It didn't matter how much power Michael wielded in city hall, or influence his mother had among the societies' elites, Henry was gone, and that was the reality of the situation. For the first time in a long time, Michael and Judith were actually forced to stay in the same house together pass eight o'clock. Normally, they each would be out, with their perspective lovers, until around midnight or so. Then they would come crawling back home, under the shadow of darkness, to kiss their two children, who were already asleep by this time, goodnight, and then scurry off to a warm bed, just to repeat the sad, pathetic ritual all over again the following day. But this night was very different. The police were in and out of the home constantly. Michael and Judith didn't get a wink of sleep, initially. Concerns

for Henry forced them to turn to one another for support, strength and the determination to hold on and not give up. Little Stanley wasn't neglected either. His father read him a bedtime story for the very first time since he was a wee toddler! For some strange reason, Michael felt it was his duty, his obligation, his responsibility to read his youngest son a bedtime story before he went to sleep that particular night. Judith turned her cell phone off completely. She wanted nothing to do with anyone, and since Henry didn't have her private number anyway, for obvious reasons, she felt very comfortable in turning it off. The two of them were acting out-of-sorts, different, changing, evolving right before everyone's eyes. There were no passing glances of hatred or disgust, but warm glares of hopefulness, for a lost son's return home. Keeping each other strong for Henry's sake was the main goal, the primary target, the priority, and each person seemed to know that somehow, without saying a single word. When Judith would break down, instinctively, Michael would step in with a comforting hug and kiss. When Michael would be near tears, it was Judith that rubbed his back, tenderly, and told him that everything would be all right. As the investigations progressed, they even found time, finally, to catch a catnap in each other's arms.

Things were terrible at the Lawrence household. Carol had been tied up and placed in the basement of the family home. She didn't tell the mysterious stranger that Susan was home also and terribly ill upstairs in bed asleep. The man proceeded to rape and sodomize her several times. Not making a single sound to alert Susan, she kept quiet and endured the terrible pain.

"You hold your tongue as well as I hold my temper," he sat and crossed his boney, hairy legs.

"Please. Let me go. I won't say anything," she moaned, blood dripping everywhere.

"I was married once, Mrs. Lawrence. My treacherous wife was caught cheating on me with the gardener. He came over to my home on Saturdays, Sundays, and even two other days a week. Now, how many times can you really water a lawn? My young, foolish wife must've thought that I was crazy, insane, a nut. She kept allowing this man to come over and help himself to the buffett, and I don't mean weed killers. Of couse I knew, and I made her pay for it, too."

"What did you do?" Carol, looking back over her shoulder, coughed a little.

"I waited until they were all alone, in the wheelhouse, and I stabbed them both. I sent a razor-sharp sickle straight through the both of them, as he laid on top of her, stroking his little brains out. Of couse, by the time she saw me standing over the both of them, it was far too late to move or explain. The plan had been hatched, and the hole was dug."

"I'm not your wife, Mister. Why are you doing this to me?" she cried.

"You are a married woman with a nice house and family. What would make you turn to the internet for sexual gratification elsewhere? What is your husband not doing?"

"I don't know what you're talking about," she moaned.

"Of course you do, Mrs. Lawrence. 'My husband is cheating on me', says you in your many postings to me. You claim that he's having this affair. Do you have any proof?"

"What you're doing here is wrong. Just let me go. I promise. I won't tell anyone. I promise," she struggled against the tight ropes.

"You can't produce any proof, can you, Mrs. Lawrence? I sat in front of my computer at home in Souix Falls and watched how you typed on and on about your husband cheating on you with someone else.

But you could never, once, produce any proof. So, I got to thinking. Maybe she's just looking for an excuse to cheat herself. Maybe this is all a red herring to make your conscience go away. Your husband has been faithful to you, hasn't he? Well, hasn't he? And, be careful not to lie. I can tell," he frowned, peering.

"Yes. I always thought he was cheating. I never had any proof of it," she gulped.

"You always thought he was cheating. What a disgrace. How many days and nights have you driven him absolutely mad with the constant naggings of infidelity that you knew were false from the beginning? I'm sure he's so very tired of it all by now," he stood, clearing his throat.

"What are you going to do?" she sniffed, fresh tears rolling down her cheeks.

"I'm simply not done with you yet, Mrs. Lawrence. There are a couple of spots I haven't had the pleasure of exploring, and I intend to absolutely plunder every single one of them before I leave," he grinned, walking towards her again.

"Please, no more. No more. No more," she sobbed, as he grabbed hold of her.

Claudine loved her husband, Thomas, however she adored her lover as well. Greg wanted to be Claudine's forever. The relationship started innocently enough. She was working on some projects for her boss, the Health and Human Services Secretary of the United States of America, and Gregory Fisher was asked to help her delegate responsibility and oversee the huge workload. The two of them grew very close during that three week period, and they kept in contact afterwards. Knowing she couldn't get pregnant, Claudine didn't ask Greg to use a prophylactic. He assured her that he had very limited contact with females in the past and that he would only use a condom on women he wasn't too sure about. This did little to ease Claudine's troubled mind, but she wanted to be with him regardless. The relationship, in Greg's mind, bloomed. He would take her out for expensive dinners and ballroom dancing every chance he got, and when she was available, of course. He was always cognicent of Thomas, too, and where he was on any given day. Knowing when to call Claudine on her cell phone, and knowing when not to drive by the residence, wave, and then park in that familiar spot, just around the corner from her house. He memorized Thomas's license plate and car, right down to the small scrape he got a few weeks back from someone rear-ending him. Greg did his homework thoroughly, and was rewarded. He was always one step ahead of a jealous husband, although selfish and greedy, very possessive and dangerous when it came to Claudine or anything else he deemed as his.

"He's not here today, right?" Greg, easing up the walkway smiling.

"You're right again. He's at work. I'm just working on some reports. Come on in," Claudine opened the door wider.

"Bingo," he entered grinning, quite proud of his record of successfully clocking Thomas.

Wayne and Jason came strolling through the front door at around 5:00 p.m. that day. Susan was already up and in the kitchen making soup. He asked where Carol was and Susan told him that when she finally got out of bed, her mother was gone. She hadn't seen her all day long. The three of them thought she may have been at the store buying something for Susan or across the street at a neighbor's house. Carol would go next door from time to time to shoot the breeze. As the evening went on, there was no sign of her. Wayne became worried and called all of their friends and family members. No one had seen or spoken to Carol that day. He then called the police. It took them some time to respond, but they finally arrived.

"I don't know where my wife is. I came home, and she was gone," Wayne paced.

"When did you see her last?" Officer Peterson pulled out a tablet and pencil.

"I saw her this morning. She got up and made me a hot breakfast. That's all," he nodded.

"I was here all day, Officer Peterson. I didn't see my mother, though, because I was in bed asleep," Susan coughed.

"You've called all of her friends and relatives," Officer Shelby looked at the group.

"We've called everyone we can think of. She's nowhere to be found," Jason slumped down on the sofa.

"We have to wait at least twenty-four hours before we can declare your wife a missing person. That's the law. Maybe she just went out to get some air. It's no law against that," Officer Peterson cleared his throat.

"My wife would never go out driving for air with Susan here sick. She's more responsible than that. You have to find her. Something's wrong," Wayne shook his head.

"We will do everything possible to help you locate your wife, but we must wait the mandatory twenty-four hours first."

"She could be in a ditch somewhere waiting to be rescued. You've got to send people out now," Wayne huffed.

"Mr. Lawrence, we understand how you may feel, but our hands are tied in this matter. Call us back if you your wife hasn't returned later. We'll come back out," Officer Shelby turned towards the door.

"You have got to be kidding me here. My mom is out there missing and the police is telling us to wait twenty-four hours. Wait until the media hears about this," Susan folded her arms and rocked from side to side, grimacing.

Michael and Judith Parker kept leaning on one another for moral support, in trying to locate their missing son, Henry. Monica, Michael's mistress, fed up with being ignored by Michael, decided to drive by the house and speak to him, outside, in private. She sent a hastily written note, by a rookie police officer, inside of the residence for Michael, but Judith intercepted it casually. It was now time to meet this mystery woman that Michael found so alluring, so magnificent, so wonderful. Judith collected her thoughts, as she watched the police officers walk throughout her home, using cell phones and talking on radios. What would she say to this woman? Judith always knew that Michael was cheating, but with whom? That was always the question. Now, she would get the chance to meet the woman, or one of the women at least. What could be said to this person? Would she even have remorse? Would she even care? There was only one way to find out. Judith took one final breath and headed for the huge front door. With her expensive, black fur coat thrown over her shoulders, she greeted the ice cold air with a raised head. Monica could see her walking from the house, and, instinctively, she wanted to jump back into her car and pull off. But something made her stay right there. Grounded her in that spot. Something made her not run from Judith. Something told her to fight for her man, Michael. Judith calmly walked towards Monica's car and started the conversation.

"You are Monica."

"I am. You must be Judith," she swallowed.

"I am. What is it you want with my husband?"

"I wanted to see him. That's all."

"See him for what purpose?"

"To tell him that I miss him, and that I'm thinking of him in this time of suffering," she nodded.

"You do realize that I'm his wife."

"I know who you are. I spend most of our time together trying to get him to stop comparing me with you. I've always played second fiddle to you, Judith. It's you he's so obsessed with," she huffed, breathing heavily.

"Don't be so melodramatic, dear. You know quite well that my husband wants to be with you. Otherwise, he never would've left our marriage bed."

"So your hands are clean in all of this," Monica frowned.

"No one has clean hands, ever. I've made my share of mistakes."

"You certainly have. I know all about Willaim Holton, Judith, and I intend to tell Michael, too."

"How would you know about William?"

"I love Michael, and I want to marry the man. Give him to me," Monica said, looking her straight in the eyes.

"You want my husband. Ask him to divorce me. See what he says," Judith grinned.

"You already know what the answer to that is. He will never leave you voluntarily, and now that Henry is missing, your filthy grip will become even tighter."

"Does Michael mean that much to you, girl? Does having him make you feel like a real woman? Answer me!"

"Why are you asking me those questions? You have no right."

"I have every right. You want my husband. Are you sure you want my husband, with all of the problems and foibles that entails."

"I know about Michael's weaknesses. You won't scare me into not wanting him."

"The question is not to scare, my dear, but to say that he won't be bothered with you. We have a history, a past. He's had his fun. That's all you were."

"Look at you. All dressed up in your fancy clothing and expensive coat. None of that matters to Michael. He wants me for me."

"He wants you for your body and nothing more. Why is it always the mistress that's the last to know these things? Why is it the mistress that never realizes that these men are not going to disrupt their pretend family lives for them?"

"You are a fool, Judith. Michael will leave you if you give him a legal, clean divorce."

"Michael can leave anytime he gets ready. He knows that. But the question is: why hasn't he?" Judith turned back towards the house.

"You're lying! You keep him dangling on a string. You won't give him a divorce," Monica waved her right fist in the air.

"How ridiculous does that sound? You yourself know all about my relationship with William Holton. Why would I ever stop Michael? You need to come to terms with the fact that he's only using you for your body and wants nothing more," she walked away.

Chapter Eight

It was now time for Lucy to go home and face her family. Unable to drive, Dorothy dropped her off. She told Lucy to call if she needed to leave the house afterwards. Dorothy patiently waited as her good friend got out and walked the miles it seemed up to the actual front door. The porch light was on, so the group had managed to make it back before Lucy did obvious. She stood on the smiling face welcoming mat, staring at the door knob. With her keys in hand, she just stood there. Dorothy started to get out and walk over to her, but decided against it. This was a demon that Lucy had to battle alone. She had to make the decision to place that key into that keyhole and turn it. That was a decision that no one else in the world could've made, so Dorothy sat in her idling car, confident, that Lucy would either go inside, or turn around and come back to the car. She stood there, on that yellow, smiling face welcoming mat, looking at the door knob trying to decide whether to even enter the house that evening. What a turn of events! To go from leaving your home, happily, for a simple book club meeting, to being afraid or even too humiliated to even enter that same house again. What would she find? Of course they're too smart to bring the filthy slut back to the family home. No doubt she's at home cleaning up the kitchen, putting dishes away or loading the dishwasher. Thinking of some immature joke Jake or Lori may have said earlier on and making a slight giggle sound to herself, quietly putting away dishes or sweeping the floor. Straightening up the living room or den after a brisk night of football and dinner, with a little ice-cream on the side. What kind of ice-cream did they finally decide on? What did Tobias want? Clearly, she was a dish on his menu. All of this, as I stand outside of my own home too afraid and embarrassed to enter. What will I find? Who will be inside? Did he manage to bring this sleazy woman back to my home? My home? I have no way of knowing it, but he can't be that stupid. I always thought that he loved me. I always felt that the children loved me, too. It's all been a shame, a lie, a farce, something not even worth mentioning in an afterthought. I hate my life right now. I deplore where I find myself right now, standing on my front porch too afraid and humiliated to enter my very own front door. I hate what Tobias and the children have done to me. But I wasn't suppose to see what I saw tonight. Think about it. Had the conductor of the book club meeting not had an emergency, we would still be sitting there, probably. I would never have been in that supermarket to see them frolicking around in the first place. But as Dorothy said, I was there, and I did see it. The question is: what will I do about it?

"Hi, honey," Tobias stopped directly in front of the door as it swung wide open.

"Hi," Lucy entered, dragging her tired, bruised ego and body along for the ride.

Dorothy immediately drove away, blowing her horn only once.

"Mom, I have a science report due in two days. I really need your help," Lori ran down the stairs, hearing the door open.

"What science report? I told you to tell me about reports in advance, didn't I?" she chided, slamming the door shut and taking off her coat.

"What is wrong with you, Lucy? Tough night at the book club meeting," Tobias frowned, moving towards her slowly with a frown and transfixed eyes.

"I actually had a very good night at the book club meeting. I learned a lot of things about myself and our family, here," she nodded, dropping her coat on the floor.

"Lucy. You just dropped your coat on the floor. Why?" Tobias shook his head, pointing.

"Does it really matter where I dropped the coat, Tobias? Will it stop tomorrow from coming, because I dropped my coat on the freaken floor? I need some air," she walked into the kitchen, sighing loudly.

"What's wrong with Mom?" Lori frowned.

"I don't know, but I aim to find out. You go on upstairs and get ready for bed," he kissed her on the cheek.

"Good luck," she scurried up the stairs.

"Lucy. What is wrong with you?" Tobias entered the kitchen, quietly.

"Where is the mayo? I want to make a sandwich," she exhaled, tapping one finger against the granite countertop.

"It's in the refrigerator," he pointed.

"I've checked already and it's not. Where did you or one of the kids put it?" she finally turned and sighed.

"I'll get it," he frowned, searching the fridge for it.

"It's not in there, is it?"

"No. But I could've sworn it was. We just had sandwiches yesterday," he scratched his head.

"Forget it!" she stomped from the kitchen.

"What is wrong with you, Lucy? Something happened at that book club meeting tonight and I think we should talk about it," he followed closely behind.

"You think we should talk about what happened tonight. Are you sure?" she laughed, covering her mouth slightly.

"What's wrong, Lucy? I'm calling your friend Dorothy. This isn't like you at all. Something happened tonight," he shook his head, walking towards the phone.

"Don't you dare call my friend. I will tell you what happened to me, Tobias," she strolled into the living room, losing the laughter and all other forms of gaiety.

"What?" he gulped, sitting slowly, eyes fixed upon her.

"The conductor of our book club meeting had an emergency tonight and allowed us to leave a little earlier than expected. So, Dorothy had the brilliant idea that we have dinner at her house tonight, but, first, she had to pick up a few items from the supermarket over on Livingston Rd and Mac Namara Ave. Can you happen to guess what I actually saw as I shopped there tonight?" she moved away from him, nearing a window.

"Oh, my God. You saw me and Cheryl, with Jake, didn't you?" he eked out the words, lowering his head, turning pale as the blood drained from his face.

"How could you do this to me, Tobias? I've given you everything. That wasn't enough, was it? Was any of it ever enough? Look at the many sacrifices I've made for you over the years. None of that meant anything, did it? You would bring that skinny harlot into our lives, and then allow our children to even meet and fraternize with her. I saw the slut touching Jake in the take-out line. I saw the three of you leave that store the way we used to leave stores years ago. Her arm draped around your waist. I stood there, motionless, hurt, angry, and scared. I watched you commit adultery. I always told you that there were only two things I would never stand for in this relationship, and the first one was always adultery. I told you, that, years ago, before we were ever married. Why? Why did you do it?!" she lashed out, running towards him and swinging her right fist, striking him across the face.

"I deserve that. I can't say why I did it, exactly. I wanted you and Cheryl."

"Cheryl. Is that the woman you told me you gave up years ago? That same woman I caught you with just before we were married. Don't tell me you've been continuing a relationship with a woman that you told me you gave up years ago? Oh, my God. You have, haven't you? Oh, Tobias. You dirty, rotten dog. This is beyond belief. I caught you with her, years ago, and this is the same woman you've been with ever since then," she gasped, clutching her chest and stumbling backwards, knocking over a few pictures.

"I made a mistake in doing things this way. I apologize for that, Lucy. I messed up big time. I even asked the kids to meet and accept Cheryl as daddy's friend. They both did. I never meant to hurt you, but I was wrong. I should've been straight and told Cheryl years ago that it was over, but the truth is: I was too weak. I wanted you and Cheryl. I wanted you both in my life. I'm sorry for being selfish and greedy, but that's the truth," he gulped, wiping his forehead and blinking incessantly.

"I want you out of my house right now, Tobias Graham. I can't even stand to look at you. The mere sight of you makes me want to vomit. How dare you use me like this for all of these years? You used me for your pleasures and then ran off to Cheryl's to be pleased again. I'm sick. I can't believe what you've done to me, this family, our relationship, our children. I can't even trust my own kids now. They both have betrayed me in the worst possible way. They have allowed someone else to take my place willingly. They have sat quietly while you've messed around and had your fun. I feel abandoned and abused. I feel cheap and sullied. What you have done to me and this family is beyond belief. Your punishment: I can't even begin to say the many ways in which you should pay for causing me this much pain and grief right now. The many years that I have laid down my wants and desires to fulfill family goals and wants. The time spent nurturing you and your career. The days of endless sacrifices for the greater good. You are just a liar. A cheap and pitiful liar. There is no way, on God's green earth, I can ever forgive you for this. I want a divorce, and I want it yesterday. You can take the kids. They seem to be loyal to you anyway. Jake is 18 now. He will do what he pleases. Lori is only 16, same for her, I suppose. My grown children keeping a secret like this from me. How could they? I'm so hurt behind that. My pain and anguish doesn't have limits when it comes to my feelings involving my children's roles in all of this. They assisted you in living this ugly lie. They helped you get away with murder. They were your alibi all the time. How could I ever believe that you would take our children to the mistress's home? Of course I would never believe a thing like that. But there they both were. There they were sitting up in Cheryl's home, enjoying her things. Forgetting about their loyalty to the woman who actually brought them into this world. There they were being cowards. Allowing you to treat me like rubbish," she paused, looking away sharply.

"You're not rubbish, Mom," Jake entered the living room crying.

"We're sorry, Mom," Lori followed.

"Why do you apologize now? Your guilty consciences have compelled you," she turned her back to them all.

"We didn't mean to hurt you, Mom. It just got out of hand, that's all," Jake cried even harder, lowering his head and falling to his knees.

"We're really sorry, Mom. This was wrong; dad was wrong. We all were wrong. Please forgive us," Lori wiped her teary face with the back of her left hand, sniffling.

"Get out of my house, Tobias. Take the children with you. I need some time to think," she turned, facing the distraught group again.

"What are you going to do, Lucy? I don't think it's wise to leave you alone right now," he swallowed hard, glancing at his nodding, remorseful children.

"You're not in a position to tell me what's good for me, are you, Tobias? Go."

The three of them grabbed their coats and left the house. Tobias drove to Cheryl's home. Jake was deeply, deeply affected by his mother's words and rarely opened his mouth on the car ride to Cheryl's. Lori was more optimistic that her mother would come around and forgive them for keeping this terrible secret from her. Tobias suddenly contemplated what a divorce would do to him financially. He was willing to give Lucy whatever she wanted, but he was going to insist on only one thing from her, and that was her total forgiveness for everything. Once they reached Cheryl's, she was waiting, with open arms, to receive and nurture them all. Jake fell into Cheryl's arms totally distraught. He was inconsolable. Tobias tried to get his son to lighten up on himself, but there was no getting through. He was in this other world all alone, trapped by intense guilt and hatred of self for what had happened for two years under his mother's very nose. There were times when he did want to tell his mother about Cheryl. There were times when they would be riding home from grocery shopping or leaving some type of event. He just thought about spilling the beans. Being open and honest with her. But he always hesitated. He always held back for fear of hurting his father and Cheryl. He didn't want to see his parents divorce. Ironically, that's what was going to happen anyway.

Back at the Graham home, Lucy sat on her living room sofa too hurt to even move. She had confronted her family about what she saw and got the response she generally thought they would give. She sat there, motionless, and full of anger. The humiliation was soon replaced by pure rage and a horrible violent tendency to destroy. The woman simply wanted to rip someone's head off and call it a night. There she sat, on the living room sofa, staring at a wall that she had intended to paint just one week later. She gazed at this unfinished, cracked wall and turned her head all kinds of ways trying to figure out the best color for that elongated, protruding spot. For just that brief moment, her mind had left the troubles of Tobias and the children and focused on something as mundane as a painting project she had set out for herself weeks ago. Back then, choosing the perfect color for this particular wall was her biggest challenge. Now, she could really care less about this wall and everything that would go on it. The countless awards and diplomas of grandeur, that would grace its beaming, bright surface. The people's names on them are what really matters, and right now, they don't matter a whole heck-of-a-lot to her. Sad to say. Look at that wall, needing attention and getting none. I guess I'm like that wall, too. Lucy would think. It sits among all the other spaces, within this room, and pretends to be great, an equal. But everyone sees its flaws, its naivety, its troubles, and look on, shaking their heads in disgust. I was going to help it become like all the other spaces in here, but, alas, it's much too late for the both of us now.

Cheryl Hampton decided that it was her turn to talk with Lucy. Her perfect little world was beginning to crumble, and Lucy was the cause. If Tobias and the kids weren't happy, she wouldn't be. So she put on her coat and drove the twenty minutes to the Graham household. She boldly parked right in front of the house. The lights were still on; Lucy hadn't gone to sleep. She had to be inside.

Walking up to the front door was easy for Cheryl. She had made herself at home anyway. Why not go all the way. She rang the doorbell and waited. The cold air hitting at her legs and feet, which weren't protected by boots. She rang the door bell again. This time, she leaned over, peering through the tiny window right next to the front door.

"Where are you, Lucy?" she huffed, ringing the doorbell one last time.

Still, there was no answer. She then proceeded to do something that many would find horrible. She reached into her pocket and pulled out the keys. On her chain, was the top and bottom lock keys for the Graham home. Tobias had given her the keys years ago and told her to only use them in emergencies. Of course this was no emergency, but Cheryl wanted to get in out of the cold and confront Lucy for spoiling a good thing. She casually opened the door and entered.

"Hello," she called out swiftly, closing the door behind herself.

There was not even a hush to be heard in the entire house. Everything was quiet. The lights were the only things blazing, screaming, telling the entire world that activity was still going on within these walls. But even they couldn't yell over the quiet that seemed to grab hold of everything within the home and hold it hostage. Nothing moved. Not even the chimes on the huge grandfather clock rang out. Everything was at a complete stand still. It was almost like a funeral had taken place, just seconds before, or in that movie where yesterday goes away, and there is a period right before tomorrow begins. This is what the scene was like. Yesterday had taken hold of the Graham household and refused to let it go. Cheryl took her time walking throughout the rooms, peering around corners and looking in closets. No one knew what she expected to find, but Lucy was long gone. There was no trace of her to be found anywhere. The master bedroom yielded no clues either. Nothing was out of place. Time was simply standing still, and Cheryl Hampton was seeing it up close and personally. She exited the home as quietly as she crept inside, with duplicate keys and all. Her bosom, still red hot with anger over Lucy's supposedly ill treatment of her own family. Cheryl had wanted to tell Lucy how selfish she thought she was to not want to share Tobias and the kids with her. Cheryl wanted to tell Lucy how she could "redeem" herself in everyone eyes, and come back into their, private family circle. Cheryl wanted to tell Lucy that her actions, alone, were causing great harm to Tobias and her own children. Evidently, Lucy robbed her of this "great" moment. She returned to her home, disgusted, yet, hopeful, in a new life with the Graham family. She told Tobias and the children that Lucy had left the home. She also told them that she had no idea where she had gone.

A few days later, Tobias was able to piece together the events of that night. He was told by a local cab company that a woman, fitting Lucy's description, was picked up from that address on that particular evening. The cab driver remembered her so well because she couldn't stop crying. He even offered her tissues, but she wouldn't take them. The lady just turned towards the window and watched, as the cab pulled away from the house. He then took her to a supermarket, where she got into another car. Her car, which was left there on the night of the incident in question. He didn't see which way she went after he pulled away.

Lucy McCain Graham was never found by her family or friends again. She completely disappeared, intentionally, the police surmised almost immediately. There was no law against wanting to just disappear, and that's exactly what she did. Jake Graham went into a deep depression, afterwards, and eventually had to be committed, by his dad, to a psychiatric institution for the mentally insane. He was forever haunted by the last words he heard his mother say just before leaving that house. Lori Graham did manage to pull herself together, and married a few years later. She would always tell each of her children about a special grandmother that sacrificed everything she had for a bunch of people that weren't grateful or even worth it. As a result of her guilt, she cut off all ties to her father, moved away, and changed her name. Tobias A. Graham ended up with good old reliable Cheryl Hampton. He did divorce Lucy, legally, marrying Cheryl a little later on. They had a son, from that union, and are reported to be living someplace in Florida.

Days passed, and there was no trace of Carol Lawrence. But suddenly this foul odor became noticeable throughout the home. Wayne and the kids would check all of the corners for dead mice or rats. They checked for any kinds of animals that may have crawled somewhere inside of the home and literally decomposed in the most horrific way possible. The stench was so bad that Wayne had resorted to opening windows to get some fresh air, never mind the cold coming in and the heat going out. Fed up with the horrible smell, Wayne took the kids to school one day and decided he was going to find out where this terrible funk was coming from. He tore the living room apart, first, and then he moved on into the dining room. After that, he went into the kitchen. He found absolutely nothing. The smell was becoming completely unbearable day by day, and if he didn't find the source of it soon, he would be forced to move himself and the kids out. He went upstairs to the bedrooms. He went into each room and tore it apart, piece by piece. He found nothing. The lingering smell was still there, hanging above everyone like ripe, juicy grapes on a vine. He went into the bathrooms and found nothing as well. The entire thing took hours. He was sweaty and tired by the time he came flopping down the stairs and fell onto the living room sofa. Then, it hit him. He hadn't checked the basement. To this day, he never understood why he didn't think to check the basement initially. But it may have been understandable why he didn't check the basement. The stairs, leading to it, were tucked way into the nook of the house. If you weren't looking, it would be quite possible to overlook the basement area all together.

As he neared the area, the smell became extremely powerful. Upon reaching the door, he could hardly stand it. He vomited almost immediately. After gasping terribly, he ran from the home, grabbing his cell phone in the process. He called the police once he was out in the cold air of the winter month. My God. What was that smell? He wouldn't dare allow his own mind to wonder on what it could've been. That thought, alone, was truly horrific in itself.

Monica Stevens wanted to speak with Michael right away. After her abrupt conversation with Judith, it was time to find out where he really stood. Judith was willing to give him the divorce. There were no more excuses.

"Why are you calling me at home, Monica? I told you never to call me here," he whispered, closing the door of the den, sitting down behind the large, oak desk.

"I spoke with Judith, Michael. She's willing to give you the divorce. Will you leave her for me?" with batted breath, she held the receiver tightly.

"You spoke to my wife. When?" he leaned forward, eyes wide open and psalms sweating.

"Just today. She is not as pure and clean as you may believe. Judith has someone else in her life. His name is William Holton."

"What?" he gasped, almost dropping the receiver.

"You must know that she has been cheating on you as well, honey. The coming home late nights, just like you. She was getting some on the outside, too," Monica grinned.

"I never want to see you again. Don't ever call my house. If you do, I'll have you arrested for harassment," he slammed the receiver down.

How could she cheat on me? Judith. My Judith. Not my Judith. She wouldn't do that. The mother of my two boys. The woman I fell in love with is cheating on me. I don't believe it. I can't believe it. All of those nights she claimed to be working late on socialite things, coming home late reeking of play. I never suspected a single thing. I never, ever would've thought that Judith would do something like this. I never knew she had it in her. To give a part of herself to someone else. This is amazing to me. What in the world was I thinking not to know. Not to expect. Not to question. Not to pause and follow her. Of course, I was too busy with Monica. Thinking I was getting away with something. The entire time my wife was doing the same thing. I can't believe it. Where is she? If I had a gun, I'd kill her, dead. I'll shoot her right between the eyes and keep on moving, running from place to place to avoid the police. Leaving my kids to live as orphans, without a mom or dad to love them. That's the road I could take. Where is that whore? Where is she? The woman who promised to give her body to me only. Where is the lying whore? Where is she? I wish I had a gun. Oh, how I wish I had a gun right now.

I would put a hole the size of Rhode Island in her head and run, run, run and run some more.

Of course, Monica wasn't going to just go away quietly. She now wanted revenge. The infatuation, turned lust, turned love, and, now, turned revenge was at the last cycle for her. She soon got started on a plan to make Michael pay for stringing her along all of these months.

Claudine hadn't been feeling well lately and decided to go to the doctor's office. After a thorough examination, she was told that she was pregnant. Unable to reconcile with the news, she fainted. After coming to, she noticed that she was in a hospital room, surrounded by family and friends.

"You're up, Mom," her cousin smiled, leaning over her.

"Hi," she blinked several times.

"How are you feeling, Mrs. Felder?" Dr. Grossman entered the room, reading a chart.

"Drained," she whispered.

"Well, you're going to be all right. The baby is fine. As I was explaining to your family members, we can't understand how this happened. For years, your charts always read that you were unable to conceive. It must be a miracle from God."

"Where's Thomas?" she looked around the room.

"He's on the way. It took us some time to get in touch with him. He was out on the road again," her niece touched her hand gently.

"Thank you all for being here," she smiled, nodding slowly.

Greg found out she was in the hospital and wanted to come over and bring flowers. On his way in, he saw Thomas. The two of them actually got on the same elevator together.

"Hi," Greg glanced at Thomas.

"Hi," he looked back at him, frowning.

"I'm here to see my wife," Greg gulped, sweating a little, gripping the flower stems tighter and tighter.

"Good," Thomas shook his head, moving closer to the doors.

"Who are you here to see?"

"A buddy. I don't know you. Stop asking me questions," Thomas grunted, as the doors opened, he stepping off on level 12.

Of course this was the floor Greg wanted, too, but he couldn't get off with Thomas and walk to Claudine's room as well. So he continued to ride the elevator until he believed it was safe enough to get off on floor 12 and hide somewhere, waiting patiently for her family to leave so he could visit her secretly.

CHAPTER NINE

The police and other personnel entered the Lawrence house and went straight to the basement area. With masks on, they were able to finally open up that door and go down into the deep bowels of the home. What they saw made two of the investigators pass out. The mutilated remains of Mrs. Carol Lawrence sat tied up in a chair. Three of her toes were missing and one finger. She had been cut so severely, that she literally bled to death right there in the basement. The new furnace was on full blast and just exacerbated the decomposition process. To combat that, an investigation showed that the door leading from the basement outside to the backyard had been propped open. This was to allow cold air to get inside and keep decomposition at a minimum. Buy some time. Somehow, the door slammed shut and no outside air got inside. Wayne was horrified. He and his children had been living in the same house as the remains of his wife/their mother. She had been chopped up in the basement the entire time. They had smelled her rotting flesh for days. The house was turned into a crime scene. Wayne and his children were allowed to take some items and move out. They went to stay with his parents, who owned a four bedroom condo on the south side of town.

"Whoever planned this was smart?" Mr. Lawrence nodded, looking at his son.

"I can't believe that we were actually living there and Carol was in the basement rotting the entire time," Wayne shook his head, crying.

"Everything will be all right, son. Let it out. We're here," his mother hugged him tenderly.

Monica put her sinister plan into motion. The babysitter would continue to take Stanley to school and pick him up afterwards. But this day was different. Monica showed to coerce Stanley to go along with her.

"Hi, Stanley," Monica approached him outside of the school on the sidewalk area.

"Hello," he looked up at her, frowning.

"Your dad wants me to pick you up. So come along with me," she extended her right hand.

"What's my dad's name?"

"Oh, that's an easy one. His name is Michael Parker," she smiled.

"No one told me that you were coming," he backed away from her.

"That's because I'm here on an emergency call, Stanley. They didn't have time to tell your teachers."

"Then let's go back inside and tell Mrs. Schumer."

"Come on, Stanley. Don't you want ice-cream and cake? Don't you want to play video games and have fun waiting for your dad to come and pick you up? Come on," she reached out to him again.

"I'm waiting for Brenda to come. She's the only person that's allowed to pick me up," he ran back towards the front doors of the school, where teachers and other kids were gathered, talking and shooting the breeze.

"Stanley," she called out one final time before scurrying back to her car and driving away.

Stanley told his teacher what happened and she told the principal, who called the police immediately.

Driving back home, Monica was very distraught. She knew the police would get involved if Stanley told anyone what happened. She just couldn't believe how calm the little boy was. He wasn't scared or anything. He just refused to go with her, and there was nothing she could do short of picking him up and carrying him to her car, kicking and screaming. But she couldn't have that, could she? How could Michael be so selfish? He just used me and threw me away. I can't believe he has done this. I've given him the best times of my life. I've had to give up other men, who were very good to me over the years, to be with Michael. That's what he insisted I do to be with him. Very possessive is what he is. I made sacrifices for him. I made all of the changes for him. He never once accommodated me. He never once asked what I wanted out of the relationship, and now, he's just going to throw me away. I won't take this lying down. Let them bring the police to my house. Let them bring the police. I'll tell the public everything I know. Oh, Michael's been very busy helping the mayor do illegal things all over this city. If they even think I'm going to jail, they have another thing coming. I'll tell everything I know to the media. I'll tell that Katie woman. I'll even go on The Oprah Show, if Oprah invites me. They better not mess with me. I've spent too many months giving and giving to this man. I love him and this is the thanks I get. He's going to just throw me away. I've been his rock when Judith treated him wrongly. I'm the one he always turns to. So this is what it's come down to. The police waiting in front of my door, as I pull into my driveway. This is what I have to face from a man I thought cared about me. I've given him so much and this is my reward. They better not put their filthy hands on me. I swear to God.

"Ms. Stevens. Ms. Monica Stevens," Officer Bellary approached her as she climbed from the car.

"I'm Ms. Stevens. What do you want?" she slammed the car door shut, locking it.

"We're you at Graceland Elementary School this afternoon, by any chance?"

"Why are you questioning me this way, Officer Bellary?" she looked at his name tag.

"There was an incident at the school today involving a student. Were you there, Ma'am?"

"I wasn't there," she shook her head.

"Would you mind coming with us downtown? We want to question you further," Officer Ricks pulled out his handcuffs.

"Am I being arrested?" she lowered her head.

"We just want to ask you some more questions downtown. You will have the right to have an attorney present," Officer Ricks turned her around slowly.

"You are making a huge mistake. I know things. I know places and events. I know names and people involved. Tell Michael that if I'm arrested for anything, I'll go on Oprah and tell the world what I know about him and his shady business practices with the mayor of our fine city."

"Miss. I wouldn't speak like that out loud. There are some people who may become very nervous behind your words," Officer Bellary frowned.

"I don't care anymore. I'd turn state's evidence. I'd go on Oprah. You see! Michael has reduced me to this. He's the one that's turned me into this horrible, savage beast. I don't want to be this way, but Michael is to blame. You must tell Michael to come and see me. Tell him that I need him. I must know that he still cares for me. He better still care for me or else!" she bellowed loudly, being placed inside of the police squad car.

Claudine's relatives eventually left the hospital. Thomas stayed behind. He wanted to make sure she was all right.

"I can stay the night," he slid a chair next to the bed.

"No. I want you to go on home," she smiled.

"Are you sure?" he frowned, looking directly into her eyes.

"I'm sure," she blew him a kiss.

"So you're pregnant now. How did that happen?" he shook his head, stunned.

"How do you really feel about this baby? Everyone is gone now, Thomas. Tell me. Do you want to keep it or not?" she gulped, sinking a little into the mattress further, hungering to hear a positive answer.

"This is our kid, Claudine. Of course I want to keep it. I didn't think we could ever have kids, that's all. This is a total shock; it has happened."

"I love you, Thomas."

"I love you too," he left.

Wayne and the children were allowed to go back into the Lawrence family home one last time before it was slated to be put on the market and sold to the highest possible bidder. An experienced cleaning crew had signed dozens of contracts to come into the home and clean it up professionally. The final costs ran somewhere in the thousands. Wayne didn't care. He just wanted to be done with the wretched, gloomy place once and for all. The kids, of course, grabbed clothes and keepsakes their mother had given to them over the years. Wayne did the same, but he also stumbled across Carol's diary, safely tucked under the mattress on her side of the bed. He would notice her writing in this book from time to time, but he never really concerned himself with it. She would write something down and then quickly hide the book under the mattress, when she felt he didn't see her. He always thought that was funny, but there was never time or cause for worrying. Too busy, too hungry, too annoyed with answering questions about being faithful. There was a terrible case of The Too's. He took the little crimson and black, gold-rimmed book back to his parents home and started to read it. And I mean, really, read it. He began to see another side to his wife of eighteen years that even he didn't know existed. She enjoyed watching football, basketball and even car racing, but dare not let anyone know for fear of being branded some kind of freak by the other ladies in the neighborhood. She didn't think her appearance was all that great and desperately wanted to get some cosmetic work done on her face and stomach areas. But what Wayne found to be the most shocking of all was when he read that Carol had lost complete affection for him. This woman didn't see him as desirable, pleasurable to be with, or manly. She wanted to fulfill all of her fantasies with another man. Wayne stopped reading immediately, dropping the book to the floor, the edges of the small room spinning out the corners of his brown eyes and the breath in his throat stuck in place. His limbs, paralyzed, his facial expression of absolute horror frozen solid in place. His wife, this other woman, this other creature, this other something has become a monster. He didn't recognize her from the pages of this diary. She had become some alien life form right before his eyes. He always knew that she was obsessed with him being with other women, but he had no idea she truly didn't care for him any longer.

This sent Wayne into a serious depression. He did love his wife. He did care for her. He always wanted to make her happy, and be her days and nights of sheer bliss. If she told him to sleep out in the rain to make any situation workable, he would've done it without question. This tiny diary was the very knife that ended Wayne Lawrence as the world knew him. The heinous last words of a woman he adored and loved. The horrible last words of a woman he worshiped and cared for. The disgusting last words of a woman that bore his children and promised to love only him. These words, these cursed words, these untenable, unloving, and hurtful words of a woman he loved was just too much to bear. Without reading the rest of the book, he got on the telephone and called the lead detective in the case. He abruptly told him that he and the children were moving away to start over. A brand new city. A brand new life, away from there. The detective asked: "Why the change of heart? Just yesterday, you wanted to hang around until the investigation was complete." He responded sharply, "Things have changed." The police were never able to catch the mysterious man who visited Carol that infamous Friday morning. They tried every lead they had but nothing turned up. Wayne never once called back to check on the case and see if any progress had been made. The kids would call and talk with the many detectives from time to time. Wayne eventually remarried, falling in love with a woman who loved him back just as much. So he hoped. They all live in the Chicago area now. Reportedly, doing well.

William Holton wasn't the kind of man to leave things to chance either. He wanted Judith and was not going to let something as trivial as a kidnapping keep him from possessing her. He immediately sent out instant messages and phone calls as discreetly as possible to try and get her to meet him. She never responded. He stoically got into his car and went to the Parker home. Instead of getting out and walking straight up to the front door, he sat there, waiting, for some hint of her. Some trace of her to peek out and notice him. He just sat there. Eventually, the police moving in and out of the residence noticed the mysterious car and approached him. He explained that he was there to see Judith Parker. He even asked if they could tell her to come out. The veteran officers told him to move on, and he did, reluctantly, in more ways than one.

While this drama played itself out outside, there was more happening indoors. Monica's arrest had made it all the way to Michael and Judith by now, and she was threatening to tell everything she knew about important deals made between the mayor and contributors to his various campaigns. She was screaming bloody murder at the police station. There was no way she could be arrested. The official word came down, from on high, to release her immediately. Michael was told to handle the situation carefully, privately and soon. An unmarked patrol car and two undercover officers were used to take her home.

Michael and Judith were now together, alone, trapped with each other's secrets. They knew all they needed to know about one another for sure. Of course each one didn't know the other knew this secret. But now came time for the intense conversation to begin.

As the police investigations kicked into high gear involving Henry's disappearance, they had the time to not only contemplate living without their oldest boy but without each other as well. The discussion started with a simple phone call from Monica. She did manage to call Michael once she was brought home from the police station. He took the call in his den.

"I told you never to call me here," he huffed.

"You will take my calls or else," she grinned, laying across the bed.

"I've heard that you've been making some very unwise threats," he leaned back.

"Not threats, Michael. Promises. I've simply told people that I will do whatever it takes to stay out of jail. I know things, and you know that I do. Keeping your mouth shut about your business affairs was never one of your strong suits."

"What do you want, Monica?"

"I want you, Michael. Judith is willing to give you a divorce."

"I can't leave Judith or Stanley now. The answer is no."

"You will leave that whore, Michael. I love you. I'm the one that cares for you."

"You care for me. Screaming how you know things that would bring down my friends and family. I don't want anything else to do with you, Monica."

"If you leave me, I'll call the Oprah Show. I'll tell them that I know things that will send the ratings through the roof. I'm sure her producers will love to hear how bribes were taken for various projects and political campaigns. And that's not all I know. I've done some digging on my on. The mayor is up to his eyeballs in so many scandals involving corruption and fraud. When I'm done with you and your friends, there will be nothing left," she laughed.

"I feel sorry for you, Monica. Good-bye," he hung up.

"Don't you dare hang up on me, Michael! You'll be sorry! All of you! I'll make you all pay for treating me this way!" she stormed throughout the house knocking things over, screaming and yelling to the top of her lungs.

Michael hung up the telephone and walked to the only window of the small den. This was his favorite time of day. At dusk, the sky was transformed into all types of colors, just before the sun dipped below the horizon for the nighttime. He stood there, thinking, and thinking some more. How was he going to handle the issue of not finding his son, Henry, or finding him dead, quite possibly? How was he going to deal with his wife, who he now knows is seeing some man name William? What on God's green earth was he going to do with Monica and her big mouth? These questions were pressing and pressing some more.

"So. Are you running away with Monica?" Judith entered, closing the door behind her.

"You heard," he never turned.

"It's all over the police station. Your tawdry affair with that vixen."

"Do I sense a tinge of jealousy?" he grinned, turning slightly.

"How can I be jealous of such a distasteful person? I've seen her up close. If anything, I should be disgusted that you preferred that over me," she rolled her eyes, sitting slowly.

"This had nothing to do with you personally, Judith. Monica always knew that. Our affair was strictly sex. That's it."

"Well apparently you're wrong. She is expecting you to divorce me and run off with her. How, oh, how will you ever manage that one?"

"Monica is a little delusional. I'm not leaving you for her. She's just confused," he turned completely.

"A little delusional. My dear boy, what are you smoking these days? Clearly, anyone can see that's she's not only delusional but insane. She's threatening to do a lot of damage to you and the mayor. What are you going to do about it?"

"I wouldn't worry too much about these matters, Judith. Monica will see the light eventually. Now, what about us? Will we survive this?" he looked into her eyes.

"I don't know. I look at you and I see unfaithfulness and mistrust all rolled up into one. How do I get that image out of my head?"

"I'm not the only one here with dirty hands, Judith. Monica told me all about this William person. Who is he?"

"A friend. That's all," she blushed, turning away sharply.

"Yeah, right? A friend. A friend that would make you turn beet red in half a second. I don't have friends like that," he scoffed.

"All right. When I found out about Monica, I turned to William for comfort. If you could cheat, why couldn't I? I wasn't going to stay at home and be the one cheated on. Oh no! I was going to get me some action, too. So I invented all of those charities and late night meetings, knowing you wouldn't care one iota. I was right. You never became suspicious, not even once. I even left William's watch right there on top of my nightstand. You never once questioned it or became curious. After that, I just did what I wanted. You didn't seem to care and neither did I," tears ran down her cheeks.

"I saw the watch, Judith."

"Stop lying. You're not scoring any points with me, Michael," she wiped her face.

"The watch was solid gold, black face, bold numbers, date on the side, Timex, across the top center. You had it face up, pointing towards the bathroom. Your side of the bed was the first thing I would see coming from the bathroom in the morning. I saw it."

"You saw that watch," she gasped.

"What do we do now?"

"Why didn't you say something? Why?" she stood, trembling.

"I don't know. But as you slept, I not only saw the watch, I picked it up. It was all a little too much at the time. I guess I just disposed of the thought and kept moving. I just never believe that you could actually be unfaithful to me," he shook his head.

Just at that moment, a police officer bursts into the room with news.

"Mr. and Mrs. Parker. Your son's jacket was found at the playground a few minutes ago. That's all I know," she nodded.

"The playground," Judith completely wiped her face with her hands and looked at Michael.

"That's good news. But where's Henry? Is there a lead on him now?"

"Come out into the living room. The lead detective wants to brief you again," she led the way.

Claudine settled back into her comfortable bed. But before she could really close her eyes and drift off to sleep, the door opened slowly. Greg, holding the flowers, entered the room and quickly shut the door.

Visiting hours would officially be over in ten minutes and he wanted every one of those minutes with Claudine.

"Claudine," he ran to her bedside.

"Gregory," she opened her eyes.

"I heard that you were in the hospital. How are you?" he rubbed her forehead.

"I'm fine," she nodded, heart pounding a mile a minute.

"What did the doctor say? What's wrong with you?"

"I'm pregnant," she whispered.

"Pregnant," he smiled.

"Yes," she became very quiet.

"Baby. That's great. You're having my baby. We can be a family, finally," he pumped his two fists in the air.

"This could be Thomas's baby, Greg. He wants to raise it with me," she gulped.

"Do you really think that this is Thomas's kid?" he looked directly into her eyes.

"It's a strong possibility. I have been sleeping with the both of you," she nodded.

"That's my baby, and I want to raise it with you," he huffed.

"Thomas knows nothing about us, Greg. Allow us to have this, please. I want to stay with my husband," she sat up in the bed.

"Are you asking me to give up my rights as a dad? This is my kid, Claudine. We both know that," he frowned, punching a nearby wall.

"All I'm asking is that you allow me the time to tell Thomas. He thinks the child is his, and he has every right to believe that. I must talk with him in private, a little later on."

"So, you want me to just fade into the background until you're done breaking the bad news to your sometimes husband. I can't do that, Claudine. What you're asking is just too much. I love you and this kid. That's my child and you know it. You can feel it, can't you? We've been together more often, lately. That's my baby."

"I want you to listen to me, Greg. This baby will be raised by me and my husband. I still love Thomas. What we had was nice, but I still love my husband."

"You just used me, Claudine. You never wanted me at all. What about all the times you would blow me kisses and tell me how much you cared. Was it all a lie?"

"This has nothing to do with blowing kisses or the countless times we were together. You knew that I was married, with a very jealous husband, when we hooked up. Now, I think we should separate. I will talk with Thomas about the child. But no matter what happens, I'm not coming back to you. It's over, Gregory. Let me go," she sniffed, wiping a tear falling from the left eye.

Back at the Parker residence, the police were giving Michael and Judith an update on the jacket found on the playground. The jacket was found by a stay-at-home dad who was taking his kids to the playground for a break. The jacket was sitting in the bushes, near a bench. You could tell it had been put there hastily. There was no care taken in laying it out. There were no blood stains or other noticeable body fluids. The lab, of course, had to get their hands on it. The jacket was the first real lead in trying to find out what happened to little Henry Parker. As the police officers gave the briefing, Michael and Judith found themselves sitting closer together and holding on to one another for moral support. Even when Judith broke down, Michael was there to hold her. This is what the disappearance of Henry Parker had done for his parents.

A few hours later, the police contacted Thomas Felder at home and told him that his wife of fourteen years had been strangled to death by a colleague named Gregory Fisher. She lay dead in her hospital bed, with Gregory's fingerprints etched indelibly around her tiny throat. He had literally crushed her windpipe. Thomas couldn't believe it. He had just been there to see his wife and sit by her side. He had no idea who Gregory Fisher was. It was later revealed to him that Mr. Fisher was her lover. This was a double whammy for Thomas! Talk about not knowing your spouse. He was speechless. How did she find the time? He was always there. She never went anywhere without him. They always traveled together. How was she able to meet with this Gregory person? This couldn't be right. His wife would never have an affair with anyone. She certainly wasn't the type. She enjoyed being home and working on various projects around the house or for other people to fill up any spare time. She would never seek outside pleasures. He kept questioning himself over and over again. Why didn't I see it? Where was I? What were the signs? I have no idea what I missed. My wife is dead because I didn't pay attention to the signs. My God. Who is this Gregory Fisher? I'll kill him. I'll kill him myself. The baby. Whose baby was it? Was it mine or his? I wonder if she knew. He knew. That's why he killed her tonight.

CHAPTER TEN

Gregory Fisher was charged with first degree murder and sentenced to life imprisonment without the possibility of parole. Thomas was given the chance to look upon the man that had captured his wife's fancies, and he simply couldn't see it. Why would Claudine leave the relationship to be with him? All throughout the trial, Thomas watched as Greg just sat there, motionless. He looked like he was from another planet. What did Claudine see in him? What was there? Why were these important things missing in Thomas? What did this psychopath have that Thomas didn't? The questions just continued to pile up as Greg attended each day of the trial. At the end of everything, after Greg had been sentenced, Thomas requested a few minutes to speak with him before he was taken off to a federal penitentiary in California.

"What did she see in you?"

"So I finally get to meet you up close, Thomas. After all those days of tailing you to get your routine down and know exactly where you were, at any given time. I finally get to see you without all of the cloak-n-dagger."

"What did she see in you?"

"You don't want to know how it all started? How we got together?"

"What did she see in you?!"

"It was very simple, Thomas. I listened to her. Something you never did," he stood.

The two fully armed guards proceeded to take Mr. Gregory Fisher away, bound and shackled from the waist down. He would never see the outside world again.

Three days later, Monica Stevens' brother, Andrew Stevens, found her lifeless body inside of her home. She was stretched across her bed, pills everywhere. The prescriptions were all in her name and signed by doctors she knew. Andrew protested that his sister was murdered by Michael and his syndicate of political leaders throughout the city. Of course he was relegated to low priority. Monica Stevens' death was ruled a suicide and the case was closed almost immediately. Andrew tried every avenue he could think of to compel people to listen to his story, but no one would. He buried his sister next to their parents. A month later, he took his sons and moved away, vowing to return when he had the evidence he needed to bring Michael and his people down for murder.

Exactly six days after the jacket was discovered on the playground within those bushes, the Parkers' received some news, in the middle of the night, that would shock even the most unshakable among us.

"Mr. and Mrs. Parker! Mr. and Mrs. Parker!" a policewoman ran into their bedroom screaming to the top of her lungs.

"What is it?!" Michael jumped up, eyes wide open, heart beating so fast it could run a marathon.

"Ah!" Judith hopped up, clutching her chest and heaving in and out, trembling from head to toe.

"What are you screaming about?!" Michael grabbed his robe, peering at the inexperienced officer as she started to calm down.

"You better have a good reason for coming in here like this, because if you don't, I will request personally that you be terminated," Judith huffed, slumping back onto the bed, letting out a huge sigh of relief, feeling her heart as it slowed in beats.

"I apologize for the way I entered the room. But there is something you must see downstairs," she stood to the side.

They both headed for the stairs and went down in a hurry. Upon entering the living room, they saw Henry. He was sitting on the sofa just as calm and well-nourished as any kid his age should be.

"Henry!" Michael and Judith ran to him.

They hugged and kissed him all over practically before the joy turned to curiosity. Where did he come from? Who had him? How was he found alive and in such good condition? These questions raced throughout Michael and Judith's minds.

"Your son was hiding out over at the Grants' home over on Travis Lane. It would seem he and their son, Kincaid Grant, hatched a plan of Henry disappearing to bring you two back together again. I was explaining to them why this was such a bad idea. It costs the city a lot of money in time and resources. It took crucial manpower away from areas that really needed it. Henry was only after saving your marriage, and he hoped that by him going missing, that would compel the two of you to lean on one another and work closer together to find him."

"How was he found at the Grants?" Judith continue holding her son.

"He was well hidden in the rear basement area; the Grants never went in their basement for anything, so on the face of it, it was perfect. But Mrs. Grant remembered seeing the family photo album tucked away in a box somewhere in that basement. She went down there searching for it and heard a strange sound coming from a backroom area. She called her husband, who of course checked it out. That sound turned out to be your oldest son."

"What do you have to say for yourself, Henry? What you did was horrible," Judith peered at him.

"Talk, son," Michael's eyebrows dug deeply into his forehead; he exhaled slowly.

"I know that I'm going to be severely punished for this. But was it worth it?" he looked at both his parents."

"Get upstairs to your room," Judith pointed to the stairs, grimacing.

"Hey," little Stanley met him at the stairs, dragging an old blanket of theirs.

"Come on, boy," he put his arm around Stanley, leading his little brother back to his room.

"I'm just curious, Officer Perkins. What happened to little Kincaid for his role in all of this?" Michael leaned forward slightly.

"Don't ask, sir. We could hear the screaming, literally, from the street. Mr. Grant was not playing," she rubbed her buttocks, walking away and shaking her head.

Henry was punished. He was ordered to give fifty hours of community service back to

the city. He was also ordered to go and speak in front of large groups of people about the dangers of pranks, for whatever reason, no matter how admirable. He was also punished by his parents. For three solid months, he could watch no television, no video games, no playground, no friends, no telephone, no movies, no arcade, no trading cards. His only existence was school and home, and at home, he was encouraged to read a book everyday to pass the time. He actually became a better reader as a result of this punishment. But it worked!

His plan succeeded. Michael and Judith did grow closer over those few weeks

of being, alone, with one another. They grew to rely on and to love one another again. Michael found himself coming straight home from work more often, finding reasons to

be home sooner rather than later. Judith spent more time around the house and less time with the other socialites. She learned new recipes and took a chance cooking different things every night. Henry's prank cost the city 1.2 million dollars in overtime pay and other resources. The unfortunate taxpayers would of course pick up the bill. This twelve year old never regretted once that he fooled his parents with that disappearance. In his little mind, at least, the end justified the means.

"All right. How do you all feel about the stories we've just listened to tonight?" Dr. Wasserman-Schulz looked around the room.

"I didn't think the situations were very realistic. Especially the one with Tobias and Lucy Graham."

"Now, I want you all to remember what I told you before we started listening to these stories. Each one is taken from an actual case I have dealt with over a thirty-five year career in counseling."

"I still don't believe kids would betray a parent like that. To give that kind of deference to a parent's lover is unbelievable," Stacey shook her head.

"It's not so unbelievable," a voice rang out from the back of the room.

"Stand up, Tamar. Tell everyone who you are," Dr. Wasserman-Schulz pointed towards her.

"Hello, my name is Tamar Ford, and I'm here because my now ex-husband cheated on me in the absolute worst possible way. I need help dealing with that," she stood.

"Welcome Tamar," the group said together.

"Tamar, why do you say that the Tobias and Lucy Graham situation is not so unbelievable? Is their situation compatible with yours," Dr. Wasserman-Schultz sat.

"My ex-husband, Jackson Ford Jr., promised that he would take care of me seven years ago, in front of an alter in my church in Montgomery, Ala. With all of our relatives and friends sitting there, he promised to be faithful, kind, and understanding towards me. We wrote our very own vows. I was young and impressionable when I met Jackson Jr. He was only two years older than I was, so I didn't see a huge problem with being with him. He would bring flowers to my home and take me out to nice restaurants and theaters," she was interrupted.

"Do you have any children?" Melissa frowned.

"I'll get to that," she nodded.

Tamar was in the process of telling her fellow companions about her life as the wife of Mr. Jackson Ford Jr. Tamar and Jackson met when they were seniors in college. She attended Spellman College and he went to Morehouse. The campuses weren't that far apart and the two would meet practically every single day. Things started off all right. Jackson said and did all of the right things. He wined and dined her. They went shopping together. He even gave up important football days to spend with her.

He stayed on the telephone for as long as she wanted to talk, which sometimes lasted for many, many hours. But he endured all of that for the woman he loved. She, in turn, gave up social dates, with fellow girlfriends, to be with him on occasions special to him. The giving and taking in the relationship was there. No one needed to come on in and direct. The two of them had figured this out flawlessly. The chemistry was absolutely amazing. Tamar Wellington stood about 5'7" tall. She had shoulder-length, straight black hair and

could fill a pair of jeans in to the tiniest air pockets. No one on her campus had words for Ms. Wellington. She was known for a sharp-tongue, quick temper and aggressive attitude, when provoked. Now, Jackson Ford Jr., on the other hand, was quite the opposite. This fellow stood 6'3" tall, short black hair and long, skinny legs. He didn't have a temper, and he certainly wasn't sharp-tongued. The two balanced each other out perfectly. Tamar had learned early on that being the boss outside of the home was all right, but when she came home, Jackson was in charge; and he took control of the running of the household. She would always have the opportunity to offer him an opinion on certain matters of importance. The arrangement worked out fine.

They both had earned college degrees and were capable of making lots of money. Tamar Wellington Ford majored in Business Finance, with a minor in Administration. Jackson Ford Jr. majored in Business Finance with a minor in Media Communications. He was constantly taking additional coursework online to help keep him abreast with the latest information in his fields of study. It was not uncommon for Tamar to come home from work and find the dinner cooked and on the stove ready, with Jackson half asleep in front of the computer. He was either attempting to read some

Chapter material for an upcoming test or answering questions posed to him by the online professor or fellow students.

The issue of children came up from time to time but they worked very hard and devoted little time to actually planning for the event. Jackson would always use a condom when performing his husbandly duties. He didn't want any slip-ups until they had talked out what a child would really mean for them and their current lifestyle. Tamar didn't have a problem with any of this. They decided that he would run the household overall, as the male figure, and she would take care of the domestic needs. Of course he would help out from time to time. Not long afterwards, they decided to have children. Tamar would give up her career, temporarily, and Jackson would be the sole breadwinner of the family for awhile. He was more than capable; his income, alone, could keep the small family sustained and mortgage paid for many, many months easily.

Tamar's mother, Justine Baker Wellington, was the glue that held their family together. She would hold down two jobs and still find time to come home and cook dinner, along with cleaning the house, making sure all of the homework or projects were done, pack lunches for the next day, make sure all notes from teachers were read and signed, and finally, talked to her husband, earnestly, about any/all problems involving the household or the children. Her austere father, Charles Wellington, worked his entire life. From the tender age of 12, he had been employed doing something for someone.

He worked three jobs at one point, only coming home long enough to eat a quick meal and take an hour or two nap. Then, it was right back out into the bitter cold of winter or blazing heat of summer. It really didn't matter; Mr. Wellington was out there, working. Working to support his family, making sure they had what the needed, along with a little of what they wanted. Tamar had two sisters. She, Tamar, in the middle. Nora Wellington Bryant was the oldest. She was the sibling that raised Tamar and Faith practically. She bore the brunt of any slack left behind by Justine, their mother.

Faith was the baby of the bunch. She basically missed all of the hard times growing up. There was little sacrificing to be done by the time Faith came chugging along. There was also an adopted girl named Stella. When Stella was a baby, her mother gave her to Justine and Charles to keep for a week. She said that she was going to New York to visit a friend and would return to pick up the child. Her mother, Henrietta Marble, disappeared. Justine and Charles decided to keep and raise Stella as their own, so she, too, grew up within the Wellington household as one of the clan.

Jackson Ford Jr.'s mother was Cynthia Ronsard Ford. She grew up very poorly in a small town called Kosciusko in the state of Mississippi. Where she once lived, dirt roads and fields were all that could be seen for miles. A small one room shack, with an outhouse or maybe two shacks with outhouses sitting tucked, nestled, dug in on a high hill or on a low plain. She was the only daughter of a sharecropper and seamstress. There were seven sons too, her older brothers, who helped out everyday. Jackson Jr.'s father, on the other hand, grew up in thriving Atlanta, Georgia. With its freshly paved, asphalt streets and huge single family homes lining nicely manicured lawns, in white neighborhoods especially. Not such a hop, skip and jump away from Kosciusko. The two young people met years later in college, their junior years, at North Carolina State University. Jackson Ford Sr. always joked, with his friends, that when he first saw that beautiful girl from Mississippi, he almost became a Mississippian! Jackson Jr. had two brothers and one sister. Curtis M. Ford, the second born, was the most stern of the group. He was very militaristic in his ways. Douglass Ford was the third born child. He was open-minded to trying new things, but absolutely hated not being informed on matters involving the family's welfare. As a result of this, Cynthia would make it her business to call Douglass first with any news at all. The youngest of the troop was Patricia or Patty Ford. She was the apple of Jackson Sr.'s eyes. She could do no wrong.

"Oh, that's terrible, Tamar," Beverly leaned back, shaking her head.

"It's all right. I've learned to move on. But there's more," she cleared her throat.

"Before you continue, Tamar, we're going to take a little break now. There are an assortment of refreshments in the back. Go and take some. We'll start again in five minutes," Dr. Wasserman-Schultz smiled.

"How do you feel?" Dr. Wasserman-Schultz touched Tamar's arm.

"I actually feel good. I've never had to open up to tell people who I am and where I came from. It feels liberating," she nodded.

"And remember we're not here to judge you. We all have our own baggage to haul."

"Thanks."

"So, what do you think about this Tamar? Do you believe any of the stuff she's telling us?" Mike looked at Kate, frowning.

"I do. There's something in her eyes, Mike. Have you really watched her while she was speaking? She's not groping for the right words; they're already there," Kate walked away, holding a thick slice of pineapple cake.

"I just wanted to say that I feel so sorry for you," Louise hugged Tamar.

"That's not what I want. I want you to learn from what I've done to help yourself or someone else," she replied, opening a soda.

"Your husband was a fool to do what he did. But is there any way you will ever forgive him?"

"I can't, Louise. What he did to me and my child was unbelievable. It's unforgivable."

"Well, I just thought I would come over and speak with you," she walked away smiling.

"All right everyone. Let's start coming back together now. Grab that last piece of cake or pie and drink. It's time to begin again," Dr. Wasserman-Schultz looked around the room.

After everyone was seated, Dr. Wasserman-Schultz turned the floor over to Tamar again. She continued telling her story.

"When my first child was born, four years ago, I suspected nothing. He was always there with a warm smile and hug. There was never a reason to doubt him. I guess I should've been more attentive. I believe that's when the affair started. Four years ago," she paused.

"Tamar. He is beautiful, girl. You did a wonderful job, baby," her mother rushed into the hospital room.

"How does he look?" she tried to sit up.

"No. No. Relax, baby. He's beautiful. Don't move. Stay right there. Jackson Jr. is on his way here," she smiled.

"Where's dad?"

"Still looking at the baby. So, have you and Jackson Jr. thought of a name for the little tot," she burst into laughter.

"Jackson Jr. wants him to be called Jackson Ford III. I like it," she nodded.

"Well I guess that's understandable. My baby just had a baby," Justine hugged her gently.

Before long, all the family members started arriving at the hospital to bless and cheer the event. When Jackson Jr. finally arrived, the celebration really started.

"Here is the man of the hour. Congratulations, young man. You're a dad now. How do you feel?" Charles, Tamar's father, asked, throwing his right arm around Jackson Jr.

"Proud, sir," he grinned.

"You should be. Tamar did great. She went straight through that birth with no problems at all," Cynthia, his mother, nodded.

"Well, it wasn't all that smooth," Tamar sat up slowly, blowing, with wide eyes.

"I know it was painful, baby, but the joys of childbirth are equal to nothing else on this planet. To bring a new life into the world is a special gift that women have," Cynthia smiled.

"I know, Cynthia. I just wish it didn't hurt so much," she exhaled, inching back against the soft pillows.

"Do you want some water or anything, baby?" Jackson Jr. held her hand.

"Yes. Some water would be fine. I ran out earlier," she glanced at the empty plastic hospital water container.

"You stay right there. I'll be back with some cold water," he left immediately.

"Where's the bathroom?" Justine looked around.

"Over there," Charles pointed, frowning.

"No. I can't use Tamar's bathroom. Germs. I'll go out to one of the public restrooms. I'll be back shortly," she kissed her husband on the cheek and left.

Outside of the overcrowded hospital room, Jackson Jr. was at the nurses' desk waiting on the container of cold water.

"I need to see you now," Justine approached him from behind.

"What about? It's not safe to be talking intimately here," he turned slightly.

"You didn't take any of my phone calls. Why are you avoiding me?"

"I can't keep doing this. You're my wife's mother," he covered his mouth a little.

"Haven't we been careful? No one will know. I'm going to call you later on after Charles has passed out. You better take the call, or I'm coming over," she sashayed away.

"Justine," he turned completely around and looked at her.

"What?" she stopped, never turning at all.

"Nothing," he shook his head, swallowing hard.

She went back to her daughter's hospital room. She went back into the arms of a girl that worshiped her totally. A girl that looked up to her. A girl that called her Mom. None of that mattered to Justine Baker Wellington. She was bent on having her way, and the one man that sent her to the moon and back in bed. Jackson Ford Jr. didn't talk at all about his manhood, but it was big and long enough for two women. And the way he worked those powerful hips and thighs, when the rhythm and grooving was just right, made any woman scream out, in several different languages, with pleasure. Any woman could have at least five or six orgasms before he could successfully have his first, with plenty more to come. He was always a gentle, slow, patient, methodical man. Hitting the same spot over and over again with such tenderness and ease. He truly believed in satisfying the woman to the hilt before he, himself, reached his climax. His favorite rule. Every woman he had a relationship with was sorry to break up with Jackson Jr. because of this one rule he lived by.

A few days later, Tamar was in the master bedroom cleaning and found a condom wrapper, just hidden behind the long bedspread that fell down to the floor. At first, she didn't know what to make of it. She knew she had been in the hospital for at least a week and a half preparing for the baby's delivery. What was a condom wrapper doing on her bedroom floor? She called Jackson Jr. at work.

"Hello, baby," he answered.

"Hi. Guess what I found while I was cleaning the bedroom?"

"What did you find?" he grinned.

"A condom wrapper. You aren't doing something behind my back that I should know about, are you?" she sat down slowly.

"A condom wrapper. Are you sure?"

"I'm holding it now, Jackson Jr., don't play games," she exhaled.

"Baby, that wrapper could've been there for weeks. We don't always throw everything away. Sometimes we may miss a wrapper here or there. Remember last winter when we stayed home and made love for days on end? How many condoms did we go through?"

"I don't know," she frowned.

"When I was cleaning up the room two weeks later, I found two open packets, didn't I? I even joked with you about not being a good housekeeper because you miss them."

"Yeah, I remember," she blushed.

"See. It's probably there from before, sometime. Stop worrying. You're the only girl for me," he smiled.

"I'm sorry to call like this. Will you ever forgive me?"

"Consider it forgiven. I'll be home around six-thirty. Do you want me to pick something up?"

"No. I'm cooking prime rib and vegetables tonight. Some dessert on the side," she licked her lips.

"What dessert?" he grinned.

"Me. With whipped cream on top," she laughed.

"That's one dessert I'll gladly eat up," he nodded.

"See you later," she hung up.

"This is crazy. We've got to stop this," Jackson Jr. hung up the phone.

"You drive me insane, Jackson Jr. What am I going to do with you?" Nora, Tamar's sister, pulled her skirt up.

"You can't come back here anymore. People are starting to suspect something."

"You're the one that started this thing with me. I can walk away anytime. Is that what you want?" Nora fixed her hair and make-up.

"No," he lowered his head.

"I'll see you back, here, in your office in a week. How I enjoy our afternoons together," she walked out.

CHAPTER ELEVEN

Jackson Jr. had his hands completely full with an affair with Tamar's mother and now, her sister. The affair with Nora Wellington Bryant started two years into his affair with Justine Baker Wellington. He always thought that Marcus Bryant, her husband, suspected something between the two of them but said nothing. Their last son also looked exactly like Jackson Jr. Right down to the dimple in the middle of his chin. The entire family was horrified with how much the male child favored Jackson Jr. over Marcus. Marcus was always suspicious of the two of them, Jackson Jr. and Nora, hanging around one another at gatherings. He would find himself following along, as they walked, hoping to catch them in the act.

"Where were you today?" Marcus slammed his book down on the table.

"I was at Eleanor's. What are you doing? Why are you spying on me?"

"You weren't at Eleanor's today, Nora. You're never at Eleanor's! She called here looking for you," he huffed, turning fiery red.

"You need to settle down before you pop. I didn't want to tell you this, but I wasn't at Eleanor's, like you already know. I was out planning a surprise party for you," she walked into the kitchen.

"A what?" he gasped, following closely behind.

"A surprise party for this Saturday night."

"You're lying. That's not what you were doing," he lost some of the grit in his voice.

"Call Steven Price. He's the manager at The Tropicana Restaurant and Lounge. He'll tell you everything," she put on her apron.

"You were out planning a surprise party for me. Why?"

"To show you my appreciation. To tell you how much I do love you. Take your pick, my beloved," she hugged him.

"I want to call him anyway. What's the number?"

"Here," she reached into her pocket and pulled out a blank, white card on one side, and Steven's business number on the other.

Marcus went to the phone and dialed the number on the card.

"Hello," Marcus said.

"Hi, this is the Tropicana. How can I help you?"

"Is there a Steven Price there?"

"He is. May I ask who's calling?"

"My name is Marcus Bryant. I need to speak with him about an urgent matter."

"He's on the floor right now. I can take a message."

"This is a very important matter, young lady. I must speak with Steven Price," he insisted.

"Hold on," she placed the receiver down, walking away.

A few seconds later, Steven came to the phone.

"Hello. This is Steven Price. How can I help you, sir?"

"Hi, my name is Marcus Bryant. My wife has told me that she's made arrangements with you for a surprise party this Saturday night. Is this correct?"

"Your wife is who?"

"Her name is Nora Bryant."

"Oh, yeah. I remember Mrs. Bryant. Sweet lady. Yeah. She came in today to finalize the arrangements. But the party was for you. How did you find out?" he frowned.

"So it's all true. The party, the arrangements, you seeing her today," he gulped.

"Yeah. Hey, is this some kind of joke or something? Is the party still on? I let a lot of business go to help your old lady plan for this party."

"The party will still happen. You'll get paid. Thanks for everything. I'll see you Saturday night," he hung up.

"See. I told you," Nora started cooking.

"I'm sorry that I doubted you. Please forgive me," he lowered his head.

"Just go into the den and watch TV, Marcus. Dinner will be ready soon," she never turned to look at him.

Charles Wellington noticed a difference in his wife. He didn't know what was going on, but she had changed dramatically. She wasn't the same attentive, loving woman she was years earlier. Her time was always spent outside of the house. He would always question her about new friends, clothes, hobbies, gifts and the like. Justine would coyly reply that Charles was being an old stick-in-the-mud. He never wanted to go out and have any fun. He wanted to be an old man before his time. This, of course, never stopped Justine from staying out all hours, running the streets, bar hopping with women fifteen to twenty years younger than she was. Charles turned to Tamar for help.

"I don't know what's gotten into your mother. She's a different woman, Tay," he shook his head, tears in his eyes.

"How long has she been acting like this?"

"It just started, suddenly. I put up with it, reluctantly, because I didn't want to cause any trouble within the family. But I'm scared. She comes home late, smelling like a street person. I love Justine, but I can't continue to live like this. What am I going to do?"

"Dad, I had no idea this was happening. You and mom look so happy together when you come to my house for visits."

"It was all an act. She's been having her way on everything around here. She's changed. My wife doesn't exist anymore. It's like something has invaded her body. The outer shell is there, but the feelings are gone. There's nothing there. No love, no understanding, no affection, nothing. I used to cry myself to sleep at night. In bed, all alone. I never went to be alone. Justine was always there. She was there, right next to me. We've been married for many years, Tay. All I want is my wife back. I want your mother back," he broke down crying.

"We'll get her back, Dad. Don't worry," she hugged him.

That surprise party for Marcus went off without a hitch. Saturday came and Marcus was suppose to pretend he was surprised. Almost everyone they knew from their perspective jobs was there. Marcus let his hair down and finally had some fun. Not keeping an eye on Nora, he danced and drank until his heart's content. The party lasted for four hours and within that time, Nora found a moment to sneak off to a nearby motel, where Jackson Jr. was already waiting.

"I thought we only met at my office," he quickly undressed.

"I can't see you this week. Marcus has been on my back like a hawk. I can't get him to leave me alone," she undressed as well.

"Why don't we just stop? If he finds out, your marriage will be over. Tamar would kill me and disown you," he slumped down on the mattress.

"He won't find out, and neither will Tamar. Just come on; do your thing that you do so well. I've been waiting for you all day long, Mr.

Long Legs," she bent over perfectly, arching her back in just the right places, and spreading her legs wide.

"Lord, have mercy. Forgive me," he swallowed, licking his lips.

Justine wasn't in the mood for listening to her own child chastise her about her relationship with her own husband. She quickly tried to put Tamar in her place.

"Where do you get off talking to me like this? I am your mother; you're not mine," Justine rolled her eyes, sucking her teeth.

"Mom, I mean no disrespect. Dad is worried about you. You're coming home all hours of the night. You have new friends and new habits. He's just concerned. Quite frankly, I'm worried too. Where are you going? Who are you with?"

"That's none of your business. I told your father to stop being an old stick-in-the-mud. I ask him to go out dancing with me. He always says no. He would rather stay at home and watch TV. We have a joint bank account, with a sizeable amount of cash in it, and all he wants to do is sit in front of the TV and snooze," she shook her head.

"That's not true. Dad just took you to New Jersey a few weeks back. You said that you had a good time."

"That's just one simple trip out of hundreds. I've asked him to travel places outside of the country. He hates the idea. I just can't stay cooped up in a house for the rest of my life. I have got to do something, with or without your father," she nodded.

"Mom, listen to yourself. You must understand how dad feels. He simply wants you to acknowledge him. Stop being so brazen with your activities. Be courteous and mindful of his wants as well. Staying home in front of a television may seem terrible to you, but that's a love he has. You must be willing to sit with him, in front of that TV, and make him happy. Are you willing to try?"

"I give in to your father all the time. He says he doesn't want to go out, so many nights I curl up with a good book and just sit with him while he's watching TV. I don't interrupt him when he's enjoying a good football game or some other program. I just go off into a corner and read. When has he gone out with me? Not once. Where's the give and take in that?"

"I'll talk with dad again, but I see that you're trying and that's good. I love you, Mom," she hugged her.

As the surprise party died down, Marcus looked everywhere for Nora. She was nowhere to be found. He search the bathrooms, the closets, the basement, the locker rooms. There wasn't a space that place had that he didn't search. He could hardly stand up, but that didn't stop him from trying to find his wife. One of his friends offered to take him home.

"Come on, Marcus. Let me take you home. You're in no condition to drive," he grabbed his arm.

"My wife is here. She is suppose to take me home. Have you seen Nora?" his words slurring, jumbling and garbling.

"She was here earlier, but she left," Rick said putting on his coat.

"She didn't leave. She wouldn't leave a party she was giving for me," he swayed from side to side, like a small sapling in a strong wind.

"Come on, Marcus. Let me get you home. Nora will see you there," he put Marcus's coat on and buttoned it up.

"Where is my wife?" he started to cry, little tears running down his cheeks.

"Marcus. Why are you crying, man?"

"Where is Nora? She left me again. Why won't she just love me, Rick? Why can't she just be faithful to me?" he lowered his head, as Rick took him from the establishment.

Regrettably, Charles never changed to accommodate Justine's new lifestyle. He still wanted to stay at home and watch TV. He would go out with her from time to time, but never to the places that Justine was now a frequent guest of. This made her so angry. She started spending more and more time out, away from the home, away from Charles. After awhile, he turned off emotionally, too. He started to miss her less and less. There were no dinners, washed clothes, ironed clothes, clean house anymore. Justine did just enough to get by and go right back out, into the night, and party. She even lost twenty-five pounds, intentionally, to fit into all of those smaller, tighter outfits. She had neglected her wifely duties towards Charles completely. Sadly, he turned to satisfying himself on a daily bases. The Wellington household was turning into a filthy cesspool you'd find on an afternoon soap opera.

Jackson Jr. kept seeing both Justine and Nora secretly. He was sleeping with Tamar at home. He had Justine, her mother, at a local motel, and Nora, he had at his job or just about anywhere they could both meet quickly without getting caught. This tawdry, filthy arrangement lasted a very long time. Marcus was still suspicious of his wife, Nora, and Jackson Jr. No matter how much she tried to prove to him that she was being faithful, he just doubted her even more. She would constantly lie about being certain places and doing things. When he questioned her further, she would try to make it look like he was the bad guy for not trusting in her. Nora was good. She always had a backdoor in her conversations with Marcus. There was always some wiggle room, just enough, for her to scurry out from under his radar. But Marcus grew tired of the lies and the games, and decided, a few years later, to see once and for all if his wife was being faithful. The result would be final for him.

Around the time Tamar and Jackson Jr.'s son was turning four years old, Marcus contacted a company called 'Infidelity'. This company sent investigators out to gather information on a spouse that was accused of cheating. After he signed all of the contracts, they went to work. With cameras and its host in toe, 'Infidelity' put a tail on Nora Wellington Bryant. On the first day of surveillance, they watched her go to work and come straight back home. Nothing. The second day was even more boring. She met up with Tamar, at a local store, and did some shopping. After that, she returned home. Day three was more exciting. She went to an office building called Transit Systems. One of the investigators followed her inside. She rode the elevator up to the tenth floor and went straight into Office 1023. He hung around the office waiting for her to come out. After about two and half hours, she emerged fixing her skirt, blouse and hair. Day four was no different. She went back to Transit Systems. She went to the tenth floor and straight to Office 1023 as usual. She stayed three hours this time. When she came out, everything was already fixed. She got on the elevator and went back down to the lobby. Day five was quiet. She stayed home most of the morning. Late that afternoon, she went out for a jog. After that, she came back home and settled in. Day six was busy. She went shopping with Faith and Stella. She bought a gold watch. After the shopping was done, she went back home to change. A few hours later, she went out again. She was tailed to a motel on Irvin Rd and Taylor Blvd. She went inside holding a package, but came back out briefly. She must've forgotten something in the car. We assumed the package she took inside earlier was the watch she purchased with her sisters while shopping. A man came outside to meet her. This mystery man, here, was identified as Jackson Ford Jr. The office building she was caught going into earlier is where this man works. His office room number is 1023. There is no doubt these two are having some type of sexual relationship. Once the investigators went over the evidence and tapes with their supervisors, they called Marcus Bryant in for a personal meeting. He was presented with all of the information of the investigation on his wayward wife. But there was an extra that Marcus didn't expect to see. While Nora and Jackson Jr. were inside of the motel room, Justine showed up. She knocked on the door. When Jackson Jr. saw her, he quickly ran out of the room and pulled her around to the side of the building.

After a few minutes of punching, screaming and yelling, Justine stormed off to her car and sped away, cursing the entire time. Surprisingly, Nora never came to the door to investigate. She stayed inside of the room the entire time. Jackson Jr. then got his breath and returned to the motel room. Marcus was floored. He saw his own mother-in-law, at this motel, in the videotape. He was having sex with her too! He couldn't believe it. The people at 'Infidelity' had earned every penny he paid them for their services. He had the option of actually surprising Nora and Jackson Jr. in the act or having a private meeting with the adulterous spouse. He chose to have a private session. But not only with Nora present. He wanted the entire family to be in the room when the videotape was played. Right after he saw the tape and other evidence of Nora's overwhelming guilt, he went out and immediately filed for a divorce and full custody of the two children he knew were his. The third child, which looked so much like Jackson Jr., was considered a bastard by him until a paternity test could be performed. Marcus returned home.

"Where have you been? Tamar called. Jackson III's birthday party is this weekend. I promised we would help her set up," Nora walked into the kitchen.

"I have some news," he followed.

"What news?" she kept looking into a cookbook.

"I have a film. A nice action movie. How about a movie night tomorrow?"

"That would be nice. We haven't had one of those in years," she glanced around.

"I was thinking of inviting the family over to see it, too."

"What?" she turned.

"The movie is the first of its kind. New for everyone. I know that when I saw the highlights, I was floored," he nodded.

"Who do you want to come over?"

"Your parents, Tamar, your other sisters, and Jackson Jr."

"Do you really want Jackson Jr. here? I know how you really feel about him."

"That's water under the bridge. He must be here. Jackson Jr. enjoys movies, doesn't he?"

"I guess he does. What man doesn't?" she went back to the cookbook.

"Good. Then tomorrow night it is. We will see this tape together, as a family," he turned, walking deliberately out of the kitchen.

The evening started off well enough. Each of the family members arrived on time. Justine and Charles did manage to put on a brave face to appear at least civil in front of everyone else. Faith and Stella came bearing gifts. Tamar and Jackson Jr. arrived last. The TV was promptly set up for a member of the 'Infidelity' team to speak to the group before the tape was actually shown. Mr. Gibbs and a few of his colleagues arrived a little after Tamar and her husband did. Everyone was being extra cordial, eating and drinking sodas or apple cider. Nora refused to serve alcohol in her home. There had been a terrible incident, a few years earlier, and she was put off of the idea completely. So, if you went to Nora and Marcus's home, you didn't get served any liquor. Most people just had their drinks before they arrived. That usually sufficed. The people from 'Infidelity' set up the tape of the incident and talked with Marcus one final time, behind closed doors, so that he would know exactly what to expect.

"Are you all right with the arrangements that we have made?" Mr. Gibbs asked.

"Yeah. When do we start?"

"Whenever you want. This is your show, sir," Mr. Tolliver nodded.

"I can't believe this. I have everyone here. After tonight, this family will never get together like this again. My wife's side of the family will be torn apart forever."

"We can still cancel everything. You're not obligated to do anything you don't want to do."

"No. We must do this. Jackson Jr. has been cheating on Tamar for far too long. She deserves to know. She's a good woman."

"So let's go and get this done," Mr. Gibbs looked at his people.

Everyone went out into the living room, where the TV was.

"Can everyone gather around the TV for the film," Mr. Gibbs motioned for everyone to come forward and sit.

"Who are you?" Nora frowned.

"I'll explain in just a second, Mrs. Bryant."

"Why are these people in my home, Marcus?" Nora shook her head.

"They are friends of mine. They are the ones that brought the tape."

"Still, I thought you said you wanted this to be a family gathering. These people aren't family," she rolled her eyes.

"Just humor me," he sighed, walking away from her.

Chapter Twelve

Two of the men ran off into the kitchen to stop the fighting in there. When everything was over, the house was a complete mess. Marcus calmly went upstairs to the master bedroom and pulled out his suitcase, which was already packed in the closet. He went into his children's rooms and got their suitcases. After coming back down the stairs, he spoke to his extended family for the last time.

"I won't be coming back to this house anymore. My two children are waiting for me at a friend's. I've already filed for a divorce, Nora. Until that youngest child has a paternity test, I won't claim him. As far as I know, he's yours and Jackson Jr.'s. I've filed for full custody of the kids. We're moving far away from you and all of this madness. No court judge in his right mind would ever consider giving you full custody once he sees what you've done to me and this family."

"Please, Marcus. I made a mistake. Just stay. I never loved Jackson Jr. It was only sex. We can work this out," she cried, wiping her face.

"Work this out. How many times did I beg you to come home and try with me? I begged you to be faithful and love me. I'm done. The good people at 'Infidelity' have given me my freedom, and I'm taking it. Tamar, you're a good woman. What Jackson Jr. did to you was unconceivable. Get out now. No more second chances. He's not worth it. Charles. You're a good man. I respect you. But any woman that would sleep with her husband and then run off for the bed of her own son-in-law is worse than ten harlots combined. She's scum! Leave and start over. You deserve better. For years, Jackson Jr. has been cheating, carrying on these illicit affairs with little to no concern for anyone else's feelings. I hope to see you Tamar and Charles, in the future, under better circumstances, so until that time, I say good-bye," he opened the front door, grabbing the suitcases and leaving. The men from 'Infidelity' left with him.

"There goes a good man," Faith watched through a window as Marcus was helped with his bags.

They loaded everything into his car, shook his hand, and they all got into their vehicles and drove away. Marcus would never come back to that house again.

Back inside, Faith offered to take Tamar home.

"How could you do this to me, Mom?" she turned to her mother, very slowly and methodically.

"Don't look at me like that. It all started very innocently enough. It's over now. Go back with your husband," she sighed.

"You don't even care, do you? You don't even care that you've hurt me more than any words every could. You slept with my husband. You were inside of my marriage bed," she sobbed.

"I never went into your bed. That's a lie," Justine wagged her finger in the air.

"I hope you get struck dead for what you've done to me. I hope God hits you with the worst possible thing known to mankind. I hope I live long enough to see it," she cried out.

"Come on, Tamar. I'll take you home," Faith put on her own coat before helping her sister with hers.

"You find somewhere else to go tonight, Jackson Jr. If you come back into my house, I'll kill you," she moved slowly out the front door.

"She's crazy," Nora rubbed her arm, shaking her head.

"Well, we might as well start cleaning up this place. It's a sty," Justine looked around the trashy living room.

Charles put on his coat and walked towards the front door, too.

"Where are you going, Charles?" Justine peered at him, placing her hands on her hips.

"Good night, Stella," he kissed her tenderly on the cheek before opening the door.

"Let me take you home, Dad. You're in no condition to drive tonight," she insisted.

"I can drive. Leave me be," he smiled, walking from the house.

"Oh, let that old fool go. If he gets into an accident, it'll be his own fault. Just let him go, Stella," Justine fanned him away, sucking her teeth, rolling her eyes.

"You don't have to be so mean, Mom. It's not his fault."

"It is his fault. Had he been there for me and not in front of that TV set all the time, this may never have happened," she nodded.

"Are you blaming Dad for what you did?" Stella gasped.

"Why not? If he had gone out with me, I may have had eyes only for him, and not that Jackson Jr.," she smirked.

"I can't believe you just said that," Stella shook her head.

"Believe it," she walked off into the kitchen, grinning.

Suddenly, there was a knock on the door. The police had finally arrived.

"Where were you earlier? The fights are over," Stella allowed them inside.

"What happened to you, sir?" Officer Henderson looked at Jackson Jr.

"I'm all right. Nothing here to see," he went up the stairs to the bathroom.

"Officers. This is my home. I am Nora Bryant. I'm the one who called," she extended her hand.

"You don't look so well yourself. Maybe we should call an ambulance," Officer Dickson frowned.

"I'm fine. Everyone is fine. My mother is in the kitchen cleaning up," Nora coughed.

"Can we see your mother?"

"Sure. Just go on back," she pointed.

"You all really did a number on this place," Officer Henderson shook his head as they walked towards the kitchen.

A few seconds later, Officer Dickson emerged from the kitchen.

"The ambulance is coming! Your mother just had a massive stroke."

"Oh, my God!" Nora ran into the kitchen.

Stella was right behind her.

Tamar was taken home by her sister Faith. She entered the residence numb to the touch. Faith paid the babysitter, who was there watching little Jackson III, and sent her on home for the evening. She also managed to put her young nephew to bed. The entire time Faith was doing these things, Tamar was lost, in another world, sitting on the living room sofa. She was just sitting there trying to grasp the concept of her husband sleeping with both her mother and her sister for years. Her own mother. The woman who had birthed her so many years ago. How could her own mother betray her like that? To be so callous and cold in the end. Not to even care that she has hurt her so badly. The bond is broken. That close bond that I had with her is broken.

I will never see her again. I will never hear her voice. The pain is just too great. If it had been another woman, a stranger, a two-bit whore, at least I could run to my mother for support and comfort. But it is she! She's the other woman. She's the other person that has caused great consternation within my immediate family. It was her doing that has made me sick with raw emotion and pangs of pure, unadulterated hatred. I want her to die. I want her to feel the wrath of God. I want her to suffer for this. I want her to know what it feels like to not be able to get relief, of any kind, when she calls out for help. I will never see that lady again. That woman, I once called my mother. That woman who took me up into her arms and kissed my tiny boo-boos and made they all seem better years ago. That woman who protected me from harm. This can't be the same woman that would do such a wretched thing. Such a horrible thing. Such a heinous thing as this. I have nothing to say about my sister. My sister, Nora, the slut. She has betrayed me, too. I will leave her fate with God as well. The two of them deserve one another. They deserve to rot forever in the bowls of the Earth, never to be seen by men again. They deserve so much unhappiness, ugliness, and pain. I hope God allows me to see it. Their suffering; their anguish and pity.

Tamar filed for a divorce and took little Jackson III with her, away from his father and

her family. Marcus Bryant moved his two children to Maryland, and they settled near the Eastern Shore area. Charles left Justine and moved in with a friend ten miles away. He calls himself 'The Happy Bachelor." Nora did have that paternity test done. Her youngest child was, in fact, Jackson Jr.'s. She quickly made arrangements for him to pay her child support, and Marcus made sure Nora paid him child support for the two kids they already had. Faith left town to start a new life. She met a young musician and had one child.

Poor Stella Wellington was stuck with Justine, who had suffered a massive stroke and was permanently paralyzed on her right side. She could hardly speak or do anything for herself. The only visitors she ever had were a few girls she used to hang out with, and the delivery boys, who would bring medicines and groceries up bi-weekly. Jackson Jr. never stopped pursuing his wife and kid. Even while Tamar had one court order after another sent to him stating that he was to stay far away from her and the child, he never listened. She always moved from one town to another, constantly, trying to keep away from him, but somehow, someway, he would track her down and just appear. One night, she arrived home from work and found him standing on her doorstep crying! She convinced him to leave and come back later that night. When he finally left, she ran again. Fortunately, he hasn't found her since that last encounter.

"And that's my story," Tamar sits down.

"Oh, my," Melissa clears her throat.

"That was tough," Mike leans back, rubbing his chin.

"How did you survive that?" Kate exhales, shaking her head.

"One day at a time," Louise answers, nodding.

"Well, we want to thank Tamar Ford for telling us her story," Dr. Wasserman Schultz claps.

Everyone else claps as well.

It was now time to leave for the evening. The small group said their final good-byes and left. Dr. Diane Wasserman Schultz locks up the building and heads down the front stairs towards a waiting car. It is her oldest son coming to pick her up.

"Oh, it's good to see you out here on time tonight. I did not feel like waiting," she jumps into the car, closing the door quickly.

"How was your group meeting tonight? Did you save some marriages?" Daniel smiles.

"It's not funny, son. I've told you numerous times that my work is very important. People have real issues, real problems to deal with," she settles back into the plush, leather seat.

"I meant nothing by it, Mom. Gee, lighten up," he frowns, sighing a little.

"How is everything at home with Stacey?"

"Why do you ask?"

"Just being concerned. I have that right, you know. I've earned it," she smirks.

"Stacey is fine. Everything is fine," he nods, making a right hand turn.

"Did you eat?" she gazed out the window, noticing all of the blazing lights inside of passing buildings.

"I had something earlier. Why?"

"Just wondering. You look so thin these days."

"I'm fine. You wouldn't believe who I heard from today," he made another turn, glancing at her.

"Who did you hear from, Daniel? And don't tell me Robert Kingsman."

"Robert Kingsman," he laughs.

"I told you not to take any of his phone calls. That poor man doesn't know how to take 'no' for an answer," she sighs, folding her arms.

"Mom, he likes you a lot. It's been six years since dad died. You have to move on," Daniel exhaled, making a final turn onto his mother's street.

"Don't you dare tell me to move on. I know how long your father has been dead. Don't you think I would know that? What I do, in my own life, is my business. Tell Robert that I'm not interested. Stop encouraging him; he's getting nowhere fast," she shakes her head.

"Mom, I didn't mean to upset you. I just thought that you should at least speak with him."

"I can run my own life, Daniel. If I need your advice, I'll ask. Agreed," she rolls her eyes.

"Yeah," his voice fades while stopping in front of her house.

"Good. I'm home. Thanks for coming to get me. I'll call Stacey later to talk. You go straight home. Call me when you arrive," she kisses him on the cheek before hopping out.

"Will do, Mom," he nods.

"All right," she taps the glass window gently before walking briskly to the front door.

"Does she have the keys?" Daniel whispers to himself; his eyes locked on his mother.

She pulled out her door keys and went inside, turning on the porch light. Daniel blew the horn and pulled away.

The house is cold, empty. Diane has come home to this every night. Feeling for that familiar switch that would light up the huge foyer area and allow her to take that all to memorable walk into the sunken living room, to turn on some soft music, and then, into the kitchen. Into the kitchen for a bottle of chilled wine and some American cheese, just on the top shelf of the refrigerator. After checking all of the messages, it's time to head

up the stairs for a bathroom crying out to be used. She runs the warm bathwater in the oversized tub and, then, turns on, yet, more soft, soothing music. Goes straight into that master bedroom, pulls out those usual pajamas, not silk or sheer. Just plain old cotton pajamas. It's time to kick back and relax. But, the phone rings.

"Yes," Diane sits on the side of her bed, holding the receiver loosely.

"I'm home, Mom," Daniel was heard.

"Good. How's Stacey? Is she there?"

"No. She hasn't gotten home from work."

"Well, it's almost ten o'clock. Does she normally work this late?"

"Sometimes. Look. I have to go, Mom."

"All right. Call me when Stacey gets in. I love you," she smiles.

"Yeah. I love you, too," he hangs up quickly.

Just as Diane starts to get into the tub, the doorbell rang.

"Who could that be at this hour?" she grabs her robe, heading down the carpeted, spiral staircase into the foyer area.

"Who is it?"

"It's Evon, Di," she calls out.

"Evon. Girl. What are you doing here at this hour?" she opens the door, standing off to the side.

"I know I'm here a little later than usual, but I was hoping for a late dinner. Have you eaten? I brought Chinese," she smiles, holding up the swollen bags.

"Come on in. You know I can't resist Chinese."

The two women are very close friends. Even though they went to separate universities, they kept in contact with one another. After their schooling was complete, they met again. This time, each woman was engaged to be married. Dr. Diane Wasserman was engaged to Dr. Frederick Shultz. Ms. Evon Hendricks was engaged to Dr. Michael Foster. They all settled down, in the same community, to raise their children together. Daniel Shultz and Eric Shultz were born to Diane and Frederick Shultz. Stacey Foster and Laura Foster were born to Evon and Michael Foster.

"I'm so glad you stopped by tonight," Diane got the plates from the cabinet, frowning.

"Why? Is something wrong?" Evon saw the expression on her face.

"Daniel called earlier to tell me that he made it home safely."

"That was nice of him."

"He also told me that Stacey wasn't home yet. I found that strange. Does she normally work until nine at night?"

"There's some special case she's working on at the firm. Some corporate boss is trying to keep his company from folding, and his head off the chopping block."

"What is he accused of doing?" Diane gasps, sitting slowly.

"Do you remember Enron?"

"Oh, my God. All of those people's funds. No," Diane shakes her head.

"Yeah. His company is paying Stacey's firm a whole lot of money to keep him looking clean and smelling like a rose."

"Well, I see why Daniel wouldn't tell me about that case. But why did Stacey tell you? Clearly her involvement with this man must be secret."

"She trusts me. Besides, who am I going to tell?" Evon grins.

"I'm starving. Pass the shrimp," Diane reaches for the box.

"There's something that I found disturbing at Daniel and Stacey's though," Evon passes the box to her before walking towards the refrigerator.

"What?" Diane took a few shrimp out.

"I was there visiting last week, and a telephone call came in. I didn't want to answer the phone, so I allowed the answering service to pick it up."

"Well, what happened?"

"It was a woman talking about bringing toys over. What can you make of that?" Evon frowns, shaking her head.

"Bringing toys over. Maybe you heard it wrongly. Maybe she said something like bringing the boys over. It could've been a mother calling to ask Daniel and Stacey to baby-sit."

"I don't know, Di. It sounded like bringing the toys over. There was no mention of boys," Evon got the wine from the refrigerator, returning to the table.

"I'm sure it was nothing. Come on. Let's eat," Diane starts right in on the shrimp.

After dinner, Evon helped with the cleaning and then left. Diane went back upstairs to her bath. She proceeded to let out the cold water and run some more hot water inside of the tub. While soaking for about ten minutes, the phone rang again.

"For heaven sake," she climbs out, grabbing a robe and dashing to the phone.

"Hello," she answers, tilting her head slightly and huffing, while rolling her eyes skyward.

"Hi, Diane. It's Stacey. Daniel wanted me to call you. I'm home safely."

"Well that's good to hear. How was your day?"

"Good. Look, Diane. I'm bushed. Can we talk tomorrow?"

"Sure. I was right in the middle of a bath anyway. Tell Daniel I said good night."

"Will do. Bye," she hangs up.

"Yeah. Bye," she sighs, hanging up as well.

The next day, Diane gets up and goes to work at her counseling practice downtown. This wasn't the same spot where the meetings are held for those dealing with adultery issues. Her practice was on the fifteenth floor of the Reeves Center Building. Her first client was a Mrs. Claire Wilson, who suspects her husband of cheating.

"Mrs. Wilson, how are you today?" Diane points to a seat, sitting down herself.

"I'm not doing well at all, Dr. Wasserman Schultz. My Marvin is at it again. He didn't come home at all last night. I waited up until about four-thirty. What am I going to do?" she yawned, sitting, covering her mouth, lowering her head slowly.

"But you told me that there was a note. Remember, you came in and told me that your husband produced the note he wrote telling you that he had some runs to make for work. He told you that he would be out most of the night," Diane flips through her tablet, crossing her legs at the ankles.

"That was all a lie. He tried to get me to believe that he wrote that note for me to find and read. There was no note. My husband is trying to drive me crazy. He leaves things out, everywhere, and blames me for being negligent. He even leaves the stove on from time to time and swears out that I was cooking and forgot to turn it off. I know he's doing these things to me on purpose. He's trying to hide his affairs," she sniffs, tears falling from her eyes.

"I want you to tell me why you believe your husband is trying to drive you crazy? Why would he want to do that to you?"

"I almost caught him the other day. I came home early from work. He wasn't expecting me. I walked right into the house and went straight upstairs to the bedroom. He was lying across the bed smoking a cigar. Now one thing I know about my dear Marvin is that he doesn't smoke a single cigar until after he's had sex, and that bedroom simply reeked with the odor of another woman. He tried covering it up with sprays and deodorizers, but nothing he did worked. That room smelled like two people being together for quite a long time. The bed was a mess and the bathroom's shower had been used. Of course I used it earlier that morning, but that was around 5:00 a.m. It was now 2:30 p.m. and the walls of the shower were still wet. Marvin was still in bed when I found him, so I know he hadn't showered. Some dirty woman was in my house, in my bed and in my shower. Of course he denied it all. He claims I'm seeing things and need to seek professional counseling. I told him we should separate for awhile if he insisted on cheating. He doesn't want to leave me," she leans back slowly.

"Why doesn't he?" Diane leans forward.

"Because I'm the one with the trust fund. My parents set up a huge trust fund in my name. I can get it upon the death of my mother. She's very sick now."

"So if he divorces you, he gets nothing. But if he drives you crazy, he gets control of everything. He will control your funds, as guardian," Diane gasps.

"That's why I believe he's trying to drive me insane. He wants to claim that I'm crazy and then get control over my inheritance."

"If you believe this, why don't you just leave him?"

"I still love Marvin despite everything. I don't want to leave him. I want to work things out. Just maybe he'll come around and feel differently."

"You know that's not true. If he's planning to drive you crazy and claim your fortune, nothing is going to stop him, but you."

"I'm not willing to leave my Marvin for anything. What do I do to save my marriage?"

"Is he interested in seeing a marriage counselor?" Diane rubs her chin, frowning.

"No. He says that the marriage is fine. I just need to trust him more. That's his answer for everything. I need to trust him more," she huffs.

"I want you to invite him to join you on your session next week. If he refuses, I want you to make it clear to him that you will be seeking outside counsel to terminate the marriage. Be firm with him. Let him know that you're not happy and if he continues to ignore the way you're feeling, you'll move on without him."

"That's what I wanted to hear, Dr. Wasserman Schultz. I've tried everything to make Marvin happy. I can't do anymore. We go to marriage counseling or I leave. That's the choice," Mrs. Wilson smiles, teary-eyed.

"Well I'm glad that I could help you. Same time next week," she stands.

"Of course," Mrs. Wilson stands, dries her eyes and leaves.

Chapter Thirteen

After Mrs. Wilson left, Mr. Gambrell came in. He had divorced his wife and was looking for comfort.

"Good morning, Mr. Gambrell. How are you today?" Diane smiles, pointing to a seat.

"I had a very rough night, Dr. Wasserman Schultz," he sits, removing his hat.

"Take your time, and tell me what happened."

"My ex-wife came around yesterday with her new boyfriend. He beats on her and I know this," he nods.

"How do you know this?"

"When she dropped off my son for visitation, her arm was wrapped up in a bandage. I believe he burned her or twisted the arm somehow."

"Those are some very serious allegations, Mr. Gambrell."

"My son tells me how Ron beats on her for not having dinner ready, for not cleaning the house properly, for not being where he thinks she should be."

"So why are you concerned about what happens to her? After all, she cheated on you with this same man, didn't she?"

"She did, but I don't want to see her mistreated. I don't want to see her hurt."

"That's very manly of you, Mr. Gambrell. I don't know what Sheila was thinking to divorce a man like you."

"It never fails. These women find a man who's willing to do whatever he can to make them happy, and they treat him wrongly. As soon a young, strong, good-looking man comes along, they drop their husbands and run off with them. I find it offensive," he shakes his head.

"Well, what is it you want me to do? Like I told you last week, if you keep this affection for your ex-wife so strong and refuse to move on with your own life, it could become a serious problem later."

"I know, but how can I just leave her alone, completely? I still love her. I still care," he lowers his head.

"It's all right to care, Mr. Gambrell. There's nothing wrong with that. But she made a conscience decision to cheat on you and walk out. You pleaded with her to stay. You told her of the consequences. Nothing made her stay with her family. She knew exactly what she was doing. This situation of abuse could be life's way of giving her what she dished out to you for so long. Just think about it. This same man that she felt was so much better than you, in every way, now beats on her for fun. You were a good thing, honestly, and no doubt, she realizes that now. If you concentrate on your life and trying to make your life better, she will really see what she lost. My advice would be to go out and have fun. Try dating again. Find someone who makes you happy."

"I think I will. Thanks, Dr. Wasserman-Schultz. Thank you very much, " he stands and leaves the office.

Around lunch time, Eric Schultz arrives at his mom's job to take her out for lunch. He pulls up to the building, in his shiny black Corvette, gets out flashing cash and sporting his five hundred dollar leather coat, with fur collar.

"Mr. Shultz, your mother is in her office with a patient now. You have to wait out here in the lobby area," Mrs. Green sighs, shaking her head, looking at the appointment book.

"What's your name, baby?" he leans over the countertop.

"I'm married," she flashes her wedding ring over and over again.

"So what? I don't care if you don't," he grins, clearing his throat, leaning in a little further.

"But I do care. Back off now before I tell your mother," she rolls her eyes, moving away a full four feet.

"No need to have a cow, baby. I was just interested in having a good time. I don't want to marry you," he hisses, straightening up.

"Have a good day, sir. Your mother is free now," she looks at a TV monitor, rolling her eyes at him, yet, again.

"You do the same, baby," he smiles, walking into his mother's office.

"Eric," Diane looks up from her papers and smiles.

"Hello Mom. I'm here to take you out for lunch. I just got paid, and I'm in the mood for some eating," he laughs.

"Well this is a welcomed surprise. Where do you want to go?" she stands, walking towards the closet.

"I was thinking Thai or Moroccan cuisine."

"Those sound great. Have you spoken with your brother today?" she pulls her coat out, putting it on briskly.

"I spoke to Daniel last night. Why? Should I have spoken to him today?"

"No. I was just curious. I wish you two were closer. I used to call your Aunt Ida everyday when she was alive. We were very close as sisters. Get my drift?" she looks at him nodding.

"I'm fine and so is Daniel. We have a great relationship," he heads for the door.

"Your father always wanted you and Daniel to be close. He would talk to me about it all the time. Call your brother later on. Please," she hugs him.

"I'll call him. Now, let's go and eat. I have all of this money burning a hole in my pocket," he grins, looking into his mom's eyes.

"Fine. Let's go and spend some of it," Diane laughs as they start to leave the office together.

Buzz, Buzz, Buzz…

"What now?" Diane runs over to her desk, pushing a little red button on a tiny speaker.

"Dr. Wasserman Shultz, Mrs. Washington is on the telephone, line two. She's holding her husband and his mistress at gun point in their home. She's wants to speak with you before she kills them," Mrs. Green stutters.

"Put her straight through!" Diane goes behind her desk and picks up the receiver.

"Hello, Lacey," Diane sits down slowly.

"Hi, Dr. Wasserman Shultz. I took your advice and decided to kill my husband. I have you on the speaker phone, so talk loudly. I want my husband and his slut to hear you too."

"You took my advice," she frowns.

"Yes. You told me to find out for sure if he was cheating on me and I did. Now that I know he is, it's time for him and his whore to die," she waves the gun around while they both sit up in the bed, naked and scared.

I never told you to kill Jerome. I just told you to find out if he was really committing adultery before you got a divorce. What you're doing now will have dire consequences, Lacey. You must put the gun down and leave the house now."

"Leave my home. You want me to leave my home. It took me twenty-five years to build up this home with Jerome. Working every single day. Going into work sick and even on holidays to make ends meet. Taking night classes to advance in my profession. I did all of this for him, for us. And this is how he repays me. I leave my job and come home early to surprise him with a special home cooked meal and a little play time afterwards, but I find he's already eaten and involved in some play time of his very own. That's why it's time to die," she points the gun directly at his chest.

"Don't do it, Lacey. Please, baby," Jerome quivers, pulling the white sheet close against his body.

"You're pathetic. I don't know what I ever saw in you. All of this should end right now," she shakes her head, tears running down her cheeks sporadically.

"I have nothing to do with this. I didn't know he was married," the woman gulps, moving away from Jerome.

"You didn't know he was married. That's rich," Lacey laughs, wiping her face with the free hand.

"I'm telling you the truth, Mrs. Washington. I didn't know he was married. He never told me," she shakes her head, glancing at Jerome.

"Well, did you tell this woman that you were married or not?"

"I didn't tell her. It wasn't suppose to be this way, Lacey. I'm sorry," he sighs.

"You're sorry. You're sorry. I don't care about you being sorry. I want you to pay for humiliating me this way. I want justice," she huffs, holding the gun firmly.

"Lacey! Listen to me. I want you to wait there until I arrive. Do you hear me?" Diane was heard over the speakerphone.

"I don't think that will be possible, Dr. Wasserman Shultz. You see, Jerome and I have

an appointment with destiny. We're going to leave this world and start all over again. Someplace new and inviting. Someplace welcoming and enchanting. There will be no distractions to keep him from wanting and loving only me. I won't be here when you arrive and neither will Jerome or this tramp," she nods.

"Please, Lacey. I want you to wait on me. I will help you to sort all of this out. It will be fine," Diane covered the receiver and told Eric to call Mrs. Green into her office.

He immediately runs out to get her.

"What is it?" Mrs. Green stands in the doorway.

"Call the police. Send them to Mrs. Washington's address. I will try to keep her on the line talking. Hurry," Diane fans Mrs. Green away.

"This isn't right, Dr. Wasserman Shultz. I need to leave this world with Jerome. Why can't you understand that?" Lacey's voice fades.

"I understand what you're going through, Lacey. My nephew, Joseph, was caught up in a situation just like yours."

"What? Your nephew, Joseph. How did he get out of it?"

"He came home one day and caught his wife in bed with the exterminator. Joseph is a

big man. He did what any husband would do. He started to fight with the exterminator. He beat him up really badly. Eventually, he let the man leave the house. He then turned his attention to his unfaithful wife, Freda. She was just sitting there, on the side of that bed, crying and begging Joseph to forgive her. He took pity on the woman and forgave her. Do you know that this incident occurred over seventeen years ago. They have been together ever since, and Freda hasn't cheated, once, in all of that time. She's there only for Joseph and vice versa."

"You're making all of that up so that I don't shoot Jerome or this whore. You want me to believe that your nephew is happily married now."

"I could give you his telephone number. You can call him yourself. Second chances do work sometimes. Nobody is guaranteeing that it will work out for you, as it did Joseph, but isn't it worth trying?"

"You want me to let this tramp leave my house. She'll go to the police."

"Let me speak with her," Diane clears her throat.

"Just speak. You're on the speakerphone," Lacey holds the gun to the young girl.

"What's your name, Miss?" Diane speaks.

"Marvel Collins," she stutters, looking at the gun.

"Listen to me, Marvel. You must promise Lacey that you won't go to the police when she allows you to leave. Will you do that for me?"

"Yes," she nods.

"Good. Tell her, now, that you won't go to the police. Reassure her that she has nothing to worry about."

"Mrs. Washington, I won't go to the police when you let me go. I'll go straight home and lock myself in my room," she cries.

"All right, Lacey. She told you. Let her leave now," Diane nods.

"Get out of here before I change my mind and put a bullet in you," Lacey grunts, looking at the bedroom door.

Marvel runs from the room, hardly taking any of her clothes. By the time she reaches the front yard, the police are already there and have surrounded the house. She is immediately covered up and taken away by a woman police officer.

"You've done great, Lacey. Now, it's time to reconcile with Jerome. But you must put the gun down first."

"I can't put my gun down. Jerome will leave. He won't listen," she shakes her head.

"Jerome. You must assure Lacey that you will listen to her if she puts down her gun."

"I will listen to you Lacey. I love you," he looks into her eyes, one tear rolling down his cheek.

"Stop it, Jerome. How could you do this to me if you love me? How can you look me in the eyes and say that you care when I catch you in bed with a girl young enough to be our own daughter? Why do you even bother to say anything loving or kind to me when you're doing things like this behind my back? What if I didn't come home early today? I would never have caught you. The lie would've gone on and on. You would be meeting girls all over the place, and I would've never been the wiser. This entire situation is so very sad. You've used me, abused me, treated me like garbage, humiliated me. There's nothing left for you to do. I've given all I can give and, yet, you take more and more."

"All I can say is that I'm very sorry for what I've done. I ask you to forgive me and give me another chance."

"Lacey. He sounds sincere to me," Diane interjects, holding the receiver firmly.

"This could all be an act, Dr. Wasserman Schultz. What if he's saying this just to keep me from shooting him."

"No one can read minds, Lacey. We have to trust that the people we love, love us back. The word trust must mean something to you and Jerome from this day forward. I don't want you to shoot him. If that happens, all bets are off and you go straight to jail. But if you just step back and look at the situation, nothing has been done that can't be rectified. Give your husband another chance. He may just turn out to be another Freda."

"Can you promise me that," she sobs.

"I can't. No one can, but I can promise you a brand new start. Either way, you'll have the chance to make a brand new start."

"Go put some clothes on, Jerome," she lowers the gun, sniffling.

"Thank you, baby," he climbs out of bed and puts on his underwear, pants and shirt.

"Thank you, Dr. Wasserman Shultz. I'll sit down and talk with Jerome. We'll try to reach some kind of understanding," she nods.

"That's good to hear."

"Don't forget about the police," Eric wrote this on a slip of paper to his mother.

"Oh, Lacey. I called the police to help bring this situation to a peaceful conclusion. Go and see if they're outside," Diane bites her bottom lip.

"Yeah. I see them," she pulls the curtain back on a bedroom window.

"You're not upset, are you?"

"No. I'll go down and speak with them. Jerome and I will go downstairs together," she smiles.

"Good. I want you to call me later."

"I will, and thanks again Dr. Wasserman Schultz," she hangs up.

"Mom, you did it. You kept that woman from killing her husband and his mistress," Eric exhales.

"Dr. Wasserman Shultz. The police are on the phone. They want to speak with you," Mrs. Green bursts into the office.

"Put them through," she waits before receiving the call.

"Dr. Wasserman Schultz. This is Officer Christopher Bell, of Police District 6, and we're standing outside of the Washington residence. I understand you were on the telephone with Mrs. Lacey Washington the entire time, calming her down."

"I was. I am her counselor twice a week."

"She has surrendered herself to us at this time. Her husband is with her as well. Will you come down to police headquarters and provide us with a statement?"

"I'll be more than happy to help Lacey in any way that I can."

"Good. We'll see you in an hour. Is that all right?"

"That's fine, Officer, good-bye," she hangs up.

"So we go down to the police station and not out for lunch," Eric grins.

"There's always tomorrow, my son. There's always tomorrow," she hugs him and laughs.

That night, Evon calls totally upset.

"Are you all right? I heard about the situation at the Washington's," she gasps, clutching her chest.

"I'm fine. I went down to police headquarters and gave a statement. Everything will be all right."

"I told you that counseling certain people would lead to this, didn't I?"

"So what do you suggest I do? I have a practice. I have to take those who come to me for help, Evon."

"You must be more discerning. Choose those who won't be psychopaths later on. The ones who won't come back to haunt you in the future."

"I took an oath as a mental health professional to assist everyone in need of care. I can't just pick and choose the people I will help. That's not right," Diane put some vegetables into a steamer.

"I want you to be all right. You scare me in this job," Evon sighs, shaking her head.

"My job is no more dangerous than yours is," Diane sits and grins.

"I work in a secured bank, managing funds. I have protection. You don't," Evon nods.

"You can have all of the protection in the world, Evon. If someone or some people decided they wanted to knock over your particular bank, nothing is going to stop them. I should be more concerned for you," Diane stands, walking back towards the stove.

"Oh, we're getting nowhere fast. Just be careful, all right?" Evon exhales, rolling her eyes.

"I will. Now, what's on your menu for tonight?" Diane opens her refrigerator and takes out some boneless chicken breasts.

"I'm having steak and potatoes."

"That sounds great. Hey, what about a movie this weekend," Diane washes off the chicken pieces.

"Fine. Do you have a picture in mind?"

"No. I guess we can decide when we get there."

"No problem. I'll give you a call on Friday. We'll make final preparations then."

"Great. Enjoy your dinner, girl. I have to go," Diane smiles.

"You too, sweetheart. Bye," Evon hangs up.

Chapter Fourteen

The next day, Diane went in to work and was confronted by another woman, who wanted desperately to speak with her about one of her clients.

"Dr. Wasserman Shultz. A Duchess Chelsea Anastasia Nicholaevna Petrovich Rothschild II is here to see you," Mrs. Green enters her office.

"My God. Royalty," Diane stands, gulping a little.

"She looks like it, too. Should I send her in?"

"By all means," Diane nods.

"You may enter, Duchess Chelsea," Mrs. Green stands to the side and bows as the duchess walks past her and into the office.

"How quaint," she looks around, clearing her throat.

"That will be all, Mrs. Green," Diane motions for her to close the door.

"Would you like to sit, Duchess?" Diane points to a chair, sitting herself.

"Thank you. I was told about you, Dr. Wasserman Schultz. I expected to see some old woman traipsing around this office in a starched, white lab coat."

"Well, no lab coat here. Older, yes, but no lab coat. How can I be of assistance to you?"

"I'm here about one of your clients."

"I'm sorry, but before we begin, I simply must ask about your name. In college, I was forced to take world history, and I must say that your name is very familiar. The Russian czar's daughter was named Anastasia Nicholaevna. How did you ever acquire it?"

"It's such a boring story, Dr. Wasserman Schultz. I tell it so much that it's etched on my subconscious permanently. My great, great grandfather, great grandfather, grandfather and father were all Russian soldiers. My great, great grandfather was a very rich and influential general in the czar's army when the revolution broke out. He never forgot his king. After they were brutally murdered by the Bolsheviks, shot to death and dumped like rubbished in the back woods somewhere in Russia, many Russians, loyal to the crown, wanted to commemorate Czar Nicholas II and Alexandra's life on earth; so they named their offspring after the monarchs or their five children. My father, a staunch loyalist to the Russian crown through his father, named me after the czar's youngest daughter. That's how I came to have that name."

"But to carry the name Anastasia Nicholaevna should be illegal. That name still has a lot of weight in Russia, doesn't it? Aren't there still Romanovs living?"

"Of course there are still Romanovs living, but I claim nothing of the past czar's. My lineage of Petrovich was fiercely loyal to his majesty. I believe all is well. Now that my life's story has been told to you, let's get down to why I'm really here."

"Yes. What is it you want, Duchess?"

"As I said before, I want you to do something for me concerning one of your clients."

"I am not at liberty to say who my clients are, Duchess. I'm sure you understand my position."

"Of course. But you must understand my position as well. My husband is Dr. Waverly Germond Rothschild IV. He and his family owns over forty-eight percent of the world's energy assets. The Rothschild family is involved in everything from politics to oil. From prime real estate, in over seventy countries, to transportation around the globe. They have funded small nations' economies and armies. They have whole villages and cities named after members of the family. My relatives are very, very powerful people, Dr. Wasserman Schultz."

"I see. But that still doesn't give me the right to divulge private information shared between me and a client. I can't even say if this client is really a client of mine."

"His name is Louis Maxwell. A commoner," she rolls her eyes, looking away.

"Why are you here, Duchess? I still have no clue."

"I want you to speak with Louis. Make him see that the affair between the two of us must end."

"Why are you telling me this? Shouldn't you have this conversation with Mr. Maxwell?"

"I have tried to tell Louis that it's over. We had our fling. But now it's getting dangerous. Waverly is due back into town today. I am to meet him at the airport in three hours. Louis must be a good memory for me by then," she crosses her legs at the ankles of course.

"Duchess, I still don't see how I can help you?"

"You are his shrink. He'll listen to you. There are people within my tight circle who have found out about my one month affair with Mr. Maxwell. They are determined to keep it a secret- even from Waverly. They have my best interest at heart. I've been keeping them at bay, trying to convince Louis that it's all over. But the stubborn fool won't take no for an answer. He insists on having me with him. He wants to provide for me. Can you believe that? My one home in Tuscany could pay Louis's rent for twenty years! He could never, ever provide for me," she shakes her head and sighs.

"I can't disclose that Louis Maxwell is my client. But I will say that this mess you've gotten yourself mixed up in is horrible. How can a woman of your stature and beauty have such an affair? It's mind boggling."

"I didn't come here for a lecture, Dr. Wasserman Schultz. I came here to save Mr. Louis Maxwell from certain death. You are the only one that can save him. I will not allow my good name and reputation to be dragged through the American tabloids. My family name of Petrovich is very important in Russia. We have status and position. To allow one man to destroy that would be very foolish. I will not be able to hold back or stop certain forces bent on eliminating Louis, should he refuse to let me go. I need your help, now, to save his very life."

"I will break my oath as a doctor to say that I have seen Louis Maxwell. I will speak to Mr. Maxwell about this conversation and hopefully convince him to leave you alone."

"I pray to God that you are successful. Well, my job here is finished. I've come to do what had to be done. Speak to Louis immediately. Waverly arrives today, and I want Louis gone. I want him out of my life for good."

"I will do my very best to accommodate you, Duchess Chelsea, but, ah, tell me please. How did you know about me? Who told you that Louis Maxwell was seeing me?"

"I have eyes and ears all over, Dr. Wasserman Schultz. Don't be shocked. I come from a very powerful and well-connected family, remember. If I need to know something, my dear, it's made known. Have a good day," she stands and leaves. Diane follows.

Her bodyguards, in the waiting room, escort her to the elevator. They all leave together, never to return again.

"Mrs. Green, get me Louis Maxwell on the telephone. I need to see him now," Diane walks back into her office.

"Yes, Dr. Wasserman Schultz," she starts looking through the files.

A few minutes later, Louis is on the telephone.

"You must come in and see me today, Louis," Diane leans back.

"But we're not scheduled to see one another today. What gives?" he frowns.

"I have some news that I must share with you. Come into my office right now to hear it."

"What kind of news?"

"You have to come into my office. When can I expect to see you? Within the hour," she waits for a response.

"Yeah. Within the hour," he hangs up.

"Is everything all right, Dr. Wasserman Schultz?" Mrs. Green enters the office carrying some folders.

"I'm fine. Have Louis come right into this office the moment he arrives. Do you understand?"

"Of course. Oh, and you have Mr. William Thompson out in the lobby. He has an appointment," she nods.

"Mr. Thompson. Yes. He's here about his daughter's divorce."

"Yes."

"Send him in," she sits.

"Fine."

A few seconds later, Mr. Thompson enters the office.

"Come in, sir. How are you today?" Diane points to a chair, sitting herself.

"I'm at the end of my rope, Dr. Wasserman Schultz. I think I'm going to pop," he lowers his head.

"Talk to me, Mr. Thompson. What's wrong now?"

"It's my daughter again. I thought I had convinced her to get a divorce from that cheating clown of a husband of hers, but he has somehow weaseled his way back into her heart. She didn't sign the divorce papers."

"What did we talk about the last time we met? Do you remember?"

"I don't have time for games, Dr. Wasserman Schultz. I need answers. What can I do to convince my daughter to leave that punk?"

"What did we talk about the last time we met? If you tell me that, the answer will not be hard to find."

"I don't remember what we talked about the last time. I need answers now. What can I do now? That person is taking advantage of my baby," he become teary-eyed.

"We talked about your responsibility and your daughter's responsibility. You can't live her life for her. This man is her husband. Until she sees the need to leave him, nothing you say or do will work. Remember we talked about that."

"I want her to listen to me. I know what he is. He's a snake. I've seen him with countless women. Giving them his phone number and offering rides everywhere. God only knows what he's doing with them. My daughter could contract a disease from him. You have got to help me. Tell me what to say that will make her listen to me."

"There is nothing to say or do. Your daughter is a grown woman, with thoughts and feelings of her own. She will never listen to you as long as your son-in-law is around convincing her not to. You must step back and look at the situation objectively. If this wasn't your daughter but a friend, would you keep trying and trying to get that friend to leave an unfaithful spouse?"

"Of course I would," he nods.

"Up until a point. When that friend keeps ignoring your advice and doing what he or she wants, eventually you will tire and give up. You would more than likely conclude that he or she will get what's coming to them for not listening to me. They will see where they are wrong. That's the reality. But since this is your daughter and not some random friend, you feel overly invested in saving her from harm. There's nothing wrong with that, but, remember, the concept is the same. She will continue to do what she wants. When will you cut the apron strings and allow her to make her own mistakes and live with them, too. You can't save your daughter, Mr. Thompson. All you can do is give her some sage advice and hope that she takes it. You know what her husband truly is. Nine times out of ten, she knows as well. Give her some time and space to arrive where you already are. That's going to be very important."

"So you simply recommend that I just back off and allow her husband to keep cheating," he frowns.

"I advise you to lay low and wait until your daughter needs and calls on you for support. Right now, her husband has taken all of the oxygen from the room. She's totally focused on him and him alone. You have got to see that by now. Give her the time and space to see her husband, really, for what he truly is. You have to back off a little and allow her to do this, on her own," Diane leans forward.

"It's going to be hard. When her mother was laying on her deathbed, I promised that I would take care of Christina. I don't know where I went wrong? I've done everything a father was suppose to do. I got up every morning and went to work. At the construction site by six o'clock every single day. I've always been a humble man. I've worked with my hands since the age of fourteen. Carrying and pulling things. Building things. That's who I am. Sometimes I believe Christina is ashamed of me. She's ashamed of what I do to make my living. She's just ashamed, period."

"What makes you say that?"

"The way she looks at me when her friends are talking about what their parents do for a living. I worked my fingers to the bone to make sure that she got into a good school and stayed there for four long years. Sometimes I even worked three jobs. I never asked her to work one day while she was in school. I provided everything. Right down to her spending money on nonsense. After she graduated from college and move in with Raul, I lost her. At the age of twenty, I lost my only daughter. She simply ran off and got married to that little idiot. She knew I didn't approve. But there she was, in Las Vegas, getting married. I'm so tired, Dr. Wasserman Schultz. I've worked my entire life for my family. I've never even bought myself a new pair of boots for work. The ones I have now are old, beat-up, and dangerous. But I keep wearing them because there's always one more bill that needs to be paid. I keep working, hard, because there's always one more item that needs to be purchased. This is my life," he nods.

"Then I want you to start a new life today, Mr. Thompson. Do you have any money in savings?"

"Why?" he frowns.

"I want you to take a vacation. Go somewhere alone. Treat yourself. You deserve it. You need it," she stands.

"I can't even think of a vacation now. There are lawyers' fees that need to be paid. I still have my construction job. I must be there tomorrow morning as usual."

"What if I showed you a picture of a casket right now? What would you do?"

"I don't know. Are you going to show me a picture of a casket?"

"I'm going to do better than that. Walk over here with me to my photo album," she starts to walk, and he stands and follows.

"What are you going to show me, Dr. Wasserman Schultz?"

"Look at this picture," she opens the album and points.

"Who is that?" he gasps.

"That was Mr. Leroy Hillman Jr. He was a client of mine six years ago."

"What happened to him?"

"He walked into my office just like you did today complaining about how his wife was being so unfaithful, and he wanted to leave her. But, she didn't want to leave him. So he played cat and mouse with her for an entire year before she finally gave in and granted him the divorce."

"But how did he die?"

"When she finally left him for good, she took half of everything they owned. Now, this was a hard working man like yourself, and he didn't have much to begin with, but he did have enough to survive on. He was left with a few thousand dollars in a bank account and a real place to call home. His boss was even going to allow him to retire, collecting his pension and any other benefits due him until he died. But Mr. Hillman outright refused to stop working. He wanted to rebuild what was taken from him in the divorce. He started working more and more, putting in unnecessary overtime. He got less sleep. His eating habits deteriorated. The man even went on job interviews looking for a second job! Well he was fortunate. He found a night job from eleven to seven in the morning. His regular job started at nine o'clock, so he had little time to prepare for that. Two months into both places of employment, he fell over and collapsed at his day job. He simply had a heart attack and died, right there at his desk. A massive coronary, I was told. When I attended the funeral, my son, Daniel, went with me. He took that picture of Mr. Hillman. At first, I was angry that he had taken the picture. I clearly saw it as an invasion of privacy for the Hillman family, but over time, I saw it as a reminder of what could happen if I don't slow down and smell the roses every once and awhile. I don't want to see you end up like poor Mr. Hillman did, Mr. Thompson. Go out, please, and smell the roses, okay," she smiles.

"All right," he nods, turning and walking towards the door.

"Dr. Wasserman Schultz, Mr. Maxwell is here to see you," Mrs. Green spoke into the speakerphone.

"Send him in, Mrs. Green. You have a good day, Mr. Thompson."

"You may go in, Mr. Maxwell," she points to the door.

"Thank you," he enters the office as Mr. Thompson exits.

"Louis, it's good to see you now. Come in and sit down, please."

"What is this all about? I have a million things to do today," he sits.

"I called you in here for a very important reason. I spoke with a Duchess Chelsea today."

"You spoke with Chelsea," he gasps.

"I did. She came into this office concerned about you. She was hoping that maybe I could help you see that the affair between the two of you must end."

"You had no right to speak to her about me. You should never have told her things that we've discussed in private," he exhales.

"I never told her anything that we've discussed. I never revealed any information you told me in private."

"What was she doing here? How did she know about you? Who told her that I was seeing you on the side?"

"I asked her those very same questions and she refused to answer. Louis. You must be practical. This woman comes from a very powerful and influential family in Russia. She has royalty in her bloodline. She has married a very wealthy and influential American leader in our society. There is no way she's giving all of that up to be with you."

"I have told Chelsea that I can provide for her. She doesn't need the expensive clothes and homes. She doesn't need the late night parties and jewelry dangling from everywhere. That stuff is superficial. We can live plainly."

"Oh, come now, Louis. Do you really believe that a woman who has been pampered her entire life by countless servants and butlers and chauffeurs is really going to allow all of that to just go away? Come back into reality. You must leave her alone. There are people who will do some terrible things if you don't," Diane frowns, looking directly into his eyes.

"Chelsea tells me those same things all the time. They won't hurt me at all. I love her, Dr. Wasserman Schultz. I'm the one she calls out for when she makes love to Waverly. I'm the one who caresses her "spot" just right, making her squirm and squeal, trembling with pleasure. I'm the one she digs her candy apple red nails into vigorously during passionate lovemaking. I'm the one who really cares about having her totally. Her husband is a fool; he knows nothing about having sex. The man doesn't even know how to please his own wife. She tells me everything. He's in and out of her so freaking fast that she doesn't even know what has happened. Me, on the other hand, I take my time and stroke. I stroke hard and stroke in rhythm and stroke to satisfy. I please her first. Waverly has no idea. While he's out making more money,

I'm in his bed pleasing his wife. She should be all mine. I want her. I deserve her. I will have her."

"Even so. These people are very dangerous, Louis. They will kill you if you don't leave the duchess alone."

"Chelsea is only saying this to scare you. She loves me. She always will. That's why she came here, to your office. That proves that she still loves me, doesn't it?" he smiles.

"That only proves that she doesn't want to see you get hurt. I don't want you to get hurt either. Leave this woman alone, Louis. Listen to wise counsel."

"She has upset you for no good reason. I've wasted enough time here. I must go and see Chelsea. I have arranged a quiet dinner for two at La Rouge."

"That's quite an expensive place. How are you ever going to afford it? A glass of water is twenty-five dollars!"

"I have my ways. Don't worry, Dr. Wasserman Schultz. This will be our last session. I don't need counseling anymore."

"What do you mean? You need to talk this out, Louis."

"I'm all right now. I see things very clearly. This is my last time in your office. Don't contact me again. Good bye," he walks towards the door.

"At least call to let me know that you're all right, Louis."

"I see no need to do such a thing, Dr. Wasserman Schultz. Chelsea has frightened you into believing something that's not true. I will be fine. Waverly will give up Chelsea to me. He doesn't love her the way I do. I'll make him see that one way or another. I'm not afraid, so don't you be," he smiles and leaves.

Chapter Fifteen

An hour later, Diane receives another visitor. A welcomed visitor.

"Dr. Wasserman Schultz, a Ms. Tamar Ford is out here to see you."

"Tamar. I can't believe it. Send her in," she stands and rushes to the door.

"Dr. Wasserman Schultz," Tamar enters smiling.

"Tamar Ford. It's good to see you. How are things? Sit," she points to a chair.

"I came here seeking your help," she sits.

"What's wrong?"

"Jackson Jr. has found me again."

"Oh no. How can you be sure? Have you seen him?"

"I arrived home from work yesterday and found him standing outside of my apartment building. Thank God I saw him before he saw me. I went to pick up little Jackson III from the babysitter and returned to the building. He was still standing there, looking around and checking his watch over and over again. I had to stay at a friend's house last night. He's found me again. What am I going to do now?"

"Why haven't you changed your name, Tamar? That's how he keeps finding you."

"I can't change my name. I love my name. My parents gave me this name, and I refuse to change it."

"Jackson Jr. will never stop trying to find you. He will track you down each time by your name and social security number. You really must look into changing everything. I know some people in government. They could assist you with this," Diane approaches her.

"I can't believe this is happening. I just want him to leave me alone. Why won't he stop looking for me?"

"Because he feels responsible. He knows that he was wrong, but soon that guilt will turn to rage and anger against you."

"What are you saying? He's the one that should be angry with himself."

"Of course he is now, but the longer you spurn his advances to apologize and try to put the past behind you, he will see you as the enemy of the relationship. He will see you as the person keeping his little family apart. That breeds hatred and revenge. Soon, he won't be looking for you in order to reconcile. He'll be looking for you in order to kill. He will reach a certain point, in his mind, where trying to say he's sorry won't be the dominant issue anymore. Getting to you, and making you pay dearly for causing him so much grief will be his main focus. You must change your name and social security number. You may have to change your appearance in some way, too. Jackson Jr. is upset and remorseful now. But later, he will become angry and revengeful. Don't ever be around when that finally happens."

"How can you help me?" Tamar looks up at Diane and cries.

A few hours later, Dr. Wasserman Schultz was sitting at her desk doing some very important paperwork when the phone rang.

"Hello," she answers.

"Dr. Wasserman Schultz."

"This is she. How can I help you?" she slips off her glasses.

"I just wanted you to know that Louis Maxwell is dead."

"What? Who is this?" she stands, legs shaking, lips quivering.

"This is the duchess. I tried to warm him, but Waverly found out about the affair. You will not hear from him again. Good bye," she starts to hang up.

"Wait, Duchess. You have to tell me what else you know. Where is he?"

"You will never find him. Waverly and his men will make sure of that. Good bye, doctor. It would seem not even you could stop the great and determined Louis Maxwell from a fate destined to occur," she hangs up.

"Oh, my God," Diane plops back down in the chair speechless and trembling.

That evening, Daniel goes to his mother's office building to pick her up.

"Are you all right?" he frowns as she gets into the car.

"No. A client of mine was murdered today."

"Murdered. What do you mean, Mom?" he drives.

"A client of mine was having an affair with a very rich and exotic woman. Her husband found out about it, and he's dead now," she glances out the window and then down at her lap filled with paperwork.

"So what are you going to do? Did you call the police and report it?"

"Report it. Report it to whom? This woman is a duchess from Russia and her well-connected husband is a Rothschild. Do you honestly believe anything will happen to those people? If anything, they'll come looking for me. I just want to stay out of it now. Anyway, I tried to warn Louis that she was trouble. The duchess wasn't worth it. But did he listen? No. He just kept moving, head first, into a dire situation. I truly don't believe he understood the gravity of the predicament he was mixed up in."

"What are you going to do tonight? Same old thing. Go home, turn on the music, eat some cheese and drink some wine, go upstairs and run a hot bath, soak for a few hours, eat something quick and then go off to bed. Do I have it down to a tee?"

"I believe you do," she grins.

"Robert Kingsman called again."

"How are you getting phone calls that come to my house?" she looks at him frowning.

"I'm not getting phone calls that come to your house. He calls me because you had your number blocked for certain calls. His included."

"I told you not to interfere. Robert is a nice man, but I'm not interested in starting a relationship with anyone right now."

"Mom. You're lonely. I know this. Why don't you just go out with him once. If you don't like it, I'll back off."

"Are you insane? How dare you say I'm lonely. Listen to me, Daniel. I'm your mother. You're not my father. Who do you think you are telling me that?" she huffs.

"I didn't mean anything by it, Mom. It's just what I see. You go home to that same big house every night. There's no one there to welcome you. I feel you should have someone there, that's all."

"Well as I told you before, it's my life and I will live it the way that I please. I want you to stop interfering," she shakes her head.

"All right, fine. I'll just tell Robert, for the very last time, that you're not interested. He'll just have to look for love somewhere else."

"Good. That's what you tell him. Maybe he'll leave you and me alone," she rolls her eyes.

"Your brother and Stacey."

"What's wrong? Why are you two fighting over them?"

"I shouldn't say. It's your brother's business. Never mind," she stands.

"What is this all about? Is something wrong with Daniel and Stacey? Are they having marriage problems?"

"No, nothing like that. It's a private matter. Let's just change the subject."

"Well, I brought Glenda over for dinner. Remember, you said two weeks ago that you wanted to meet her."

"Oh, yes. The new girl. When are you going to settle down and find one woman to be with, Eric?" she grins.

"I believe Glenda is the one."

"Where is she?"

"In the living room waiting."

"I can't wait to meet her, but, first, let me wash my hands and start cooking something."

Chapter Sixteen

The very next day, Diane went into work on public transportation. She enjoyed catching the bus and riding on the subway system. It was about a twenty minute trip from her home. When she entered her office, a basket was sitting on the desk. She immediately opened the card and saw it was from Mr. William Thompson. He was sending that gift basket as a thank you for giving him the advice to go on a trip. He was on his way to Florida for an entire two weeks! He decided to take some of that money he had saved for lawyers and spend it on himself. He used up just a fraction of the mountains of leave he had accumulated on his construction job over the years. Diane was tickled pink.

"Oh, this is so wonderful," she giggles to herself.

"Mr. Thompson is such a good guy. He hand delivered that himself very early this morning before setting off on his trip to Florida," Mrs. Green enters the office smiling.

"He is a sweetheart. The basket is filled with oils and gels. Bath items that I simply adore. Fresh herbs. This is such a treat," Diane went through the items one at a time.

"You have your first appointment of the day. Mr. Russell Gilmore. His wife has divorced him because he was the cheater."

"Send him in."

"Yes, Dr. Wasserman Schultz," Mrs. Green leaves grinning.

"Good morning, Dr. Wasserman Schultz."

"Hello, Mr. Gilmore. Come on in and sit," she points to a chair.

"I just thought I would come by and talk about my wife again," he lowers his head and sits slowly.

"Russell Gilmore, you come in here, on your appointment days, to only talk about your ex-wife. Let's talk about you for a change. What have you done lately to take care of yourself?"

"I don't know what you mean. Iris is my life. I was wrong to cheat on her, Dr. Wasserman Schultz. I messed up a good thing, and she won't forgive me. She won't take me back," tears stream down his cheeks.

"Mr. Gilmore, you have got to move on. This obsession, with your ex-wife, is unhealthy. She has told you, through her actions, that she's not interested anymore in you, as a friend, or having an intimate relationship. Why can't you take 'no' for an answer?"

"I love her too much. I never knew how much I loved and needed Iris in my life. She's my everything, Dr. Wasserman Schultz.

"But doesn't it concern you that she has moved on with her life. She's met someone else, and according to you, they will be married next spring. Why are you so bent on getting her back? Clearly she has gone on without you."

"She will not marry Thomas Riggs. He is a punk! He doesn't know what she likes or dislikes. She wants things to be a certain way. Only I know how to do things for Iris. She will be with me, Dr. Wasserman Schultz."

"Mr. Gilmore, what you're saying sounds like you're going to force your ex-wife to return to you."

"I will not allow her to marry Thomas. She will not leave me like this. I have messed up badly. I know this. She has given me the evil eye. She screamed and fussed. I've taken

a lot from her, but now I want a little sympathy. I want her to see that I'm sorry and that I've truly changed. That woman that Iris caught me with is long gone. I kicked her to the curb months ago. She cost me my marriage. I want Iris to see that I still love her. She can't just leave me behind and run off with Thomas Riggs. He's a fool. She needs a real man like me," he nods.

"Your words are frightening me, Mr. Gilmore. Your wife has already told you through her plans to marry this Mr. Riggs that she's moving on without you. Why won't you accept that?"

"She doesn't know what she's doing. She needs me there to show her the right way to go. I love my wife, Dr. Wasserman Schultz."

"I know you love your ex-wife, but this conversation is not going the way that I thought it would. You must stay completely away from your ex-wife, Mr. Gilmore. Do you understand?"

"You can't tell me to stay away from my own wife! She's a part of me. I'm a part of her. We are one, intertwined," he smiles and nods.

"Stop smiling like that. It disturbs me," Diane sits, finally, not taking her eyes off of him.

"You have nothing to fear, Dr. Wasserman Schultz. I have been working on our second wedding plans. I want to marry Iris all over again. She doesn't need Thomas Riggs to make her happy. She doesn't need him for anything. Will you come to the wedding?"

"I must say that I'm really afraid for you and your ex-wife, Russell. I want you to sit here while I go out and get a friend," Diane stands.

"What kind of friend?"

"The kind that will talk with you further about this stubbornness you're determined to have."

"You can't allow another doctor to know what we're discussing. That's illegal," he stands, frowning.

"Russell. I'm afraid you will hurt your ex-wife and yourself. It is my duty to tell someone else. Maybe they can reach you where I haven't."

"I won't be here when you return. I will leave your office and never come back."

"Russell. You are not willing to let Iris go. You are determined to harm her if she doesn't come back to you. Am I right?"

"Dr. Wasserman Schultz, I would never hurt Iris. I love her too much. Haven't you been listening to me? Iris is my whole world. She's my rising sun and glowing moon. She's my up and down. She's everything. I made a mistake. I just have to allow her the time to deal with that."

"What if she never comes around to seeing things your way, Russell? What will you do then?"

"I will make her see that I'm the only man for her. I love my wife. She will be with me again. I was stupid. I made a terrible mistake when I slept with Georgina. That girl was just a child practically. I was wrong. I seduced her. Iris never allowed me the chance to explain everything fully. She just stormed out after she found us in bed together. I can't let things just end like that. She must see that I'm lonely and depressed without her. Dr. Wasserman Schultz, can't you see that I'm remorseful?"

"That has nothing to do with it, Russell. If she doesn't want to take you back then you must find a way to move on and leave her alone. Can you leave her alone? Just walk away from her forever," Diane gulps.

"I can't just leave her alone. She's my wife. I still love her. How can you ask me to stop seeing my own wife? I love her so very much. The bond between us shouldn't be broken. It should be tight and steady. I messed things up. I know this, but Iris must see that I'm dying inside. She must see that I'm in so much pain over what happened. I want her to come back to me, Dr, Wasserman Schultz. I want her to be with me again. She has to see that I'm the right choice for her. This other man has nothing good to offer her. He's only stepping in to fill a void that I've left by leaving temporarily. I want him out of her life. She deserves better. I am her husband. She should be with me."

"Russell. You keep calling Iris your wife, but she has filed for a divorce and you signed the papers, too. You no longer have a wife. Stop calling Iris your wife."

"I can't stop calling her my wife. She's my everything."

"I want you to know something, Mr. Gilmore. I am very uncomfortable with this conversation and where I believe your actions are heading towards your ex-wife if she doesn't quite see things the way that you do. I will have to contact the police."

"The police. Are you serious?" he laughs.

"Yes. I see no choice. Iris has moved on. She will not come back to you under any circumstances. Why are you insisting on being with her?"

"Because she is my wife! Nothing you say or do will ever change that."

"Calm down, Russell. I want you to sit down and relax."

"I'm not sitting down anywhere! You just threatened to call the cops on me because I want to see my wife. What kind of counselor are you?"

"The kind that can clearly see you're heading for more heartbreak and eventually trouble. Iris isn't safe around you anymore. She will ignore your proposals to get back together again, and you will be beyond furious. Not a single soul will be able to tell you anything. When you see Iris and Thomas somewhere together, and you will follow them from one place to another, seething with rage and jealousy, you will snap. Perhaps you will try to harm her and yourself. Maybe you will try to harm both Thomas and Iris. I don't know, but I've seen this sad movie play out too many times, in my past, to simply stand here

and allow you to just walk right out of this office without telling someone of authority what I believe you will do to your ex-wife when she refuses to come back to you, which she unquestionably will do."

"Oh, Dr. Wasserman Schultz. You're so filled with ideas. You believe you know everything. I won't try to take Iris's life. I love her too much. Haven't you been paying attention?"

"That love you feel will turn into an uncontrollable rage. She will surely reject you for Thomas, and you won't stand for it. You will want to get revenge, and the next thing I know, you've done something terrible, irrevocable. And I'm reading about it on the front page of every city edition's morning papers. Please, Russell. Let Iris go. She has moved on with someone else. She's marrying Thomas. You have got to see what's out there for you. There is someone out there for you."

"Iris is the only one for me. You must understand that, Dr. Wasserman Schultz. I better be going now. I don't feel so good," he grabs his stomach.

"Are you all right?" she rushes to his side.

"My stomach has been giving me problems lately," he falls over to the floor, wincing in pain.

"Mrs. Green! Mrs. Green! Call the ambulance!" Diane screams, rubbing his head.

Evon was fed up with Diane refusing to take her calls. She just couldn't believe things ended the way that they did on the telephone. She decided to pay Diane a little visit.

"I'm sorry Mrs. Foster, but Dr. Wasserman Schultz is in her office waiting on the paramedics," Mrs. Green shakes her head.

"What happened?"

"A client has terrible stomach cramps. She's holding his hand and waiting for the ambulance to arrive."

"Oh, good. They're here!" Evon looks towards the main doors of the suite.

"Through that door," Mrs. Green points.

"Thank you," the paramedics enter and start to work on Russell Gilmore.

"What do you know about him?" a paramedic asks taking his blood pressure.

"He's a client of mine. We were in here talking and then he started complaining about stomach pains. He bent over and fell to the floor. I screamed for my secretary to call you all. I have never been so shaken up in my life. Is he going to be all right?"

"We have to get him to the hospital, pronto. Is there someone we can call?"

"Call me once you're done delivering him. Give the hospital my number, too. Here is my business card," she hands the woman a card.

"We will pass that information on. You are his what again?" she asks, frowning.

"I'm his counselor. He has no wife and children. His parents died when her was a teen-ager. There are no other relatives either. I will be the contact person. Call me for anything he needs," Diane smiles.

"Thank you, Dr. Wasserman Schultz. Will do," they carefully place Russell on a gurney and wheel him from the office.

"Well, I came down here to squash our drama, but it looks like you've created a little more on your own. What is going on?" Evon looks at Diane.

"What are you doing here?" Diane hisses.

"Can we talk in your office and not out here in the lobby?"

"I don't think we have anything else to say to one another, Evon. You made that quite clear when you took Daniel and Stacey's side in that seedy behavior they're basking in so joyously," she scoffs, turning her nose up at her.

"I took no glory in that and you know it. Stop being so melodramatic. I want to talk with you in private," Evon walks straight into Diane's office.

"Do you want me to get security?" Mrs. Green picks up the telephone receiver.

"No, that won't be necessary. Go back to your work. I'm fine."

"Are you sure?" she swallows hard.

"I know this woman very well. She wouldn't physically hurt me," Diane walks into her office, closing the door behind herself.

"Now we can really talk," Evon sits.

"Why are you here? I've said all I needed to say and so have you," Diane walks to her desk and stops.

"We need to speak about this Daniel and Stacey issue. Why are we fighting with one another? This isn't our problem."

"Evon. Our children are living in sin. What do you plan to do about it?"

"Diane. Do you remember when we first moved into our homes?"

"Yes. I remember. Why?"

"What did you do to Mrs. Lindstrum?"

"Oh, what does that have to do with anything?"

"Everything. You talk about sin. What you did to her was sinful, and, yet, you made an excuse for it."

"What I did to her was payback. She harassed my boys. There was no way I would allow that. She was this evil, sadist, old prude who never wanted to reach out and compromise on anything. She was just stuck in her own ways. It made me so angry," Diane huffs.

"You may not be evil and sadistic, but you can be an old prude at time," Evon laughs.

"I am not. I like being with one man as much as the next woman. But to be with multiple partners, in this troubled world we live in, is foolish. Our Daniel and Stacey are opening themselves up to an array of things that will be harmful. Can't you just back me on this?"

"Don't you think the two of them have counted the cost of this behavior? Like I said before, I don't approve of what they've decided to do, but I will not stop speaking to

my daughter because of it. I'm sorry, Diane. The line has to be drawn somewhere."

"Then there's nothing more to say, Evon. You have made your points crystal clear and so have I. Now, I have clients coming in shortly. You know where the door is," Diane points.

"You can't just dismiss me like this, Diane. I came here to make peace. Let's not allow this situation to stop us from being friends," Evon gulps.

"Stop us from being friends. Oh, my dear, Evon. Friends back one another up. Friends are there to help when the chips are down. Friends take the fall, sometimes, when need be. What you're doing now is not acting like a friend."

"I'm so sorry that you feel that way, Diane. It must be so lonely up there, where you are, on the top of that pedestal. The perfect Dr. Diane Olivia Wasserman Schultz. The great mediator and all-knowing. The Alpha and the Omega. The one who grants all things to everyone. The one that should be worshiped. Do I bow, now, Diane? Do I? Living with you must have been hell for Fred and those boys. Trying hard to live up to your perfect standards. Always doing things Diane's way. Well this time, I'm not going along for the ride," Evon leaves the office in tears.

That evening, Eric came to pick Diane up from work. He takes her to the local shopping center to get some dinner items. On the way out, she hears Daniel calling out to her.

"Mom!" he calls out from across the parking lot.

"Hey, Mom. It's Daniel," Eric waves back.

"Put the bags into the car, Eric. Hurry," she never turns.

"But it's Daniel. He's coming over," Eric smiles.

"Hurry. I want to go home," she runs to the passenger side of the car, but the door is locked.

"Hi, Eric. Hi, Mom," Daniel walks up to them smiling.

"Hi, big brother. What are you doing out this way?"

"Stacey wanted a few things at the last minute," he frowns, noticing that his mother never turns to look at him.

"Mom," he approaches her.

"Eric. Put the rest of those bags into this car so we can go," she clears her throat.

"Yeah, Mom," he frowns, too.

"Mom, what's wrong with you? Why won't you turn and look at me?" Daniel exhales.

"Daniel. I want you to promise me that you won't live in sin anymore."

"Mom, what are you talking about?"

"I know all about you and Stacey's love life. I wish I didn't, but I do. I want your word that you'll stop it," she never turns to look directly at him.

"What me and Stacey do in our own bedroom is our own business, Mom. How can you ask me to stop that?"

"I'm your mother. Me and your father didn't raise you to carry on this way," she finally turns and faces him.

"How did dad get into this?"

"Just promise me that you won't do that horrible stuff anymore, and I will forgive you. God will forgive you," she looks into his eyes.

"I can't promise that, Mom. What you're asking is something that I and my wife should decide together. I can't make that decision, right now, standing in the middle of a grocery store's parking lot. You can't expect me to give you a satisfying answer."

"Well there's nothing more to say. Eric, open the car door and take me home. I must start dinner," she turns her back to him.

"It's open, Mom," he hits the main lock, and the tiny, square latches, on all four doors, pop up instantly.

"What about the barbeque on Saturday? Is it still on, Mom?" Daniel looks at her, dreading the response.

"Take me home, Eric. I'm very tired," she completely ignores him, opening the car door slowly.

"Why are you doing this to me, Mom? Don't do that, Mom. Don't do that. Please don't do that," Daniel raises his voice slightly.

"No you don't, don't do that! Me and your father didn't raise you to live a debauched life. You grew up in a religious household. Why are you embarrassing me and God this way?"

"I'm not embarrassing anyone. What me and my wife do in the privacy of our own bedroom is our business. No one should be privy to that, Mom."

"I wish I wasn't, Daniel. God knows I wish I didn't know this, but I do. You must come to the conclusion that this lifestyle is wrong for you and Stacey. You must do that soon, son. Call me once you're ready to talk. Do you understand?"

"You are blackmailing me, Mom. You are placing conditions on how and when I am to contact you now," he frowns, with teary eyes.

"I want the Daniel back that I knew as a young man. The decent and God-fearing young man. The man who made me and his father very proud. I know that Daniel is still in there somewhere. Get rid of the new Daniel. I don't care to see him anymore. I want my Daniel back. When he reappears, call me," she gets into the car, slamming the door shut.

"See you around, Daniel," Eric waves before driving off.

Chapter Seventeen

The next day, Diane decided to stay home from work and do some baking. She was tired and called Mrs. Green early enough to have all of the appointments for the day cancelled.

As she was baking and pondering over the situation involving Daniel and Stacey, the door bell rang.

"Now what?" she walked from the kitchen into the foyer area.

"Who is it?"

"It's Robert Kingsman, Diane. May I speak to you, please?"

"Robert," she opens the door.

"Hello. I called into your place of business this morning to try and get an appointment but your answering service said that the office was closed and would reopen tomorrow. I came straight over."

"Why did you come straight over?" she sighs.

"I was concerned, besides, I wanted to speak with you about an important issue."

"An important issue," she shakes her head.

"It is rather cold out here. May I come in for a few minutes?" he rubs his hands together, looking at his breath in the cold morning air.

"All right. But only for a few minutes. I'm in the kitchen baking," she stands to the side as he enters.

"Thank you," he smiles as she closes the door.

"Follow me," she leads him into the kitchen.

"You have a huge house here. Lots of space for roaming," he looks around nodding.

"I like it. Me and Fred bought this house many years ago, when the boys were small. I thought we would have more children, but two seemed to be quite enough," she walks over to the oven and pulls the door open slowly.

"What are you making? It smells great."

"Oh, some cakes and pies. I always bake when I'm trying to sort out things. Now, what is it you needed from me?" she closes the oven door and turns, facing him fully.

"I had a talk with Daniel late last night. He was very upset about your encounter in the grocery store's parking lot."

"What me and my son discussed is not your business, Robert. How dare you show up here, at my home, to question me about a personal family matter. I want you out of this house immediately," she gasps, looking away sharply.

"Before you throw me out on my ears, Diane, I want you to hear something," he reaches into his pocket and pulls out a small tape recorder.

"What's that?"

"Something I think you should hear," he hits the start button.

"Mom, this is Daniel. I know you didn't want me to call you, so I decided to send a message by Robert. I'm sorry that you're disappointed in me, but I won't stop living my life the way I want to live it. Stacey and I love you very much; we look forward to the day when we can be reunited again. I guess that's it. When you're ready to talk to me, you call. Bye," he stops abruptly, his voice fading.

"Where did you get that?"

"Your son made it last night and brought it over to my home early this morning before he went off to work. Diane. He loves you very much. You should've seen the expression on his face when he brought this tape to me. He was visibly and emotionally a wreck. Call him."

"Don't tell me how to handle this situation. No doubt you're aware of what's happening here," she turns away slightly.

"I am. Of course I don't approve, but I'm not willing to throw my good friendship with Daniel and Stacey under the bus because of it. They are grown folks, Diane. They are capable of making their own choices and mistakes. Could this be a huge blunder for them? Maybe so. But it's their blunder not yours."

"Don't tell me about blunders. I've raised my boys to be good and God-fearing. That behavior is frowned upon."

"What people do in the privacy of their own bedrooms is nobody's business but theirs. Haven't you heard that saying before?"

"God is watching that tawdry, filthy behavior. My Frederick would be appalled. He'd never stand for such a thing. He would've taken our

Daniel out to the woodshed a long time ago over this nonsense," she nods.

"Maybe so. But Frederick George Schultz is not here. He's dead and gone. You are the parent that's still here. You are the only parent that Daniel has left. Don't throw away your good relationship with one another based on this nonsense."

"Who do you think you are? You waltz in here saying you have a situation, and it turns out that very situation is about my family. I would never have allowed you in here had I known your real motive, Mr. Kingsman," she huffs.

"Is that the garage?" he points.

"Why?!"

"Just curious. Frederick had a brand new car he drove around town before he died. You still have it, don't you?"

"I still have many of Frederick's things. That's none of your business, Robert."

"May I see his car?"

"No," she shakes her head.

"Those are his keys, right?" he looks at the wall next to the door leading to the garage and see a pair of keys dangling from the small key rack.

"I want you to leave now. You've said your piece, and I'm working," she swallows hard.

He walks over to the door, unlocks it and grabs the keys from the wall. He proceeds to go through the door and step down the few stairs into the garage area. There was Frederick's car. It was all covered up and sitting idly. He quickly uncovers it and hops inside.

Diane follows him into the garage.

"What are you doing? You have no right to come into my home and do this. You are trespassing, Robert Kingsman! I want you out of my home now!"

"Go back into the house and turn off the oven. Get your coat and ride with me. I want to show you something," he steps from the car, momentarily, and looks directly at Diane.

"I will not! If you don't leave, I'm calling the police," her chest heaving up and down with such force that it looks like she's going to explode.

"No one is hurting you, Diane. I simply want to show you something. Go back inside and shut your home down for a few minutes. That's all," he gets back inside and starts up the car, which takes no time to rev itself up, back to life, after a long, brutal slumber.

He then raises the garage door by pushing a button inside of the car. Diane reluctantly goes back inside and turns the oven off. She then walks into the foyer area and gets her coat from the rack. Griping the entire time, she turns off the lights and closes the door of the garage to the house behind herself.

"Get in," he lowers the window on the front, passenger side.

"You're kidnapping me!" she hops in, slamming the door shut.

"I want to show you something," he backs out slowly, lowering the garage door after he's a considerable distance away.

"Why am I doing this for you?" she shake her head.

"There's a special place I've been meaning to take you. Just sit back and relax. It'll take us a few minutes to get there," he nods.

"You have no right driving Frederick's car like this. You're kidnapping and stealing," she rolls her eyes.

"He had great taste. This car rides smoothly."

"My Frederick was the best. He always did things first class," she smiles a little.

"Morning traffic," Robert makes a few turns and uses some convenient back roads.

"Where are you taking me? I demand to know."

"Demand," he glances at her, one eyebrow up and the other digging deeply into his forehead.

"I want to know," she clears her throat.

"You'll see," he makes a few more turns.

"This is crazy. I should've called the police when I went back inside."

"You were never going to call the police."

"How can you be so certain?"

"Because you know that I'm right about your son and Frederick's car. Everything. And you're just a little bit curious about where I'm taking you right now," he smiles.

"You think you know so much Robert Kingsman. Oh, you men!" she huffs, folding her arms tightly.

"Well, here we are," he makes the final turn into Harmony Cemetery.

"You just brought me to a cemetery. Why?"

"You'll see. He drives inside and proceeds to move around the maze like structure. Snaking slowly over the thinly laid pavement, he arrives at a patch of gravesites.

"Come on. Don't forget to button up," he gets out quickly, taking the keys with him.

"Why did I ever allow this man into my home this morning?" Diane wonders out loud before stepping from the car.

"This is what I wanted to show you," he motions her over.

"What?" she walks slowly towards him.

"This was my beloved wife. Mrs. Charlotte Rae Kingsman. She died three years ago from

breast cancer. The doctors caught it too late. We tried everything to keep her alive. From chemotherapy to home remedies, nothing worked. I stayed up many nights cursing God and begging him, at the same time, to spare my wife's life. But on March 14th, 2004, she died at Bethel Grace Haven Memorial Hospital at 12:37 a.m. from complications. I was very hurt, but a small part of me was at peace. For a very long time, I blamed God for what I was going through. Many people say that God doesn't try us out with evil, horrible things. I don't know what to believe. But my wife had suffered terribly, and I watched her die. She melted away right before my very eyes. This vibrant, young, beautiful woman, so full of zest and life. She was reduced to this small, weak and shriveling shell of a person. I didn't even recognize her when she died. Her looks had faded so badly that it was like looking at a foreigner. I toiled around the house for many months afterwards. I cried and cursed. I cried and cured some more and some more and some more. But then I decided one day to live, Diane. I decided to live not only for me but for our son."

"You have a son," she gasps.

"Yeah. You didn't know I had a son," he grins.

"I had no idea."

"Have you ever heard of the writer John Harvey Kingsman?"

"The renowned psychologist! The one who writes the journals every year," her little eyes opened widely.

"Yes, that's him."

"Your son is Dr. John Harvey Kingsman! I read his work all the time. His seminars are standing room only. Why didn't you tell me your son was Dr. John Harvey Kingsman?"

"I didn't think it mattered."

"Oh, my God. This is so amazing."

"How do you feel?" he smiles at her.

"I still don't know why you brought me here."

"You have got to learn how to put the past behind you and live for those who are still here with you now. My wife was a huge part of my life and losing her was especially hard, but we had a son that needed me to be there for him, too, so I couldn't be a recluse forever. Find your own way of dealing with the past, or it will consume you totally. I still come up here every now and then to see Charlotte's grave, but I know that she's not here anymore. She's gone, Diane. She's been gone for three long, agonizing years. I had to find a way to deal with that pain and move on. The 'living' simply needed me more. Just like your two boys. They loved their father very, very much. But he's gone. You are the only one left for them, and they both need you, now, more than ever. Don't close the door on them. Either one," he looks into her eyes and then slowly walks back to the car and waits for her.

On Saturday, everyone shows up at Diane's house for the huge family get-together. Daniel shows up last with two uninvited but interesting guests.

"Mom," he enters carrying a lot of grocery store plastic bags.

"My goodness. Did you buy out the entire place?" she laughs, shaking her head.

"Oh let us help you, Daniel," Evon, Ruth and Patty come running up to them.

As the women help bring the bags inside, Daniel speaks with his mother further.

"I was in the store shopping and ran into a good friend."

"Who did you see?" Diane frowns.

"Me," Robert steps into the doorway.

"Robert. I should've known."

"And I'm not alone, Diane. This is my son, John," he motions for him to step out into the doorway as well.

"Oh, my goodness! Dr. John Harvey Kingsman! I read all of your medical journals. I love your work," she jumps for joy, clasping her hands together and smiling broadly.

"Thank you so much, Dr. Wasserman Schultz. My father has told me some very good things about you."

"Call me Diane, please," she smiles, unclasping her hands and swallowing hurriedly.

"Well Mom. I knew they weren't invited here, but I did happen to see them in the store. Neither one had anything else planned for today. Can they stay a while?" Daniel starts to take off his coat.

"Of course they can stay. Come on in," she nods, motioning the men to enter quickly.

John enters right away and joins Daniel. The two begin talking as they move casually through the foyer and into the warm, crowded and bustling kitchen beyond.

"I see someone took some very good advice," Robert clears his throat, looking around.

"You and your son just happened to be at the same store where Daniel was shopping," she folds her arms with a crooked smile, never taking her eyes off of Robert.

"Well let's just say that me and John were in the vicinity of the grocery store, and Daniel just happened to pick us up on his way over here to be with you."

"What am I going to do with you, Mr. Robert Kingsman?" she exhales, grinning proudly from ear to ear.

"I don't know, but I hope it starts off with a long, cozy drive up the coast to a small cabin, with a roaring fire, near this frozen lake that I know. It's simply breathtaking this time of year," he grins, unzipping his black leather coat.

"Get in here," Diane laughs heartily, closing the door behind him.

Chapter Eighteen

Veronica Deloris Green was Dr. Diane Wasserman Schultz's secretary. She handled everything for the doctor. When Diane gave her family get-together, Veronica was one of the first people invited. She showed up early but stayed just a short time. Her husband, Curtis Green, was home sick with the flu, and she wanted to get back as soon as possible. After saying her good-byes, she left.

"I'll see you in the office on Monday, Dr. Wasserman Schultz. Thanks again for inviting me," Veronica smiles, walking to her car.

"Don't mention it. Give my love to Curtis. Drive safely now," she waves.

"Good-bye, Mrs. Green," Robert waves as well, standing on the huge porch with Diane.

"Nice woman," Robert looks at Diane, as Veronica starts up her car and drives away.

"She's one of the best," Diane nods.

"Let's get back inside. It's cold out here," Robert stands to the side as Diane hurries back inside, and he follows closely behind.

As she drives, she suddenly remembers that Curtis has only a small amount of medicines at home. She quickly pulls into the nearest drug store parking lot.

"I need some medications for the flu. Can you tell me the best kind to buy?" she looks at a young clerk, holding an adding machine.

"I use this," she picks up a bottle.

"But is it really good?" she examines the bottle closely.

"It works for me. This is the very best," she nods, smiling the entire time.

"All right. I'll take this and some chicken soup. Where is the soup aisle?"

"You'll find what you're looking for in aisle number two," she points.

"Thank you," Veronica walks away.

Once she got the medicines, soups and juices, it was time to head home. Their adopted daughter, Su-Lee, had volunteered to stay home and look after her father while Veronica was at the gathering of Dr. Wasserman Schultz. Her best friends had invited her out to a movie, but she declined. Veronica felt extremely guilty and decided she would allow Su-Lee to drive her car on Sunday to a football game at the local college. That was the least she could do. When she approaches the house, she sees that Curtis's car has been moved.

"I hope nothing happened," she says to herself, quickly parking and running up to the front door with the bags.

When she enters, the house is quiet. No televisions or radios are playing. This is not like Su-Lee. She usually has the radio playing in the living room at least. Veronica walks into the kitchen and sits the bags down. She proceeds to start cooking a can of chicken soup for Curtis. After taking off her coat, finally, she heads up the stairs to the bedroom. The house is unusually quiet. As she approaches the master bedroom door, she hears what sounds like tiny grunts and moans. She can't quite make out what's being mumbled but

it is definitely the sound of a woman. Who could this be in my bedroom with Curtis? She grabs the door knob and turns it ever so quietly. As the door opens, she sees through the crack that's formed. Su-Lee is on top of Curtis straddling him like she's riding on a horse. The two are so caught up in their illicit passion that they don't even notice Veronica has entered into the room. She stands by the door a full minute or so just watching, horrified, sickened, gasping, wanting to jump out the nearest window. Suddenly, Curtis turns his head slightly toward the door and sees her. He immediately throws Su-Lee off of him and pulls the covers over himself.

"What did you do that for?!" she screams, hitting the floor on the other side of the bed.

"Veronica! I didn't see you standing there. This is not what it looks like, baby," he gets out of the bed, grabbing his underwear.

"You and Su-Lee. You have been sleeping with Su-Lee behind my back. This is our adopted daughter. How could you sleep with her?! She's seventeen years old, and your daughter!" Veronica speaks, gasping a little and turning very pale.

"I know this was stupid. Please don't jump to any conclusions. I still love you very much," he puts his pants and shirt on, coughing some.

"I went to the store and brought you some medicine back. I brought you soup and juice. Everything is downstairs waiting. I call myself coming home to take care of you because I felt guilty going to that get-together at Dr. Wasserman Schultz's. I came home to be with you, and this is what I'm rewarded with. You're having sex in our bed with Su-Lee! I just don't know what to say next. You are disgusting, Curtis."

"Please baby. I didn't mean for any of this to happen. She came in here and seduced me. Su-Lee came into this room and flaunted herself around me, half-dressed. I didn't want to do it."

"You're sick! It was not her responsibility to be moral here. It was yours. I don't care if she walked into this room wearing nothing but a smile. You are the adult. You should've told her to get out and wait for me to come back home. I would've handled the situation. But what did you do? You gave in to those selfish, illicit desires and now you're stuck with the consequences," she turns and leaves.

"Where are you going?" he follows.

"First, I'm going to the kitchen to turn off that burning soup and, then, I'm going over to my mother's house. I want you out of here by the time I return."

"You want me out. Where am I suppose to go?" he coughs.

"I don't care where you go, but it better be far away from here. Su-Lee will stay here with me," she goes into the kitchen.

"So you're punishing me. Nothing will happen to Su-Lee."

"You are the adult, Curtis! How many times must I remind you of that fact. I will deal with Su-Lee in another way. I want you out of here," she turns off the burning soup and throws the pot into the sink.

"You want me out of my own house. What if I refuse to leave?"

"Then I will call the police and have you arrested for statutory rape. You're just lucky I'm not in the mood right this very moment to call the cops. I want to talk with someone I trust first," she huffs, turning toward the sink and the burnt, smoky pot.

"It's not my fault," he picks up a cast iron black frying pan, laying on the kitchen's island and smacks Veronica across the back of the head with it.

She immediately falls down to the floor like a side of beef freshly cut after the saw.

"What have I done?!" he stutters, coughing, nose running and shaking from the chills.

"Curtis!" Su-Lee runs into the kitchen.

"Don't start with me, Su-Lee. Veronica was throwing me out of here. I had to do it."

"Is she dead? Did you kill her?" her eyes open wide.

He then drags her body through the basement door and down the stairs. He lays her out across the middle of the floor and leaves. After returning upstairs, Su-Lee starts to panic.

"You fool! What have you done?"

"I didn't mean to kill her. I just didn't want her to call the cops on me."

"You didn't have to kill her. What are we going to do now?"

"I don't know. I have to think," he rushed back upstairs to the master bedroom.

"The two argue over whether to dump her body in a ravine or bury her in the woods somewhere. As they discuss and argue, Veronica comes out of the stupor. There is a huge lump on the back of her head. She doesn't remember quite what happened very clearly but she knows enough to want to get out of that house immediately. She stands, steadying herself against the wall which extends to the top of the stairs. Her vision still quite blurry, she makes her way up the steps, one at a time. She slowly opens the basement door into the kitchen area. She then sees the iron frying pan laying lifelessly on the cold, unyielding floor below. She can faintly hear yelling back and forth coming from the bedroom areas. She quietly goes out of the back door, not locking it back, but shutting it behind herself. The cold evening air envelops her, thoroughly, and she gets a second wind, so-to-speak. Staggering onward out the backyard's gate and moving slowly by the side of the house, she finally makes her way to the grayish sidewalk in front of her home. She can see that her neighbors are all home, because their lights are on. Instead of going to a neighbor's home, she walks two blocks to a corner store. Mr. Phillips is the man who always speaks to her when she come in.

"Mr. Phillips," she collapses, falling across his three items or less display.

When she finally wakes up, she is in a cozy hospital bed, with her mother beside her.

"What happened?" she tries to sit up, looking around the room with a slight frown.

"Don't move, baby, you're ill," June Avery takes a cool rag and places it on her forehead.

"Where is Curtis?"

"He's been called. The police are bringing him here to see you."

"No," she shakes her head rather gingerly.

"Why? What's wrong? What happened to you, Veronica?" June frowns, staring at her daughter sharply.

"It was Curtis that did this to me. He hit me with something. I believe it was a frying pan," she starts to cry.

"Curtis did this to you. I don't believe it," June stands, gasping for air.

"I didn't think he would do anything like this either. He put me in the basement and I escaped. I believe he thought that he had killed me."

"Oh, Veronica. We must tell the police. Why would Curtis do such a thing?" June sat slowly, shaking her head.

At that very moment, there was a knock on the door.

"Who is it?" June stands again.

"Diane and Robert. May we come in?"

"Yes. Come in, Dr. Wasserman Schultz," June nods.

"Oh, my God. What happened to you, Veronica?" she enters quickly with Robert in toe.

"Hello, Dr. Wasserman Schultz."

"Call me Diane. We're off the clock now," she grins.

"You know I can't do that, doctor," she smiles.

"What happened?" Diane looks at June.

"Veronica just told me that Curtis did this to her. He hit her across the head with a frying pan."

"Curtis did this! He hit you with a frying pan. I don't believe it."

"It's true. He hit me, hard, and I went down. That's what happened."

"How do you know it was a frying pan?" Robert rubs his chin, never flinching an inch.

"When I came around, I was in the basement. I got up and walked up the stairs. When I emerged into the kitchen, there was the cast iron frying pan laying right there on the floor. I went out the backdoor, not to disturb anyone, because I heard them upstairs talking."

"My God. He could've killed you, Veronica," Diane hugs her tightly, exhaling abruptly.

"I'm all right now, Dr. Wasserman Schultz. I'm just glad he left me in the basement."

"So what happens now?" Diane sighs.

"The police are bringing Curtis here. They don't know that he did this to her. Veronica was found in a corner store, not at the family home."

"We'll just have to tell them what really happened, won't we?" Diane looks at June.

"This is so terrible," Veronica shakes her head.

"What led to all of this anyway?" Robert finally asks the question.

"Yes. What happened to cause him to hit you like that?" Diane scratches her head.

"I caught him in my bed with Su-Lee. The two of them were having sex when I walked in on them earlier. I threatened to call the cops if Curtis didn't leave the house by the time I returned from my mother's home. That's when he hit me."

"Curtis was having sex with Su-Lee. My God!" June gasps, eyes wide open, and clutching her chest.

"Oh my goodness. Are you sure, Veronica? This is very, very serious. Are you really sure that you saw the two of them in that bed together?" Diane swallows hard, not even stopping to breathe.

"I know what I saw, Dr. Wasserman Schultz. The two of them were engaged in sexual intercourse. I walked right in and caught them. That's what happened," she coughs.

"Well, it would seem Curtis has a lot to account for here," Robert exhales quickly, rubbing Diane's shoulders and peering intently at a very gaunt and pale-faced Veronica.

"I can believe that snake would do such a thing. I warned you not to marry that fraud. That man was after your money from the very beginning. Oh, that terrible louse!"

"What money, June?" Diane frowns, glancing at Robert briefly.

"Veronica's father left her over four hundred fifty thousand dollars in a trust fund. It's made up of cash, bonds, mutual funds, etc. It's probably more than that now. No one can touch that money but Veronica. He has been urging her to dig into it ever since they tied the knot," June rolls her eyes, clawing on the thick bed sheets of her distraught daughter.

"Is this true, Veronica?" Diane looks at her, with eyes hungering for an answer totally different from what her mother just espoused.

"Yes. But I thought he loved me. I see, now, that my mother was right from the beginning. He was only after my money and our daughter, apparently."

"If you have so much money, why are you working as a secretary?" Robert asks.

"I enjoy working for Dr. Wasserman Schultz. I couldn't imagine staying home and doing nothing. Going to the office everyday is what I love doing. It's not that I need the salary, but I want to be around people. That's why I work for the good doctor."

Knock, Knock…

"Come in," June looks at the door, releasing her nails from the warm confines of the thick bed coverings.

"Hello, Mrs. Green. I'm Officer Bates and this is Officer Regent."

They enter with Curtis and Su-Lee.

"Hi," June looks at the men.

"Baby," Curtis runs to her bedside.

"You stay away from my daughter! This man hit her across the head with a frying pan."

"What?" Curtis frowns.

"Don't stand there and deny it. Veronica told us everything. You tried to kill her," Diane looks Curtis directly in the eyes.

"Is that what she told you?" Curtis starts laughing.

"What's so funny?" Officer Bates frowns.

Everyone in the room is dumbfounded. Curtis is standing there laughing. Su-Lee cracks a smile as well.

"Veronica was walking up to the house carrying a bag of items. She slipped on the last step and fell back, hitting her head severely on the pavement. I ran inside to get Su-Lee. I wanted her to help me get Veronica inside. By the time we both came back out, Veronica had disappeared. Me and Su-Lee went searching for her. That's why we were outside walking when you both pulled up to our home."

"Your wife slipped on the stairs," Officer Regent glances at Veronica, his eyes immediately shifting off slightly in the distance.

"Go back to the house and check the pavement where you go up the last few steps leading to our front door. You'll see her blood," Su-Lee added, clearing her throat.

"They're lying! I was hit across the head with a frying pan or something very hard. He took me into the basement. Go and look at my blood on the frying pan and inside of the basement," Veronica points, her chest heaving and her words dagger-like.

"Baby, why are you doing this?" Curtis sighs, turning away with faded voice.

"Don't call me your baby. I'm not your baby anymore. You tried to kill me, Curtis. I caught you in my bed with Su-Lee. Don't even try to deny it."

"I was in bed with the flu when I heard your car pull up, so I decided to come down and meet you. That's when I saw you fall. Why are you saying these lies to the police and your mother?"

"They're not lies. I know what I saw you doing. Don't try to make me look like I'm the crazy one here. It's your fault. You were caught screwing around with Su-Lee."

"Su-Lee. Have you ever been in a sexual relationship with Mr. Green?" Officer Regent asks.

"No. He's my father. Why would I do something like that?" she frowns.

"I can't believe this. They're standing there lying to all of you," Veronica gasps.

"I don't know what to believe," Officer Bates looks directly at Curtis, who by now has tears in his eyes.

"Why would Veronica make this up, Curtis? If she loves you as much as I know she does, why would she say such horrible things?" Diane peers at him, tilting her head forward a little.

"I don't know, Diane. Maybe it's the bump on her head. I have no idea, but my wife has taken leave of her senses. I want your help to cure her," he frowns, gingerly wiping his eyes.

"Dr. Wasserman Schultz. You've known me for three years. This is crazy. I know you don't believe Curtis over me," Veronica looks at her directly, exhaling firmly.

" I believe you, Veronica. There is no way you would make this all up. Su-Lee, where were you in the house when Curtis went back inside to get you?"

"In my bedroom. Why?"

"Well, how long did it actually take for him to go and get you from that bedroom? I've been to your house on many occasions, Su-Lee. The front walkway leading to the final four stairs that puts you on the landing where the front door is isn't that long at all. Your bedroom is the first door on the right at the top of the stairs. It shouldn't have taken a very long time for Curtis to get you and make it back outside before Veronica had time to really disappear from view. It's amazing you both didn't make it back outside in order to see her anywhere within a ten to thirty feet radius of the house. A woman with a severe concussion wobbling down a street. Your house sits in the middle of your block. You didn't see her in any direction. That begs the question: How long did it really take for you, Curtis, to go back inside and get Su-Lee from her bedroom to help with Veronica?" Diane frowns, looking around the room as if she were in a courtroom of law.

" I can't really say. Being sick and all, I moved as fast as I could. My body is still very achy and tired. My voice is weak, as you can hear. Obviously it took some time."

"I don't care if you moved like a snail with a turtle on its back. You still should've been able to get back outside to see Veronica. You should've saw the very direction in which she traveled after that severe fall. Clearly she couldn't have run or skipped away."

"I can't account for that." Curtis coughs, thick yellow mucus emerges from his lungs.

"Well there's nothing we can do. I'm sorry, Mrs. Green," the two cops leave.

"I want you out of here. Get out!" Veronica yells as loud as she possibly can.

"Just go," June turns away.

"I love my wife, Dr. Wasserman Schultz. I don't know why she's saying these things about me and Su-Lee." Curtis finally leaves with Su-Lee.

"They lied. They both stood in this very room and lied. What am I going to do?"

"You will get better, Veronica, and then decide what happens next. I want you to rest now. This has been enough excitement for one day," Diane holds her hand.

"Thank you for coming." June looks at Diane and Robert, taking their hands into hers.

"Anything we can do, for the both of you, please, let us know," he smiles, nodding.

"You get some rest." Diane hugs and kisses her on the cheek.

"I will, Dr. Wasserman Schultz."

"Good-bye, June. I'll call later to check up on her." Diane and Robert finally leave.

The room was now semi-empty. June was left staring at her distraught daughter lying in the hospital bed. Veronica was totally beside herself. But there was nothing the police could do. Veronica wasn't hurt or found inside of the home at the time of the attack, so there was little evidence that Curtis tried to kill her, from the policemen's point-of-view. Of course this was all false. Curtis was desperate and wanted Veronica to just accept his foolish explanation for why Su-Lee was caught in their marriage bed having sex with him. When she wouldn't go along with the program and threatened to put him out of the house, he snapped. That's what really happened, but to everyone, not in the home at the time, it could've seemed like Veronica was suffering from a bad bump on the head, due to an unfortunate fall. Could she really have fallen and just don't remember what actually happened? Could Curtis be telling the truth in all of this drama? Robert had his doubts. Especially after the superb performances of both Curtis and Su-Lee. Even Dr. Wasserman Schultz doubted, for a second, that Veronica was getting the facts straight. But then she remembered her friend. The woman who had worked so closely with her for three whole years. There was no way this woman would make up a story like this. She loved Curtis Green with every once of her being, and to come out so boldly with claims like this was not only shocking but had to be the truth. June had mixed feelings about everything that took place. She knew her daughter had suffered some calamity. The question was: How did it happen? Was Curtis and Su-Lee to blame or did she, in fact, slip on some concrete stairs and fall back, hitting her head severely? The only way to know the truth was to examine the evidence. June called in Veronica's nurse and asked her to give her daughter a sedative. Once the nurse did that and left the room, June left the hospital altogether.

On her way over to Veronica and Curtis's home, she allowed her mind to wonder some. What if I find the evidence that incriminates Curtis? He's not going to allow me to leave. I must come up with a plan. There has to be a way to find out if Veronica was telling the truth or just making up the story due to the fall. As she neared the residence, she suddenly saw a parking space midway the block. She took it right away. Getting out quickly, the bitterly cold air met her fiercely, as it always did, announcing its dominance over the outside domain and standing as strong as a prized fighter ready for the boxing ring. With chattering teeth, she walks toward the house. Sensing a strong vibe of Veronica taking these same steps, but in the other direction, away from her own home, away from safety, away from protection, into the cold evening's night. How utterly appropriate that June would walk that sidewalk to the house. Just that past summer, June and Veronica walked to that same corner store, where Veronica was found. June commented on how such a nice, brisk walk was beneficial. Little did they both know, at the time, they would each be making that same walk again, on that same stretch of sideway. One, towards the safety of strangers. The other on a journey to find the truth.

June walks to the rear of the house, remembering what her daughter had said. Just maybe the backdoor was still open. After all, who would think to lock a door that's already closed. She crept inside and walked deliberately to the basement door. The house was quiet. Apparently, the two attempted murderers weren't home yet. Remembering where Veronica kept the full-faced flashlight, she carefully moved towards the cabinet and opened it. After taking out the object, she turned it on, grateful it was actually working. Going down those steps was brutal. She could recall the many other times she would dash down to the basement to get something from the deep freezer or to help wash a load of laundry. Those times, when looking at those stairs, were a headache because of having to climb them again the get out. But this time the stairs were so inviting. They were so welcoming. They were screaming out for someone to walk down them and see. See what the two attempted murderers had done. Remarkably, not one of those stairs squeaked. June was able to descend quietly without so much as a peep from them. Like a gentle breeze on a calm day settling over everything, June made her way effortlessly down those stairs and onto the cold basement floor below. Unannounced and unnoticed, she made her way through the boxes and other items that seem to jump out at her all of a sudden. The things her daughter had accumulated over the years closed in on her. After taking a deep breath and exhaling slowly, she went about the searching for the blood. The light blazing high in the full moon mode. The floors looked clean, that freshly scrubbed appearance. Things seemed to be put in just the right places. June had been down here many times over the years and never quite remembered everything basically stacked, neatly organized and positioned. Even the big, bulky things sat quietly in their own spaces not making so much as a peep. It seems Curtis and Su-Lee were very busy cleaning up their mess. Was Veronica right about being down here and bleeding onto the floor? The place did seem extra clean for some reason and one thing Curtis was never known for was his neatness. Not seeing anything incriminating, June headed back for the stairs, but suddenly, she heard the front door open. They were back. The two attempted murderers were back and she was caught in their basement. What to do? What to do? That's what raced through her mind. Not finding any blood on the basement floor meant she was trespassing, and this could be trouble for her in a court of law. But she had little time to think about court proceedings and the like. The obtrusive sound of two attempted murderers was heard on the squeaky floor just above her. They didn't waste any time going to the kitchen for a drink or maybe cooking something to fill those guts of theirs. They tore into laughter and joking about getting away with it. Su-Lee was the loudest. This girl that I had called my own granddaughter. I held nothing back from this person. I treated her just as I would a grandchild that actually came from the womb of my own daughter. I never once thought that she could be so evil and vile as to betray the woman that visited her in her homeland of China more than twelve times. Veronica went through many hoops to get Su-Lee here, as an American citizen. She toiled day and night with immigration and customs. With the Chinese and American governments. The daily and demanding stresses of adoption from its very beginning to the final signature on the dotted line is horrendous. The peaks and valleys that one must endure is riveting to say the least, and I, June Ruda, stood quietly by and watched my Veronica go through all of this for this ingrate of a girl called Su-Lee.

She withstood the many trials and tribulations that came with securing a little girl that she thought really deserved a chance to live in the United States and be taught the good old U.S.A. creed. I stand in my daughter's drafty basement shocked and horrified at what I'm hearing happening right above me. That harlot is in fact sleeping with Curtis. The proof is right here in front of me now. I did, for a brief moment, doubt my own daughter. I did believe that maybe she wasn't quite as clear about the events surrounding her being in the hospital. After all, how could Curtis be able to do these types of things to a woman who I know he loves. This was my line of thinking. Maybe Veronica got it wrong. Maybe she was confused. I just didn't see Curtis as this evil henchman on a quest to kill my child-my only child. And who would ever have suspected Su-Lee? This girl, now a teenager, of so many affable qualities. Honor roll student in high school. Made the Dean's List many years in a row. Very respectful and studious. She would make you question whether it's raining outside when clearly you see the drops hitting your bedroom window. That's just how good she could be. The tongue of a sweet, innocent salesman bent on selling you something he and you know is not needed. At any rate, I doubted her and for that, I will never forgive myself. But, now, what do I do? Getting out of the house would be fairly easy. The house doesn't have an alarm system and the back door is still open. The two of them have, by now, slinked upstairs and into Veronica and Curtis's marriage bed. I'm sure of it. The laughing and joking around has quieted down a lot. The two are not in the living room anymore. It's time to leave this godforsaken house and never step back into it again. Never dart its doors with even a whisper of my own daughter's name. No reference at all to this horrible place I once enjoyed coming to. I'll leave this terrible place and never return. June makes her way up the stairs and is able to now turn the flashlight off. Entering the kitchen, she notices the infamous frying pan. There it sat on the stove. There it was. Just sitting there available for the touch and the examination. There was the frying pan that Veronica said she had been struck with. Should I even dare to pick it up? Should I even dare to hold it and see if there is even a trace of human blood on it? Should I even dare to suppose that the two attempted murderers cleaned it up, too? After all, it brazenly sits openly on the stove face up. There it is. No hiding in the crevices of a dusty back drawer under the sunken white sink. No out of sight location where the human mind would even dream of looking. It sits so openly and self assuredly on the stove announcing to the world that it has nothing to hide. It sits there telling the world that it's only use is frying things and nothing more. It sits there as if nothing at all has happened. June reaches out her hand and grips the handled firmly. I will be the judge of that. I will see if you have anything to hide. She picks up the pan slowly and flips it over. The smears of blood can still be seen on the bottom of the pan. It was as if someone had just placed it back on the stove and neglected to clean off the bottom of it. The evidence was damning. It was truly damning. Here was the proof that Veronica had been telling the truth the entire time. Here was the proof that she had not gone crazy and lost her mind. Here was the actual proof that that no good husband of hers was not only having an illicit affair with their adopted daughter, but he had in fact tried to kill her and cover it all up. What on earth would June do with this information? The two shameless lovers were upstairs, in the master bedroom by this time, enjoying the delectable fruits of one another yet again. This was a horrible thing to imagine, but it was occurring all the same.

The thought of going to the police did cross her mind, but then she would have to explain how she got into the house and on and on and on. The situation could easily be spun to Curtis's advantage. That was never going to happen. Not to June and her daughter. She places the frying pan down on a counter and then discreetly turns on the stove. Making sure the pilot light isn't lit, the gas pours out of all four of the eyes. June now makes her way to the back door and then stops, suddenly, and turns. She takes one final look at the house where she once stayed an entire week while her daughter and husband were away on vacation. She took one final look at where she had finally learned how to make blueberry muffins with her daughter. She took one final look around at everything and then left. The next morning brought terrible news from the police.

"Mrs. Green, we're sorry about this. It looks like a suicide."

"Officer Trenton. Are you sure?"

"Yes. All of the stove's eyes were turned on and the two of them simply slipped off into a deep sleep together. There is no doubt that they were sleeping together."

"How were you informed of the suicide?" June sat completely still, waiting for the response.

"A neighbor smelled the gas and called the police. When we responded, it was much too late to save anyone in the house. It was completely engulfed with gas."

"Thank you," she finally moved, glancing at her daughter.

"If there is anything we can do, Mrs. Green, let us know."

"I will. Thank you, again."

"Goodbye," the two officers left the room.

"Dead. Mother, I can't believe it."

"Well, believe it. No more Curtis and Su-Lee to cause you pain."

"Mother. I woke-up late last night and noticed that you were gone. Where did you go?"

"I went out to get some dinner."

"Dinner," she paused, swallowing hard and quickly.

"Yes. Why?"

"Then how do you explain that?" she pointed to the full-faced flashlight sitting in a nearby corner next to June's coat.

"Never you mind, my dear. Never you mind," she sighed, turning away slowly and squinting just a little.

Geraldine Margarite Holland was face down on the floor of her penthouse apartment.

The police swarming all around with guns drawn and screaming frantically for the man, Carlos Hernandez, to drop his weapon. This wasn't how Geraldine expected her life to turn out when she married Theodore Winston Holland thirty-eight years earlier. The couple had little time for children because of the constant traveling. But Theodore had a secret that he hid from Geraldine for many years. Secretly, he lived a double life. Across town from where he and Geraldine lived was another family of his. He was illegally married to a second woman named Carla Sampson Rodgers Holland. She was a housewife with two children fathered by Theodore. Carla knew all about Geraldine, but didn't mind sharing him with her. Theodore, a wealthy commodies broker and private attorney to those within his own circle, made more than enough money to keep both families living in a lifestyle worthy of the Joneses. Geraldine, by occupation, was a successful and accomplished doctor in her own right. She spent many of her later years specializing in pediatric medicine. Helping children all over the world in developing countries to get the care and assistance they needed to simply go to school. Whenever Theodore went on out-of-town conferences, Geraldine spent that time traveling to Africa and South America. She would venture into sparsely populated villages and small towns in need of her medical expertise. The sex between Geraldine and Theodore had settled to a low ebb a few years earlier, but the two found time to enjoy each other's company in other ways. Vacations to Hawaii and often to the Carribian Islands were special. Theodore always found time to spend holidays with both families. Carla and the boys saw him mostly at Christmas time and during special occassions within the kids' lives. Geraldine always had him at awards' dinners/banquets and gatherings, where spouses of the doctors were invited for weekend retreats. Theodore was very happy with his life and enjoyed traveling back and forth for a good fifteen years, but that all came crashing down when one of his children became seriously ill while out at the playground with his nanny. He was taken straight to the same hospital where Geraldine Holland was on duty. It just so happened that Geraldine was scheduled to be off that Saturday, but a fellow doctor's wife was having a baby, in that same hospital, and wasn't going to be on duty when that event took place. Geraldine decided to come in and take over his rounds. This would be a day she would never forget.

"What's wrong with him?" Geraldine enters the room almost breathless.

"The nanny brought him in. He simply collapsed at a playground," a nurse read line by line from a chart.

"Let's take a look at you, young man," she calmly walks to the bedside and frowns.

"What's the problem?" the nurse notices the frown almost immediately.

"This child looks so familiar to me. The eyes and nose. Strangely familiar," she shakes her head and touches his forehead.

"What do you want me to do, Doctor Holland?"

"Leave me with him. Go and find out where his parents are," she never takes her eyes off of him.

"Yes, Doctor Holland," she leaves in a hurry.

Outside of the hospital room, Nurse Stafford meets with Carla, who by this time has just arrived, and Henrietta.

"I am Nurse Betty Stafford. Doctor Holland is in with your son now. She should be done momentarily. You'll be able to get more information then. But, now, your son is stable."

"I hate hospitals."

"Quiet Henrietta," Carla touched her arm, biting her bottom lip continuously.

"I'll send Doctor Holland to you once she's done," Nurse Stafford walks away.

"I'm going to finally get a chance to meet her up close," Carla sighs, turning towards a wall and grimacing.

"Meet her. What are you talking about, Sis?'

"Geraldine. She works here."

"Oh, my God. Geraldine Holland is the same Doctor Holland that nurse was talking about. She's attending to Chris!"

"Yeah. Go figure. She doesn't know me of course, but I know all about her."

"Hello. Nurse Stafford pointed you two out to me. I'm Doctor Geraldine Holland. You are Mrs. Carla Holland," Geraldine walks over and extends her hand.

"I don't use Holland. I'm Mrs. Rodgers," Carla swallows hard, looking around subtly.

"Oh, well. Mrs. Rodgers. Your forms say Holland," Geraldine smiles, glancing at the clipboard.

"Tell me, Doctor Holland. How is my son?"

"There is absolutely nothing to worry about now, Mrs. Rodgers. He was suffering from severe dehydration. He is now hooked up to a drip that will hydrate him completely. Just a couple more hours and he should be ready to leave."

"Thank you. What a relief. Oh, I'm so sorry. This is my sister, Henrietta Sampson."

"Hello Ms. Sampson. Well, if there is anything else I can do, let me know," she smiles again and walks away.

"She's nice."

"They all seem that way until they find out you're sleeping with their husbands," Carla exhales walking towards the waiting room.

Little Christopher Holland was given the drip and released from the hospital. His mother quickly took him from the hospital and scurried pathetically back to their home. Carla was enamored with Geraldine. This accomplished doctor using her time to help children all over the planet. There was a quiet dignity about that. She saw Gerri as a woman of taste and integrity. Even though she knew about Geraldine and was all right with the relationship that Theodore had set up, she was still a wee bit jealous. She hadn't gone to college and there were no fancy degrees hanging on her walls. All she had to show for what she had was a rich husband, and he wasn't even her husband technically. The money in the accounts said that Carla Sampson Rodgers Holland could play in the game with the big boys and girls, however her background truly kept her from really belonging. With all she had, there was still this outside looking in mentality that she could never seem to overcome. Her family was from the seedy part of town and nothing good ever grew there, the rich would say between cocktails and the occasional five course meal at the most expensive restaurants around. Carla would often complain about still not quite fitting in and Theodore would try to calm her fears and inhibitions.

"Why do you believe you don't belong?"

"You just don't understand. You come from privilege and position. Your parents were in politics."

"Carla. My parents have nothing to do with why you're in here feeling sorry for yourself."

"I saw Geraldine today. She actually waited on Christopher when he became ill," she sighs.

"You never told me that you saw Geraldine there. You didn't say anything, did you?" he gulps, standing up immediately.

"I would never jeopardize what we have here, sweetheart. That's not the point. I know that you have set me and the kids up for a very long time, but I need more. I want to be someone. I want to have something that's really mine."

"What are you talking about? You have a beautiful home and two very good children. A husband that loves you. What more could you want?"

"I want what Geraldine has."

"What?"

"Yes. I want what Geraldine has. She has a career and people who really depend on her to make their lives better. She has a life outside of being your first wife. She travels and speaks at conventions. Very important people listen to every word she says. I want that. The degrees hanging from my office walls. I actually went to her office today and saw where she went to school."

"You went to Geraldine's office at the hospital."

"Yes. I wanted to see what else I could learn about her. She invited me in just before Christopher was released. We talked about her college years at Wellsely and then her medical training at Yale. I was very impressed."

"I've told you about Geraldine before. Why did you need to go to her office?"

"I had to see for myself. I wanted to see the degrees hanging on the wall. That's what I want, Theodore. You must not deny me," she looks into his eyes.

"Well what do you want me to do?"

"I want to go to college. I have my high school diploma. I want to go to a nice college and study something important."

"What would you like to study?"

"I don't know. I've always thought about social work. What do you think about that?"

"Social work is noble. You could do a lot of good things with a degree in that. I will support you one hundred percent. Get all of the college information ready and we'll register you," he smiles.

"Thank you, baby. I knew you wouldn't let me down."

"But what about the boys? You are a stay at home mom, remember."

"We could hire a nanny that can care for them full-time during the weekends. After all, they are in school most of the day anyway. It's only in the late afternoons and evenings when the nanny will actually be needed. I can see to the details."

"I'm sure you can, my dear. Well, I have to go now. Gerri will be home soon and I promised to have dinner waiting," he kisses her on the lips.

"Running off to be with her. Why don't you just divorce that slut!"

"Carla. Now, now. You know I can't divorce Gerri. We have an agreement. I have to go. You be good. I'll be back tomorrow morning," he smiles and leaves.

Geraldine couldn't get over the fact that the twelve year old boy she saw earlier that day looked so familiar. She couldn't quite put her finger on it but he was very familiar in a gentle, kind sort of way. The kind of way you long for. His face told a story of passion and history all at the same time. Where have I seen you before? I know that I've seen you somewhere. She goes over the boy's face in her mind. Nothing triggers. But the nagging thoughts are there. Where have I seen him? She hops into her car and starts out of the hospital parking lot. The day passes issued to doctors were late yet again and she has to show her identification to avoid paying the fees. You would think a hospital this size would have the decency to give its doctors their passes for the parking facilities on time. God only knows they demand that we turn in things on time and according to regulations. Getting our passes on time for once would be nice. But I digress. The roads are simply packed with people trying to get home to love ones. Nothing is moving. Everyone seems to be going in the same direction. Just as she starts to hit the main highway that would take her home, the thoughts crowd into her head like passengers hurrying for that last train leaving the station. Hurrying to pick-up that last newspaper on a busy news day morning. That's where I've seen that boy's face. That's where it was. In Theodore's old picture album. That's where that child resides in the recesses of my mind. He sits there in that picture album. I will have to get that album and see. Get that album and see if I'm really correct. The nagging and prodding won't go away. I've seen that child's face and the thoughts won't leave me be until I have satisfied them. The car finally picks up speed. Geraldine is able to reach a good stretch of highway which brings her ever closer to her home. Brings her ever closer to finding that boy in the picture album. But how could some strange boy's picture be in Theodore's picture album? How crazy of me to ever believe this. What am I saying to myself here? A strange boy's picture will actually be in my Theodor's picture album. The thoughts were becoming stronger and stronger as the car neared the palatial home. Geraldine quickly parked and literally hopped from the driver's seat of the car. She hurried to the front door and scrambled for her keys. The very keys that would allow her to enter the house and see if her perdiction was correct. She opens the door without force and gains entry. Now, where is the picture album? That's what races through her mind again and again. She hurries to the den and searches the many cabinets and bins. Nothing. She then goes into the library and searches the shelves and various cabinets in there. Still, nothing. She then goes into the living room and searches the coffee table and end tables. Nothing. Where on earth can that picture album be? I know Theodore didn't move it anywhere special, did he? That would surely be preposterous. He would have no reason to hide the picture book.

As soon as her mind started to wonder on where the picture album could be, she immediately thought of the bedroom and the little sitting area just off the bathroom. Geraldine keeps many books there. Here is where she thinks and meditates on things. Here is where she reflects on past events and prepares for future endeavors. The picture book is more than likely to be here. That famous sitting room of sorts. Where Theodore told her of his promotion and their trip to the Carribean Islands to celebrate. Where his aunt announced that she would be leaving all of her worldly possessions to Theodore upon her death from complication with cancer. This one room which has seen so many good and bad times. Where Geraldine received the news that she couldn't have children from Doctor Witherspoon, a trusted friend. Geraldine ran to the bedroom and flung the grand doors wide open. She walked what seemed two miles to the little sitting room off the huge bathroom area. And there it was. The very picture book she had been fantasizing about looking through to find that boy's picture. Not wasting any more time, she hurries over and grabs the book. She sits slowly and gulps. What am I doing? This is crazy. What do I mean to accomplish? That boy has nothing to do with me or this family. Why is this so important to me? Not daring to put the book down, she opens it slowly and almost by instinct knows just what page to turn to. She flips the pages slowly at first but then picks up the pace. What am I doing? This boy won't be in this album. He couldn't be. But there he was. The exact replica! It was as if the boy jumped out of this very book and presented himself for inspection in that hospital bed earlier. My God. Where did he come from? The two were exactly alike. Right down to the small dimple or some would say a minor cleft above the top lip. This was a picture of Theodore at age eleven. He looks exactly like that boy in the hospital bed. How can that be? I'm sure there are millions of people who look alike but what are the odds that they look this much alike without being related. Oh, listen to me. I'm being silly. I'm being very silly now. My thoughts are running away with me. How can this boy be related to my Theodore? That doesn't make any sense. Oh, well, I just need to leave this entire situation alone. It makes no sense. By the way, where is Theodore? He was suppose to make dinner tonight. Not ten minutes later, Theodore comes walking through the front door. He calls out several times before heading into the kitchen.

"Hello," Gerri comes back downstairs and joins him in the kitchen.

"Hi. Sorry I'm late. I had to see a client just before coming home, but I will have dinner done very soon."

"Theo. I have to ask you something. I don't want you to get angry."

"Why would I get angry?"

"I had a very interesting patient today, and he's still on my mind."

"Should I be jealous or worried?" he smirks, reaching into the refridgrator.

"Nothing like that. It was a young boy. His name was Christopher."

"Christopher," he swallows hard, reaching into the refridgerator once more.

Yes. It seems rather odd that he looks exactly like you did many years ago. I saw him and almost froze solid. His face was the mirror image of yours."

"Some people look alike all over, Gerri. What are you implying?" he closes the refridgerator door and looks at her.

"I'm not implying anything, Theo. It just seems so strange that this boy would look just like you did at age eleven. How utterly curious," she snickers, shaking her head.

"I would think. Now, what about spagetti and meatballs with garlic bread and wine?"

"That sounds heavenly. I also met a very strange woman today."

"Strange woman. How was she strange?"

"Well it was her son that I saw. She came to my office and literally forced herself upon me. Asking questions about my life and family. I didn't want to be rude but she was very pushy."

"How did you deal with her?" he walks to the stove and pauses briefly.

"I was kind. What I could tell her about myself, I did. But I felt sorry for her on some level. Here child had fainted on the playground due to deydration and she was a nervous wreck when I first saw her. You know how compassionate I can be for those who are in need."

"I do."

"I hope she doing well tonight. Can I help?"

"No. I have it. Just relax."

"You're so good to me. What would I ever do without you?"

"I don't know, but I love you, too," he smiles filling a pot with water.

Geraldine walks into the den and starts to clean up the mess she made earlier searching for the picture album. As she puts things back in place, the phone rings.

"I'll get it," Gerri yells out.

"Hello."

"Is this Geraldine Holland?"

"It is. How can I help you?"

"You don't know me well, my dear, but I'm a relative of Carla Holland's."

"Who is this person you speak of? I have no knowledge of such a woman."

"Carla Holland."

"I don't know anyone by that name. I'm sorry. You have the wrong number."

"I don't have the wrong number. Carla Rodgers Holland's son was admitted to your hospital earlier today, suffering from dehydration. She was in your office, too, I recall."

"Who are you? Why are you calling me?" one eyebrow raised and the other shifting.

"Get with it, lady. Your husband has been cheating on you with Carla Holland for years now. He has even married her illegally. That child you saw today is your husband's son."

"What?!"

"You were thinking it already, weren't you?"

"You're lying. None of this is true. Why should I ever believe this filth?"

"I'm lying. You don't really believe that. But I guess it would be very convenient, seeing you're so content on staying with your husband no matter what. To just dismiss all of this as foolish talk and return to that toad of a man, Theodore, pretending everything is fine."

"Who are you? How do you know these things about my family?"

"I told you that I'm a friend of Carla Holland's. Of course I'm not acting like a very good friend now. She refused to give me that two thousnad dollars she promised if I did some work for her. That woman is a liar and cheat."

"What do you want from me?" Geraldine gasps, grabbing her chest and exhaling slowly.

"Just to tell you that your faithless husband and Carla have been together for over fifteen years and that he has two children with her. That boy you saw today is his and there is another son. His name is Matthew. Carla lives on the other side of town. I can tell you her address and telephone number. Do you want them?"

After dinner, Geraldine made up an excuse to leave the house. Theodore went to bed early and paid little attention to what his wife did in her spare time anyway. She took a ride over to where the mystery woman said Carla Holland lived. The drive was scary and life-changing. What would I actually see out here? Will I see that woman I met today as a stranger? Was that mystery woman lying, or was she telling me something that I needed to know? I can't even begin to know what to think. Theodore and I have been married for thirty-eight years. He couldn't do something this heinous to me. Could he? Could it be that the man I've loved all these years is sleeping with someone else? Is he giving his affections to another woman? Is he the father of two children? So many questions and not enough answers. Do I really want the answers? Can I truly handle what the answers would be? This wreched car takes me closer and closer to this address and I repel the cruel thoughts that race through my mind. It started with seeing that boy today and now I'm on my way to his home. How utterly shocking. Can it be that Theodore is the father of two sons and this Carla woman is his second wife? I can't believe that. The town car eventually comes to a stop in front of the address of Carla Holland's home. It wasn't a grand place. Very ordinary and usual. You would think with all the money that Theodore has he would at least buy something more ostentatious for his illegal second wife. The many negative thoughts raced, with great speed, throughout Gerri's mind. She sits in her car looking around at all of the other showcased cars perfectly parked in front of the well- manicured lawns and darkened windows of their upper middle-class owners. Many have gone to bed by now. Some are still wide awake. A few lights are on here and there. The quiet of the cold night. The giant streetlights glaring and announcing that nighttime has arrived yet again to the area, and it's time for them to lend a helping hand in showing natives, as well as visitors alike, the way. Gerri sits there wondering if its all a cruel joke at her expense. Maybe this so-called mystery woman was lying to get a rise out of me. What if this isn't Carla Holland's home and I've shown up here for no good reason? I am such a fool. What am I doing here? I better get back home. I have an important surgery in the morning. Rest is needed. Why am I so stupid? Listening to some strange woman about my own husband. I do know Theodore Holland better than anyone else ever could. He would never cheat on me, let alone father two children and carry on a fifteen year relationship. How pathetic of me to believe such lies. I know my husband. He is a kind and gentle man. He loves me. He always will. Time to get back home and slip into bed beside my beloved. This has been a total waste of time. These purely negative thoughts have kept me going. They have kept me wrapped up in a quandary. They have allowed the decent and moral thoughts to be relegated to backseat status. I must leave this place and get back home to the man I love. He must be worried sick about me now. Waking and not finding me in the house after all of this time has gone by. He may call the police if I'm not home this very instant. Oh, God. Who am I kidding? What planet am I on? I know things haven't been very good between me and Theodore lately. He's always at a conference and away from home. The sex isn't what it used to be, but I always thought we did our best to make sure the other was satisfied. What if the mystery woman is right about all of this? I've been that fool I detest so much?

Maybe I should investigate and find out if Carla Holland lives here and what her ties are to my husband. Maybe I should.

Geraldine gets out of her car and slowly walks up to the front door. Not fearing any man or thing, she sternly knocks and waits for an answer. The whispering winds are blowing subtly but briskly. The sound of healthy dogs barking in the distance and leaves rustling are very distinct.

"Yes," the front door opens partially, obscuring the owner's face.

"Are you Carla Holland?"

"I am," the feminine voice replied, while looking out focused, methodically.

"I am Doctor Geraldine Holland. We met earlier at the hospital."

"Doctor Gerri Holland. What are you doing here?"

"May I come in? We need to talk, Carla."

"You found out about me and Theodore. Did he confess it all to you?" she stands to the side, head up high, as Gerri enters boldly, eyes peering around every corner.

"There was nothing said by my Theodore. I simply figured it out. I must give you credit for the brazenness and utter disregard for my feelings. You forward hussy!"

"Is that the very best you can do? Oh, come on, Mrs. Holland, the first, or should I say, Mrs. Naïve, the hopeless. I must give you credit. Being able to finally grasp what our husband has be up to all of these years. Why are you here? To get revenge, no doubt."

"To see if it was really true. To see if my thoughts were just foolish thoughts or was there a hint of logic involved. You seem very content to live, here, with my Theodore, knowing his situation. I must confess to you that I wouldn't be as bold, my dear. There is simply not enough love in this world to endure such a heinous thing as a kept woman."

"I'm not kept, and this has nothing to do with being bold, Geraldine. I have asked our Theodore to leave you and come be with me. That shouldn't sound so amazing."

"It doesn't, coming from the likes of you. It would seem my Theodore thinks otherwise. I want to know one thing and after knowing it, I will leave this house, never to return."

"What would you like to know, Gerri?"

"Do you really love my husband? I don't mean infatuation or a casual love affair. Do you love him enough to sacrifice for him and be there for him through thick and thin?"

"I love Theodore with every once of being I have. There is nothing I wouldn't do for him."

"I love him, too. I must admit that being here, now, has me very perplexed. I thought we were happy. I thought we could work through any problems that presented themselves. This proves that I was wrong-totally misguided."

"Your husband fell in love with me some years after you two were married. What didn't you do to please him? What would make him turn to me for love and affection? I often ask myself those questions. I look at you, now, and I see success and power. I see grandure and the epitome of what women our age strive for, and, yet, your own husband has reached out of his marriage to take another wife. I find that totally astonishing."

"I find that sad, Mrs. Rodgers," Gerri says walking towards the door.

"I'm glad this is out in the open. Maybe now Theodore can leave you for me. We can be together without incident," Carla nods.

"That's up to Theodore. I wash my hands of it all," Gerri leaves.

The car ride home was indeed solemn. How could Theodore do this to me? How could he give himself to another woman like this? That woman. That infamous, tawdry woman. I see nothing redeeming in her at all. She openly reveals her love affair with my husband and practically dares me to do anything about it. How odd she is? I've never seen anyone like her. This Carla Rodgers Holland woman. Calling herself a Holland. How does she even have the nerve? Why didn't I take my fists and beat her to within an inch of her life? Why didn't I pick up something and crack her skull open with it? Why didn't I take my long fingernails and scratch her beady little eyes out and stomp on them? I am filled with so many emotions right now. I feel anger and frustration. I feel saddness and hurt. This is not normal. A husband or a wife has to be made of absolute steel not to be affected by this. I hate this world sometimes and the people in it make it difficult to deal. It's that plain and simply. I drive home right now shellshocked. I can't believe my Theodore is involved in all of this. He has disgraced me and our families. To have a second wife and kids. Living as a dual husband. How could I have been so blind over the years? Where the hell was I when all of this was going on? Why didn't I see this other life happening right under my nose? This has been an eye-opening dilemma for me. It's plain and simple what I must do now. I have to leave Theodore and all of what I thought we had behind. I have to find the inner strength from somewhere to confront him and leave him to this whore. Leave him to her, the slut. Give him up in order to have a peace of mind. Give him the way out he so desperately wanted. I am hurt. I am very hurt and disappointed in the man I thought loved me no matter how tough times were. He will move on and so will I. Things won't always be this glum. Geraldine pulls into her driveway and parks the car. The hot engine stops and she gets out. The night sky is brutally cold by now. The moon is shining, partly hidden by the clouds enveloping the skies above. She calmly walks up to the front door and inserts her key. No fumbling around or searching for a set of keys this time. There they were, at the ready. Entering, the warm air hits her face, first. It feels good to be back home, but it is a hollow victory. This home is now tainted. It is tainted with the stain of adultery.

Theodore has been unfaithful to me and now things are chaotic. How different I feel right now from when I entered this same house earlier today. The entire mood has completely changed, and my attitude towards everything involving my relationship with Theodore is one of dread. She walks up the stairs to the master bedroom and enters quietly.

"Theodore. I must speak with you," she shakes him thoroughly.

"What is it?" he rubs his eyes, turning on the bright light next to his side of the bed.

"Do you love me, Theo?" she sits on her side of the bed slowly rubbing the bed spread.

"What?" he sighs.

"Just answer, please."

"Of course I love you, Gerri. What is this about?" he shifts to get a better look at her.

"I just left Carla Rodgers Holland's home," her voice almost in a whisper.

"What?!" He sits straight up, stammering for what to say next.

"I know all about your second marriage to Carla and the two sons you have with this woman. It would seem the boy I examined earlier today is your son, Christopher."

"Let me explain, Gerri," he gets out of bed quickly, reaching for his pants.

"There is nothing to explain. You have made your choice, my dear. Carla says that she has asked you to leave me numerous times. Do you want to leave me, Theodore?"

"No. I love you, and I want to be married to you," he gulps, sliding one leg into the pants.

"You want to be married to me. Why? Why would you still want to be married to me?"

"I don't want us to end like this, Gerri. I've made some mistakes. Yes. But that's no reason to end what we have here. We love one another, don't we?" he slips the other leg into his pants and pulls them up.

"I thought we did. I thought we had something special. There was always this feeling I would get from time to time about you straying away and being with someone elses, but I would dismiss it as nonsense. You have proven me wrong."

"You must understand why I turned to Carla all those years earlier. Let me tell you."

"Will it matter? Will it really matter, Theodore?"

"I have nothing to hide, Gerri. You must give me the chance to explain why I did what I did. I still have deep passion and love for you inside of me."

"I owe you nothing. You must undertand that I have to leave now. How you deal with Carla and those kids is your business. Give me a clean, quiet divorce."

"I will not give you a divorce. Allow me to explain, Gerri. Let me tell you why I did what I did. I still love you."

"You still love me. How terribly opportunistic. There isn't enough groveling in the world that will cause me to live with you a minute further. I will divorce you, Theo, and that's all to it," she walks to the bedroom doors, tears in her eyes.

"You can't just walk out on me like this! I won't allow it. Do you understand?!" he runs over and grabs her arm.

"Let go of me! I owe you nothing! You have lied to me constantly. There is another spouse and even children out there. Do you really think that I can just forget all of that and continue living with you? Even you can't be that dunce," she shakes her head, pulling away from him firmly.

"I won't allow you to embarrass me like this. I have a reputation and business to uphold. You can't do this to me, Gerri."

"Your business and reputation. That's what you're so concerned about now. Well that figures. I am leaving this house. You can have it," she storms out the double doors.

"You won't get away with this! You won't get a dime of my money!" Theodore follows, hitting the walls as he trails her from a distance down the ghostly lit hallway.

"I have my own money. I never, ever, asked you for a single thing. Even when we were first married, I paid my own way. How truly pathetic that sounds to me now. How utterly ridiculous! Why didn't I see through you then? Why? Good-bye, Theodore," she hurries down the stairs and towards the front door.

"I will not be gracious during the divorce! You old witch! I won't give you a single penny. Get out! Get out, now!" Theodore huffs, smacking the railings over and over again.

"Oh, what a pity, Theo. All that so-called deep passion and love for me all pent up and hidden inside of you. Go fly a kite, you creep!" she opens the door and slams it shut on her way out.

"You stupid @$&%!" he makes a fist, gritting his teeth, hard.

Theodore tried many times to convince Geraldine not to get that divorce but she was determined. When all else failed, he turned to a hit man to discreetly kill her and make it look like a suicide. The man recruited to carry out the murder was on probation for armed robbery and decided to go to the police and cut a deal in the hopes of staying out

of jail permanently. A plan was hatched, and when money exchanged hands, Theodore was immediately arrested. The man, Carlos Hernandez, testified against him. Theodore Winston Holland received thirty-five years to life for the attempted murder of his soon-to-be ex-wife. Geraldine left that penthouse apartment and moved back into the palatial family home she once shared with Theodore. A few years later, she found someone else and married him. They currently live in that extravagant home together, traveling around the world from time to time helping sick children and all those in need of other care.